POPPY HARMON FINDS A BODY

Poppy followed the sound of the music toward the living room, where she was finally able to recognize the familiar voice belting out a classic song on an old CD player set up in a corner.

It was Elaine Stritch.

How appropriate, Poppy thought, given the majority of women who resided here in the Palm Leaf Retirement Village, most of whom spent their days golfing during the morning and enjoying cocktails in the afternoon, during their typical, like clockwork, daily three-hour lunches.

She had moved farther into the living room in order to turn off the CD player when she caught something out of the corner of her eye.

Poppy spun around, gasping, her right hand flying to her mouth as she stared at the body lying facedown on the floor…

Books by Lee Hollis

Published by Kensington Publishing Corporation

Poppy Harmon Investigates

LEE HOLLIS

KENSINGTON BOOKS
www.kensingtonbooks.com

KENSINGTON BOOKS are published by

Kensington Publishing Corp.
119 West 40th Street
New York, NY 10018

All Kensington titles, imprints and distributed lines are available at special quantity discounts for bulk purchases for sales promotion, premiums, fund-raising, educational or institutional use. Special book excerpts or customized printings can also be created to fit specific needs. For details, write or phone the office of the Kensington Special Sales Manager: Kensington Publishing Corp., 119 West 40th Street, New York, NY, 10018. Attn. Special Sales Department. Phone: 1-800-221-2647.

Kensington and the K logo Reg. U.S. Pat. & TM Off.

ISBN-13: 978-1-4967-1389-6
ISBN-10: 1-4967-1389-3
First Kensington Hardcover Edition: August 2018
First Kensington Mass Market Edition: December 2019

eISBN-13: 978-1-4967-1390-2 (ebook)
eISBN-10: 1-4967-1390-7 (ebook)

10 9 8 7 6 5 4 3 2 1

Printed in the United States of America

For Brigitte Kirsch
Both a friend and an inspiration

Chapter 1

Poppy frantically banged on the door of the house, but there was no answer.

She waited a few moments and then tried again. Still no answer.

A foreboding sense of dread filled her entire body.

She had learned at a very young age to trust her intuition.

And she instinctively knew something was seriously wrong.

Poppy jiggled the door handle.

The door was unlocked.

She waited, debating with herself, and then sighed, making a quick decision. She pushed the door open slightly and poked her head inside.

"Hello? Anyone home?"

The single-level house was eerily quiet except for some soft music playing from somewhere not too far away.

She couldn't tell who was singing, because the volume was too low.

Poppy pushed the door all the way open and slipped inside, looking back to make sure none of the nosy neighbors on the idyllic, sleepy street saw her sneaking into a house where she did not live.

"Hello?" she tried one more time, but there was still no answer.

She was hardly surprised.

Poppy had guest starred in enough TV crime shows in the 1980s to know this was usually the point in the show when an unsuspecting woman found herself in the wrong place at the wrong time and suddenly fell prey to a mad killer or a treacherous villain seconds before the commercial break.

Still, her burning curiosity won out over her innate cautiousness, and she shut the door behind her and slowly, carefully, tiptoed farther into the foyer, looking around to be absolutely certain no one was lying in wait to suddenly jump out at her with a rag soaked with chloroform or, worse, a sharp weapon, like a carving knife or a rope cord from the curtains, which he could use to loop around her neck and strangle her to death.

Again, she had played a lot of damsels in distress during her years of acting in film and on television.

So her imagination tended to run a bit wild.

There was hardly that kind of violent crime to be found in California's Coachella Valley, her home for the past ten years.

And yet there were alarm bells suddenly going off in her head.

She had never felt such a strong sense of imminent danger.

Poppy followed the sound of the music toward the living room, where she was finally able to recognize the familiar voice belting out a classic song on an old CD player set up in a corner, on a small wooden desk adjacent to the fireplace.

It was Elaine Stritch.

The brassy, ballsy late Broadway legend.

And the song was "The Ladies Who Lunch," from the hit 1970 Stephen Sondheim musical *Company*.

How appropriate, Poppy thought, given the majority of women who resided here in the Palm Leaf Retirement Village, most of whom spent their days golfing during the morning and enjoying cocktails in the afternoon, during their typical, like clockwork, daily three-hour lunches.

She had moved farther into the living room in order to turn off the CD player when she caught something out of the corner of her eye.

Poppy spun around, gasping, her right hand flying to her mouth.

She struggled to steady herself as she stared at the body lying facedown on the floor, next to a cracked coffee table.

A small pool of blood seeped slowly into the pristine white carpet.

Chapter 2

Two months earlier . . .

Poppy Harmon was speechless.

Perhaps, for the very first time in her life.

And she was sixty-two years old.

Poppy had always been known for her enviable ability to bravely respond to a crisis with a calm, focused demeanor. She was never rattled or flummoxed or prone to overreaction, which was what made today such a momentous occasion.

Poppy Harmon was at this moment completely freaking out.

With her mouth hanging open, she finally managed to reclaim her power of speech and leaned forward.

"What the hell are you talking about?" Poppy wailed, suddenly light-headed, desperately trying to steady herself before she fainted and tumbled off the flimsy chair that faced her lawyer, Edwin Pierce, in his spacious, well-appointed office in Palm Desert, California.

Edwin's face was drawn, his complexion as pale as pasteurized milk, and his eyes were bloodshot, with the lids hanging at half-mast. The poor man was obviously sleep deprived, having probably been up all night, dreading this unavoidable and supremely uncomfortable meeting with his client.

"As I said, Chester, unfortunately, had accumulated some debt before he passed away, and according to my calculations, the sum total he owed . . ." Edwin's voice trailed off as he punched a few numbers into a calculator program on his computer screen. Poppy noticed his hand shaking as he brushed the keys with his crooked, bony fingers.

He was a bundle of nerves.

"How much, Edwin?" Poppy urged, wanting to get the bad news over with so she could begin dealing with the situation.

Edwin blinked at the screen, almost in disbelief at the final total, and then he cleared his throat before continuing. "Roughly six hundred and seventy thousand dollars."

Poppy stared blankly at Edwin.

She must have heard wrong.

Maybe he said six thousand dollars, which would be bad enough, but surely, he could not have possibly said . . .

"Six hundred and seventy thousand," Edwin repeated.

"That's impossible. How on earth did he . . . ? I would have known if he was spending that much!"

"It seems Chester had a small gambling problem. . . ."

"He played poker with the boys twice a month. I would hardly call that a gambling problem," Poppy scoffed, still in a state of denial.

"He played more than poker, I'm afraid. There were dozens of weekend trips to Las Vegas, according to my records. . . ."

"Those were business trips," Poppy quickly explained, as if saying the words would make them true.

Edwin gave Poppy a sad look of pity.

The wife was always the last to know.

"Chester was fired from his job a year ago."

"What?" Poppy screamed.

"I'm guessing from your reaction that he never told you."

Poppy shook her head, now on the verge of tears. "I don't understand. Why wouldn't he tell me something like that?"

"He was probably too embarrassed. You know, Chester, he was a very proud man."

Poppy stared at Edwin. "Actually, I'm beginning to suspect that I never actually knew Chester."

"I'm sure the stress of hiding all of this from you contributed to his heart attack."

Chester had died suddenly three weeks ago.

He and Poppy had been dining with friends at Wang's in the Desert, a popular Asian-fusion restaurant in Palm Springs.

As dessert was served, Chester complained of indigestion and excused himself to go to the restroom. When he hadn't returned twenty minutes later, Poppy sent his buddy Al, who was at the table, to go check on him. Al found him slumped over on the toilet in a stall, dead.

The days following Chester's sudden death were a blur.

Calling friends and relatives.

Making funeral arrangements.

Providing emotional support for her daughter, Heather, who was inconsolable over losing her favorite stepfather.

There had been two others after her biological father.

But Chester was her absolute favorite.

The last thing on Poppy's mind during all the grief and tears was their finances.

Chester had never given any hint they were in any kind of trouble.

In fact, they had just splurged on a cruise to the Greek islands.

Bought a new Chrysler Pacifica Hybrid.

Remodeled a guest suite in their five-bedroom, three-and-a-half-bath home nestled in the hills above Palm Springs.

The house.

Poppy absolutely loved their house.

"I'm not going to have to sell the house to pay off this debt, am I?"

Edwin swallowed hard.

She could see his Adam's apple move up and down.

That was not a good sign.

"Not if you can make the payments on the mortgages."

"Mortgages? But the house is paid off."

"Chester took out two mortgages against the value of the property, each in the amount of two hundred thousand dollars."

The blood drained from Poppy's face.

"There isn't much equity left, and with what you owe on the credit cards and personal loans . . ."

"I'm going to have to sell."

"I think that would be a wise move," Edwin said quietly, eyes downcast.

"What about his pension?"

"Gone."

"Our savings?"

Edwin hesitated but then opened his mouth to answer, but she beat him to it.

"Gone."

Edwin nodded.

"There is some good news, Poppy. You still have your SAG pension."

During the eighties and nineties, Poppy had dabbled in acting, scoring small parts in a string of TV shows and feature films, even nabbing a supporting role as a secretary on a private-eye series that lasted three seasons on ABC. She had made enough income before she left the business in order to get married and have a kid and enjoy a small pension when she turned sixty.

Small being the key word.

Her monthly check was five hundred and forty-eight dollars.

Before taxes.

What was she going to do now?

The thought of Chester's betrayal was overwhelming.

And she wanted to kick herself for being too stupid not to suspect.

She knew what she was in for now.

Pitied to her face, laughed at behind her back.

Poor, ding-a-ling, aging starlet Poppy.

She hadn't had a clue about her gambling-addicted wash-out of a husband.

And her fourth one, at that.

After four times, you would think she would get it right.

Edwin stood up from his desk, walked around, and placed a comforting hand on Poppy's padded shoulder.

"You will get through this, Poppy. I've known you a long time. You're a strong woman," Edwin lied.

"Are there any more secrets you need to tell me? We might as well get it all out in the open now."

Edwin flinched and opened his mouth to tell her something, but for some reason, he changed his mind at the last second and shook his head.

"No. Nothing."

She knew he was lying.

If she pushed hard enough, she was convinced she could get him to spill the beans about what he was still holding back.

But she was too emotionally battered at the moment to even try. At this point, there was a part of her that just didn't want to know.

Poppy stared straight ahead, her mind racing, bile rising in her throat.

"Penny for your thoughts," Edwin asked softly.

"A lousy penny isn't going to help me much right now, Edwin."

"It's best to let it all out. Tell me what's going through your mind."

"If I had known the bastard had wiped me out, I never would have chosen such an expensive casket!"

Chapter 3

"The only reason I married Chester was so I could have a stable, stress-free life in the desert and not have to worry about my financial security anymore," Poppy moaned as she sipped her cosmo at the 19th Hole, a popular bar located in the clubhouse of the Whispering Palms Golf Course. She sat at a table with her two best friends: Iris Becker, a very sturdy and direct German woman, her white hair beautifully coiffured and her makeup picture perfect, in a bright yellow–colored polo shirt and white capri pants; and Violet Hogan, Iris's polar opposite, quiet and demure, bordering on mousy, but constantly trying to change that impression with her bold fashion choices, like today's leopard-print sleeveless top and clashing black-and-white polka-dot shorts.

"Well, yes, that, and you loved him," Violet said, gently nudging Poppy between sips of her Grey Goose and lemonade.

"Of course I loved him! But after three failed marriages, I wasn't in a big hurry to rush right into another one! Chester was the one who convinced me that by marrying him, I would never have to worry about anything ever again. I could focus on my charities and political causes."

"That was obviously to keep you in the dark about what he was really doing. Never trust a man who offers to take care of you, because the opposite will happen, and you will be stuck taking care of him!" Iris said matter-of-factly, never one to mince words, in her heavy German accent.

She continued. "In my twenties, there was a filmmaker I met through Fassbinder, who I went barhopping with in Munich. Well, he fell for me instantly and begged me to be in his next film, but I said no. What do I know about acting? All my friends thought I was insane to turn down such a once-in-a-lifetime opportunity, but I did not want to be tied down in one place, making a movie. Besides, I found something better to do. So he found another muse, made his film with her as the star. They impulsively married the night of the film's opening. But then the movie flopped. He never directed another film again, and she wound up supporting him by doing soft-core porn disguised as French art films!"

"I don't think I could have turned down a starring role in a film," Poppy said. "What could have been better to do than that?"

"I hooked up with Mick Jagger at a beer garden in Berlin and spent the summer touring with the Stones."

Poppy sat back in her chair, impressed. "You're right. That is better."

"You've lived such an interesting life, Iris," Violet said wistfully. "So full of fascinating stories."

"I suppose so, compared to you," Iris said, nodding.

Violet was a retired high school principal from Massachusetts.

Not the most exciting past, but she did have a library named after her, and she continued to this day to receive letters from dozens of former students, heaping praise on her and gushing about how much of an influence she had been on them, which, in Poppy's mind, was just as impressive as Iris's wild jet-setting tales of yesteryear.

"I do not understand how he took out two mortgages against the house without you knowing about it!" Iris said. "I assume the house was under both your names?"

"Yes." Poppy nodded, supremely embarrassed. "Edwin showed me the loan applications. My messy signature was on both of them. Either Chester had me sign them without me knowing what they were, or he forged my name. It doesn't really matter. Either way, I'm responsible."

"And you had no idea what he was up to?" Violet asked, placing a comforting hand on Poppy's arm.

"That's the most humiliating part! No. I had no clue what was going on. Chester isn't what you would call a masterful con man. It was pretty much what you see is what you get. I always knew what he was thinking. There weren't a lot of layers, if you know what I mean. Which means I just wasn't paying attention. I was caught up in my own activities, blissfully ignorant of the fact that my husband was leading a secret life behind my back."

"What are you going to do now?" Violet asked.

"Well, I'm meeting with a Realtor tomorrow to put the house on the market. It's going to be a short sale because I can no longer make the payments, which means it will probably sell quickly, and then I have to find another place to live."

"You will stay with me until you find a place," Iris said, deciding the matter without even waiting for Poppy to accept her kind offer.

"You can stay with me, too," Violet offered, feeling left out.

"Don't be silly, Violet," Iris said. "My house has more room, and the patio has a far superior view."

Iris was never mean-spirited.

Just brutally honest.

"Thank you, both of you," Poppy said. "I couldn't ask for better friends."

"I know," Iris said, nodding.

"And then, I suppose, I'm going to have to find a job."

Poppy caught Iris and Violet exchanging concerned looks.

"What was that?" Poppy asked.

"What?" Iris and Violet said in unison.

"That! That worried look between you two."

"It was nothing!" Violet lied in a valiant effort to protect Poppy's feelings.

Iris, however, was not one to protect feelings.

The hard, bitter truth was always best.

And she had no problem dishing it out.

"What skills do you have? You haven't worked in over twenty years," Iris said gruffly.

Iris was right.

Poppy's last serious job was as a Hollywood actress.

But once ABC canceled her only steady gig after three seasons, she struggled to find acting roles. All the sexpot roles that seemed to have rained down upon her in her twenties had long dried up, and she never managed to get cast in a part that required any serious acting chops. When she was just shy of forty and her youthful looks began to fade, despite some nips and tucks and scary injections, no one was willing to give her a chance anymore.

When she left Hollywood on her fortieth birthday, she never looked back. And never worried about working ever again, especially since her third husband at the time, Ira Greenstein, was a successful entertainment attorney.

"Maybe I could get back into acting. I always said, when I was more mature, there would be so many roles I could finally play."

"I just heard they are holding auditions for *Steel Magnolias* at the Palm Springs Playhouse," Violet said excitedly.

"How much are they paying?"

"They didn't say anything about money."

"Which means there is none!" Iris said, waving off Violet's useless suggestion. "She's not going to pay her rent by playing a part that Shirley MacLaine performed better in the movie!"

"Maybe I could go back to Hollywood . . .," Poppy said, trying to convince herself this was a plausible course of action.

"Forget it," Iris said. "All those mature roles you are finally ready to play are going to go to Meryl Streep, believe me."

"I think we should try to stay positive, Iris," Violet scolded.

"I know! I am positive Poppy going back to acting is not the answer," Iris said. "We need a good idea!"

That one stung Poppy.

But she certainly couldn't argue with it.

"What am I going to do? I've never balanced a checkbook, let alone stuck to a budget, in my life!" Poppy moaned.

"We are here to help you," Violet said. "And so is Heather."

Poppy gasped.

Her daughter, Heather.

She was still in the dark about the whole situation.

"Tell me you told Heather what is going on," Iris said.

"No. I drove right over here from the lawyer's office. I didn't want to call her in the car and fall apart on the phone. Not until I can come up with a plan."

"You have to tell her. If you don't, she is going to find out from someone else, and that will not be good," Iris warned.

"But she is so high strung and emotional, and she was so close to Chester and always held him in such high regard. How can I tell her he squandered away all our savings, including her rather sizable inheritance, before he kicked the bucket?"

A waiter appeared at the table with a piece of paper.

His face was tight, and his movements were stiff.

It was obvious he was pained to have to do this.

But he took a deep breath and powered through, handing Poppy the paper. "Your bill, ma'am."

Poppy stared at the paper for a long moment and then calmly looked up at the nervous young waiter.

"It says I owe four thousand five hundred and

thirty-nine dollars. Now, I know you raised your prices, but three cocktails and a plate of stuffed mushrooms shouldn't cost this much."

"I know, ma'am," the waiter said, clearing his throat. "But your late husband, and I am so sorry for your loss, he paid for a lot of meals he had with his golf buddies over the past year or so and ran a tab, which he, unfortunately, never had the chance to pay, and now the owner is insisting you pay it off, or forfeit club membership."

"I can't pay it," Poppy said, slumping in her chair.

Then she quietly picked her purse up off the floor next to her chair, stood up, and forced a smile. "I always thought golf was boring, anyhow. There. Now I can say it."

"Where are you going?" Violet asked.

"To tell Heather," Poppy said, glancing around the room, noticing several tables of club members either staring directly at her or averting their gaze to avoid eye contact. "Iris is right. If I don't get to her first, there are about a dozen little birdies right here in this clubhouse who will happily do it for me."

Chapter 4

Poppy went over in her mind the conversation she was about to have as she sat at a corner table at Las Casuelas, a popular Mexican eatery in the heart of Palm Springs. She had promised herself not to indulge in the basket of salty, greasy taco chips that would greet her at the table when she arrived and was seated, but the stress of breaking her troubling news to her daughter that she was broke quickly dissolved any remaining vestiges of self-control. There was only a handful of crumbled chips left in the basket after only five minutes at the table, and the waiter had to scurry off for another serving of salsa so she could finish them off after he delivered her Cadillac margarita on the rocks, the first of several she would be downing during the course of the meal, for sure.

She had practiced silently to herself just how she was going to tell Heather, and she had imagined her daughter's response, starting with the inevitable shock, which would soon give way to a self-pitying "Why is this happening to me?" crying jag, and would finally wrap up with unadulterated sheer panic once it sank in that her inheritance was entirely gone.

Poppy would try her best to remain a calming influence, but the fact that at the moment she was screaming and hysterical on the inside didn't bode well for her playing the role of supportive and reassuring mother.

A three-man mariachi band snapped her out of her thoughts as they weaved through the tables, singing "El Rey." The lead singer was lean and handsome, with a pencil-thin mustache, and was enjoying the attention from the room as he crooned, aiming his velvety chords toward the female patrons, including Poppy. He broke into a wide smile as he passed by, serenading her, and for a brief moment, Poppy thought he might have recognized her from her TV work, but then the reality of his age—late twenties, at most—settled in, and she figured he was just doing his job charming all the eye-batting, enamored older ladies in the house.

She was halfway through her first margarita and keeping an eye out for the waiter to be prepared to fetch another when she spotted Heather by the hostess stand. Poppy had to wave a few times before Heather noticed her, but when she did, her daughter beamed, bright and happy, not a care in the world. Poppy dreaded the idea of the cold, hard slap in the face she was about to deliver.

Heather bounded over to the table and plopped down in a chair after a quick air kiss with her mother. She was wearing a flattering pink print sundress, her hair had recently been curled and styled, and there was a generous amount of makeup covering every blemish. Poppy had never seen Heather go to such efforts to look pretty for a night out with Mom. But she didn't question it.

In hindsight, she probably should have.

"Sorry I'm late. There was a lot of traffic on the one-eleven," Heather said, scooping up a chip and dipping it in the fresh bowl of salsa the waiter had just dropped off.

"Was there an accident?" Poppy asked.

"No. Just your typical Palm Springs traffic jam, which we both know is a bunch of old people driving too slow."

Poppy smiled. "You look lovely tonight, dear."

"Thank you," Heather said. "I wanted to look nice for this special occasion."

Poppy suddenly panicked.

Did she forget Heather's birthday?

No.

Heather was born on December 22.

That was still months away.

"Special occasion?" Poppy asked, giving up trying to figure it out.

"Yes," Heather said slyly, glancing around the restaurant, as if looking for someone. "I've invited someone to join us for dinner."

Oh no.

The last thing Poppy wanted was a third party at the table. She had steeled herself to do this, and she could not put it off any longer.

"Heather, I thought it was just going to be the two of us. I have something I need to talk about, and it's very important—"

"There he is!" Heather giggled, waving her arms frantically at a young man who had just breezed into the restaurant and was glad-handing the hostess and apparently talking her ear off.

He was average height but movie-star hand-some, with dark, close-cropped hair, a goatee that was bordering on ironic, and an air of self-assurance, which the hostess, at least, found intoxicating.

She pointed at their table, and with a big grin plastered on his face, the young man practically jogged over, arms outstretched, as Heather jumped to her feet and fell into his embrace. They hugged for what seemed like a whole minute, before pulling just far enough away from each other to gaze into the other's eyes, then concluded their touching reunion with a long, sloppy wet kiss.

Oh, God, Poppy thought. *Heather has a new boy-friend.*

The handsome young man quickly turned his attention to Poppy and, with a hand over his heart, said dramatically, "You must be Poppy. I've heard so much about you. . . . All bad!"

"Excuse me?" Poppy asked.

He broke out into a fit of giggles. "Kidding, kidding."

"You'll get used to his weird sense of humor," Heather felt the need to mention as she slapped him playfully on the arm and told him to sit down.

He reached over, grabbed Poppy's hand, and after a short struggle, with Poppy fruitlessly trying to withdraw it, he managed to pucker up his lips and smack the back of her hand with a loud kiss. When he finally let go, Poppy yanked her hand back, grabbed the stem of her margarita glass, and took a generous gulp.

"Mom, this is Matt Cameron. We met at yoga class," Heather said.

"I was in a downward dog position, spotted her

through my legs stretching that glorious body of hers, and presto, I was immediately hooked," he said, winking at Heather.

"Matt's an actor," Heather said proudly.

The information was coming fast and furious.

Poppy didn't know where to start.

Having been married to two actors in her lifetime, not to mention the dozens that she had dated back in the day, Poppy was reasonably sure the last kind of man she would ever want her daughter mixed up with would be an actor.

Poppy's hopes of having that serious discussion with her daughter about their uncertain future was going to have to be postponed. Especially since from the moment the topic of his chosen profession was introduced, Matt Cameron never stopped talking about himself.

How he wowed his hometown in upstate New York with his indelible performance in *Evita*, playing the rabble-rouser anarchist Che to packed houses at his local community theater, before taking the train to New York and the Great White Way, never looking back. He never mentioned any Broadway shows he had ever appeared in, only a "gritty, bare-bones" production of a decades-old play called *Fortune and Men's Eyes*, in which he played a persecuted juvenile delinquent under the thumb of a sexually aggressive fellow inmate. Poppy knew how to translate his words. *Gritty* and *bare-bones* meant that the play was put on in a Lower East Side garage, that it had very few props, that nobody got paid, and that they were lucky if half of the twenty hard-back chairs lined up in front of the stage were filled every night.

If Poppy was good at one thing, it was interpreting "actor-speak."

By the time they ordered their food, Matt had covered his starving actor years in New York, his therapeutic road trip out west to find himself, and his first role as Surfer #3 in an episode of *NCIS: Los Angeles*, which secured him his SAG card.

Heather was besotted, laughing too hard at his jokes, melting whenever his eyes rested on her, constantly glancing at Poppy to see if she was as charmed by this delectable vision as she was.

Poppy, ever the actress herself, managed to deliver a believable, understated performance as a woman marginally interested in what this self-absorbed idiot had to say. For the sake of her daughter's feelings, she was not going to put a damper on this impromptu "Mom, meet the man of my dreams" dinner.

"The second Heather told me you were once an actress, I looked you up on IMDb. You had quite a career way back when," Matt said.

Way back when?

His stock was plunging further and faster.

"I think I remember my parents watching that detective show you were in when I was little. My mom had a huge crush on the star."

"Rod Harper."

"Yeah. Whatever happened to him? He still alive?"

"I believe so, yes. He's only sixty-five."

Matt chuckled. "That's funny."

"What?"

"Only sixty-five . . ."

He didn't linger on the moment, completely unaware he had just insulted her. Instead, he bravely plowed ahead, oblivious to how close he was to having a margarita thrown in his face.

"And I actually remember seeing you in that Disney movie about the talking car, *Speedy Goes to Le Mans*, and you played the pretty French girl in the pit crew, Genevieve. . . ."

"Yes. You have a good memory," Poppy sighed.

"Well, not really. I watched it on Netflix the other night, after Heather and I planned this dinner. I wanted to study up on you."

Poppy looked at her daughter again with pleading eyes that could not be sending a more clear and unequivocal message: *You can't be serious!*

When Matt began to roll out the idea for his one-man show, Poppy begged the waiter to hurry back with another round of drinks. At least she was feeling a comfortable buzz to help dull the pain of dining with this moron, who was sucking up all the oxygen in the room. Thank heavens for the Uber app, which she could use to get home safely.

She started to mentally go through her to-do list for tomorrow as he prattled on and on until the bill mercifully arrived. She waited a few minutes for Matt to at least pick up the check, in order to impress his possible future mother-in-law, but no such moment came. She had finally picked it up to check the damage and to suggest they split the tab when she heard Matt say, with all sincerity, "Thank you, Poppy. That's very generous of you."

She bit her lip hard and told herself he was a struggling actor, probably a few months behind on his rent.

She handed her American Express card to the waiter and silently prayed there was enough credit left on there to pay for the meal.

Was Heather really falling for this sketchy character?

She liked to think her daughter had better taste.

Then again, when Poppy was thirty, she was not exactly making exemplary choices when it came to men.

In fact, upon reflection, she realized she had dated a few Matt Camerons herself.

Actually, when she really thought about it, given her current situation, marrying Chester was probably also a disastrous choice.

Maybe she had cursed her own daughter by passing along some kind of "terrible taste in men" gene.

Thankfully, the waiter returned with two slips of paper and a pen, which meant the card had mercifully gone through. As Poppy calculated the tip and signed the receipt, Matt leapt from his chair and raced over to the mariachi band, nearly knocked the young lead singer into a potted plant as he wrestled some maracas out of the surprised man's hands, and began belting out "Volver, Volver." The good news was Matt had a nice singing voice. The bad news was Matt was singing. In front of the entire restaurant, much to the consternation of the mariachi singer with the pencil-thin mustache, who was glaring at him after having been so rudely shoved out of the spotlight.

Matt was in his element.

When he finished, the entire restaurant burst into applause, and feigning modesty, Matt bashfully waved them off as he marched back over to the table, reached down, and planted another big wet kiss on his new gal's mouth. He was about to do the same to Poppy, but she quickly stood up and brushed past him for the door, passing the mariachi singer, who could tell she liked Matt even less than he did.

They shared a look, both silently agreeing that the mad attention whore was utterly distasteful and downright irritating.

Now, if she could only get her daughter to see past her new beau's insincere charm.

But that was a future battle.

The more pressing issue was breaking the news that Heather was no longer an heiress, thanks to Chester.

But on the bright side, the fact that Heather was suddenly penniless just might do the trick in scaring off this D-list Ryan Gosling wannabe.

Chapter 5

When Poppy arrived back home, her head was pounding. Not from too many margaritas, mind you, but from having to endure an achingly long meal with Heather's obnoxious new boy toy.

She couldn't help but hope that the fire in her daughter's latest relationship would quickly burn out, and the whole sickening romance between the two of them would soon become just a painfully bad memory.

However, she also wanted Heather to be happy, and if this egotistical man-child was somehow inexplicably making her smile and feel all warm inside, then who was she to object?

It was not as if Poppy herself had to spend any more time with him.

Or at least she hoped that would be the case.

If, God forbid, Heather were to marry the guy, then there would be holidays and birthdays and Sunday family dinners to contend with, and she just couldn't bring herself to picture that awful reality just yet.

Poppy undressed, slipped into a baby blue silk nightgown and matching furry slippers, and then padded to the kitchen to pour herself a nightcap. As she sat down and gulped down her drink, enjoying the little kick before bedtime, she made the decision to call Heather first thing in the morning and plan to meet for coffee, this time just the two of them.

Poppy worried if she waited much longer to break the news, Heather was going to find out some other way, and she didn't want her blaming her for keeping her in the dark for so long. This situation had to be dealt with swiftly and carefully.

She had recorded *60 Minutes* while she was out dining with Heather and Matt, and was looking forward to settling into her recliner and watching that adorable Anderson Cooper report on a story about smartphone addiction when her doorbell rang.

She checked the Swiss clock she had picked up on a trip to Zurich a few years ago on the wall. It was almost nine thirty.

Who would be dropping by at this hour?

For a moment, her stomach lurched, as she feared it might be Heather and Matt with a carton of ice cream to share since Poppy had rushed out of Las Casuelas before they had a chance to order dessert.

But she was enormously relieved when she opened the door to find Iris and Violet. Violet carried a covered casserole dish wrapped in tinfoil in her hands. Iris had her checkbook.

"What is this?"

"Chicken and biscuit casserole. My mother's recipe," Violet said, handing the dish to Poppy.

"I just ate, but thank you. I'll have some for lunch tomorrow. So you came all the way over here to bring me a casserole?"

"Yes," Violet said, twitching and nervous.

Iris sighed. "You're a terrible liar, Violet."

"I know," Violet wailed. "I get so nervous."

"The casserole was just an excuse. We figured if we told you the real reason we're here, you wouldn't let us in," Iris said.

"Now I'm intrigued," Poppy said. "Come on in."

Iris and Violet didn't need further prodding.

They marched inside and made a beeline for the kitchen, where Iris helped herself to a shot of cognac and Violet poured herself a glass of lemonade from a pitcher in the refrigerator, being the teetotaler that she was.

Or at least that was what she told people.

But usually only before happy hour.

"Are you hungry? I have a chicken and biscuit casserole I can serve you," Poppy playfully offered, holding out the covered dish.

"No, that's for you. Now, let's get down to business," Iris barked, sitting on a high stool next to the island in Poppy's kitchen.

"And what business is that?"

"Iris, I thought we were going to ease into it . . . ," Violet stammered.

"Why? There's no time. She's broke. She's got bills to pay," Iris argued.

"You do realize I'm here in the room with you, right?" Poppy asked.

Iris nodded and then opened her checkbook and began scribbling. "Will eight thousand be enough to get you through the next few months?"

"I beg your pardon?" Poppy gasped.

"Violet and I have pooled our resources, and we're going to float you a loan to get you through this rough patch."

"You're going to give me eight grand?" Poppy asked, incredulous.

"I knew we should have offered ten," Violet whispered quietly.

"No! I can't take your money!" Poppy exclaimed.

"Why not?" Iris growled, personally affronted. "It's not like we stole it!"

"I just don't want to accept any handouts. I'll figure this out on my own," Poppy said, touched that her two best friends were prepared to be so generous.

"This is not the time to be proud, Poppy. We're your friends, and we want to help, so stop fighting us on this," Iris said as she finished signing the check and tore it off the pad with a flourish. She handed it to Poppy, who immediately handed it back to her.

"I'm sorry. I can't," Poppy said.

"Then what will you do?"

"Look, this is all just starting to sink in. I need to meet with the lawyer again, talk to some debt consolidation advisers, and then go from there. And I appreciate your sweet offer of allowing me to stay with one of you, but I don't want to be a burden."

Violet gasped. "That could take weeks. How are you going to feed yourself in the meantime? And what happens when the house sells? Where will you go if you don't stay with one of us?"

"I can always stay with Heather while I look for a more permanent situation," Poppy said.

Iris and Violet exchanged dubious looks and then burst into uncontrollable laughter.

"That is the dumbest idea I have ever heard," Iris said. "You two will be at each other's throats before you even have a chance to unpack your bag."

"I think I'm capable of living with my daughter for a couple of weeks, while I look for a place," Poppy said, trying to convince herself.

Iris was having none of it.

She stared down Poppy, whose confident exterior began to crack almost instantly. She knew Iris was right. "Maybe I'll be lucky and find a place really fast, like in a week or so."

"You know, on second thought, I bet Heather will love having you stay at her place. I get the feeling she's been lonely lately, and the company would surely do her good," Violet said, always in search of a positive note.

"That's not a problem anymore. She has a new boy-friend," Poppy sighed, not even making an effort to hide her scorn.

"Uh-oh. So you've met him?" Iris asked.

"Yes. Tonight. But I'd rather not talk about it," Poppy said.

"That bad, huh?" Iris shook her head sympathetically.

Violet snatched the check out of Iris's hand and tried shoving it toward Poppy again, who adamantly waved it away.

"I appreciate the thought, but you girls need that money, and I wouldn't feel right taking it. Stop worrying about me. I can find a way to buy my groceries."

"How?" Iris asked, challenging her.

"I'll think of something . . . ," Poppy said, knowing her worry lines were probably showing on her forehead.

"What about a babysitter?" Violet piped in excitedly.

"I haven't done that since I was sixteen years old," Poppy said.

"Not a babysitter, really, a companion. I've seen a lot of postings at the senior center where I take my self-defense class, looking for a part-time paid companion for wealthy elderly people who need to be looked after during the day, until a family member can come home and take over at night, after work."

"What would I have to do?" Poppy asked.

"Prepare lunch, take him or her for a ride in the car, play Scrabble once in a while, maybe light water aerobics in the pool once a week. It sounds like the easiest job in the world," Violet said.

"I could do that," Poppy agreed.

Finally, some hope.

Perhaps she had found a temporary solution to keep the lights on in her home . . . her home that was about to be sold by the bank for a fraction of its value.

Looking after an eighty-year-old a few times a week.

Seriously, how hard could that be?

Chapter 6

"What do you mean, you can't find her?" Clifford Wentworth screamed over the phone at Poppy.

Poppy stood outside the elegant multimillion-dollar home nestled against the mountain in the tony area of Las Palmas, just west of downtown Palm Springs. Her cell phone was clamped to her ear.

"I was in the kitchen, making her a sandwich for lunch, and she gave me the slip," Poppy said, out of breath, having frantically searched inside and outside the expansive property. "I caught a glimpse of her running past the window outside, near the pool, and came out to catch her, but now she's gone again!"

"You were tasked with keeping an eye on my mother for three days a week, not with playing hide-and-seek with her!" Clifford huffed angrily.

"I know, Mr. Wentworth, but she's very difficult to corral."

Poppy was just being polite.

Estelle Wentworth, the eighty-nine-year-old matriarch of a wealthy family who had made their fortune selling sandwich condiments was a living, breathing nightmare to behold.

Poppy had actually been afraid she might be bored when she accepted the position as a companion to the spry octogenarian three days a week, while her son and his wife flew back east to take care of the family business in Pittsburgh.

But Estelle had turned out to be much more than just a handful.

She was demanding, paranoid, and perhaps certifiably crazy.

Estelle believed that Poppy was a spy for her older sister Janet, who left the family business to start a rival company, and she was convinced that Janet was using Poppy to try to steal company secrets for her own company's gain.

The only problem with that theory was Janet had been dead since 2004. And the rival company she started had gone bankrupt after the 2008 financial crisis and was no longer in existence.

On her first day at the fancy Las Palmas estate, Poppy had tried to entice Estelle with some board games, only to be pelted with Monopoly pieces when Estelle began to suspect Poppy of trying to cheat her out of Park Place, which she was convinced rightfully belonged to her.

A shopping trip to El Paseo in Palm Desert had resulted in Poppy having to beg the manager of Ann Taylor not to call the police when Estelle tried walking out of the store wearing a plaid split-neck drawstring dress she had only moments before taken into the dressing room to try on.

In fact, that wasn't the only store where she had

attempted to shoplift that morning, but when Estelle first tried walking out of El Paseo Jewelers with a diamond necklace she hadn't paid for, Poppy simply chalked it up to her forgetfulness, which undoubtedly came with her advanced age. But after the Ann Taylor incident, Poppy was now convinced the old bat was a full-blown kleptomaniac.

Since shopping was no longer an option on their list of activities, Poppy had decided to take her to a movie.

Unfortunately, they hadn't made it past the first five minutes of the film, once Estelle realized Dame Judi Dench was in the cast. The old woman had a peculiar hatred for the Oscar-winning legend, and she spewed a litany of insults at the screen at the top of her lungs, claiming Judi had once brazenly stolen a boyfriend of hers while she was studying abroad one summer in London during the 1950s.

Not caring whether or not this was true, though based on her privileged, colorful past, there was no reason to doubt her, Poppy dragged Estelle out of the theater so the other patrons could enjoy the rest of the show without having to listen to a cranky old woman yell four-letter words at the screen.

And then there was Estelle's aggravating determination to drive.

She hadn't been allowed to drive since she was eighty-four.

But driving was her favorite pastime, and she missed it terribly.

Poppy had once found Estelle trying to pickpocket her car keys from her front pants pocket and had had to slap her hand away.

When they had stopped for lunch at Spencer's, a picturesque spot with a sunny patio at a tennis club near Estelle's home, Estelle tried conning the valet by telling him that the Ferrari he had just driven up to the restaurant entrance belonged to her. She was actually behind the wheel and ready to take off before Poppy realized what was happening and quickly intervened.

All that had happened on day one.

After she had got home and made herself a drink and plopped down, exhausted, in her re-cliner to catch up on the day's news, Poppy had contemplated quitting.

Why put herself through another day of tor-ture?

But her bills were still unpaid, and she couldn't face herself in the mirror if she quit a job after just one day, so she'd resolved to stick it out.

And now it was eleven o'clock in the morning on day two.

And she had lost her.

Poppy's sole responsibility was to look after an eighty-nine-year-old woman, make her lunch, and keep her mind occupied for a few hours, and she was now nowhere to be found.

Poppy had dreaded calling Estelle's son Clifford in Pittsburgh, but she'd felt she had no choice. She had to tell him his mother was missing. He was not at all pleased to be bothered. Poppy had the feeling Clifford found his mother to be a nui-sance, but he had to keep her happy so his posi-tion in her will would remain secure. When he interviewed Poppy for the job, he'd taken great pains to explain how it was his personal mission to be a devoted son looking after his dear mother.

Poppy didn't buy it for a second, especially since he was pawning her off on a paid caregiver to keep her out of his hair. But at least he put on a good show and made it appear as if he actually cared.

"She couldn't have gone too far! I mean, she's eighty-nine!" Clifford yelled over the phone. "It's not like she can outrun you!"

Poppy wasn't so sure.

Suddenly, out of the corner of her eye, she saw movement inside the house. She whipped around to see Estelle waving at her from the kitchen window, contentedly eating the tuna sandwich Poppy had prepared for her.

"Wait! There she is! She's in the kitchen!" Poppy yelled, racing over to the large sliding glass door and grabbing the handle to open it.

It was locked.

"Oh no . . . ," Poppy said quietly.

"What? What's happening?" Clifford demanded to know.

"She locked me out."

"What? You have to get inside! She can't be left alone! There's no telling what she'll do!"

"Is there another key hidden away somewhere in case you get locked out?"

"No. Nobody has ever been stupid enough to get locked out of the house before," Clifford said, letting the words hang there in order to make Poppy feel like an even bigger imbecile.

"Well, I don't know what to do!" Poppy wailed, peering in the kitchen window, trying to locate Estelle, who had suddenly vanished again.

"I'll call the housekeeper. She has a key. She can probably be there in ten minutes. In the meantime, make sure she stays inside the house and doesn't try to go anywhere!"

Poppy heard a rumbling sound.

She tried to make out what it was and where it was coming from.

"Poppy, are you still there?"

The rumbling stopped, and then she heard a car engine roaring to life.

Oh, dear God, no.

The rumbling sound had been the garage door opening on the front side of the house.

Clifford's prized Rolls-Royce was parked in there.

Estelle had found the keys and was hell bent on going for a joyride.

Poppy gasped and raced around the pool, out the gate, and around the house, toward the street.

She could hear Clifford screaming faintly through the cell phone that she clutched in her right hand. "Poppy, what's going on? What is she doing?"

Poppy couldn't bring herself to raise the phone to her ear and tell him as she helplessly watched Estelle Wentworth speed out of the garage in a vintage 1972 Rolls-Royce Silver Shadow, tires squealing, make a sharp turn onto the street, and broadside an unsuspecting Mercedes that happened to be passing by, minding its own business.

Clifford heard a honking horn, the grueling sound of crunching metal, and the angry yelling from the driver of the Mercedes and pretty much surmised what had just transpired.

Poppy stood in the driveway, sick to her stomach, but on some level relieved her career as a

caregiver was about to come to an abrupt and mer-
ciful end.

At least she wasn't going to have to quit.

Because she heard the faint voice of her employer, Clifford Wentworth, screaming through
the cell phone from Pittsburgh, "You're fired!"

Chapter 7

Poppy pushed off from the tiled wall of the pool and swam through the cool chlorinated water, alternating between freestyle, breaststroke, and backstroke, before touching the other side with her hand and turning her body around to head back to the other end.

After ten laps, she hauled herself up the metal ladder, water dripping off her turquoise one-piece swimsuit, and padded over to Iris and Violet, who were comfortably ensconced in some plush cushioned patio chairs around a round glass table that was shaded from the blazing sun by a giant yellow umbrella. Iris was drinking a Bloody Mary, and Violet was sipping an iced tea, and the two were embroiled in deep conversation. Other than a rotund, abnormally hairy, balding retiree who was wearing a far too small swimsuit that showed off way more than was appropriate for polite society and who was snoozing on a lounger nearby, none of the other residents of Violet's gated condo community were anywhere to be seen, so the ladies mostly had the pool to themselves.

As Poppy grabbed a lukewarm bottled water from her bag next to an empty chair, she noticed Violet scribbling something down on a pad of paper as Iris looked on approvingly.

"What are you two up to?" Poppy asked.

"We are coming up with a list of your attributes in order to help you find a position more suitable to your skills," Iris said, checking Violet's work. "Read what we have so far, Violet."

"Honest, loyal, responsible, compassionate . . ."

"You two are going to make me blush," Poppy said, smiling.

"Well, they may speak to your character, but they won't help you land a job. How many words per minute can you type?" Iris asked.

"I never learned to type," Poppy said, embarrassed.

"She didn't have to," Violet said. "She was working as a model by the time she was sixteen."

"And after that, the acting parts started to roll in, so I was too busy to finish college."

"You were an actress, so you have experience working with people. I would say that's a plus," Violet said, trying to remain upbeat.

"Great. That makes her qualified to become a greeter at Walmart," Iris said, shaking her head at Violet.

"I basically have no skills," Poppy said, grabbing a towel draped over the empty chair and wiping herself dry. "Which does not bode well for a future that does not include homelessness!"

"Let's not panic just yet," Iris said. "You have to be good at something besides acting!"

"Frankly, there was a *TV Guide* critic back in the eighties who would argue even that. I remember his quote verbatim in the fall preview issue the year my series premiered on ABC. He said, 'Poppy Harmon's physical gifts, including her shapely legs, her firm buttocks, and her ample chest, work hard to help the viewer overlook her stiff line readings and vacant stare as the hero's breathlessly sexy, devoted secretary.' "

"You must have been devastated reading that," Violet said, frowning.

"Not really. I worked hard to get that body, and I was making five grand a week. I didn't let it get to me. But now that my legs aren't so shapely, my buttocks are not nearly as firm, and my ample chest has suffered from the unforgiving forces of gravity, his words hurt a hell of a lot more."

"Think. There must be something, anything you're good at," Iris said, concentrating between gulps of her Bloody Mary.

"This is really starting to get depressing," Poppy whined, dropping her towel and plopping down in the chair.

"You're an excellent gift wrapper!" Violet blurted out suddenly. "You always make a present look so pretty with flowers and ribbons and glitter. I didn't even want to open the gift you gave me for my birthday last month, it looked so pretty."

"That would actually be helpful, Violet, if the Christmas season was not months away!" Iris barked. "There is not a shortage of professional gift wrappers this time of year!"

"So did you finally open it and read the book I gave you?" Poppy asked.

"Yes, and you were right. It was a real page-turner," Violet said. "It had me guessing right up until the end."

"I figured out who the killer was after the first twenty pages, but I still enjoyed it," Poppy said.

"That's why I refuse to go to a movie with you or watch a TV show that has some kind of mystery to solve," Iris said. "You always ruin it by blurting out the answer!"

"I can't help it! Chester loved all those true-crime shows that played late at night on cable, but he would wait until I was asleep, because he hated watching them with me. I always knew who did it, how, and why before the first commercial."

"Where do you think that comes from?" Iris asked.

"She's always been hyper observant," Violet said.

"If she was hyper observant, she would have known Chester was frittering away their life savings," Iris said before noticing Poppy was crestfallen. "I'm sorry. I just speak the truth."

"Have you always been good at solving puzzles, Poppy?" Violet asked, trying to change the subject, after shooting Iris a stern look.

"As far back as I can remember," Poppy said. "When I was playing Daphne on *Jack Colt, PI*, we had this producer, Sam Emerson, who had gone to law school and then opened his own business as a private investigator in New York before he realized his true calling was writing scripts for television, so he chucked it all and moved to Hollywood and wound up on the show's staff. Well, whenever he would write himself into a corner, he would take me to lunch and pick my brain, and I would always come up with the solution. He was the only one who didn't see me as a brainless starlet. He actually liked me for my mind. That was pretty much the first inkling I had that I had a knack for that kind of stuff."

"That's it! The answer is right in front of you, Poppy!" Violet shouted, almost startling herself.

"What?" Iris wanted to know.

"That's what you should do! Solve mysteries!" Violet exclaimed, quite pleased with herself for coming up with this brilliant thought on her own.

Poppy sat back in her chair and laughed.

What a sweet but utterly ridiculous suggestion.

Did Violet actually think Poppy could become some kind of crime investigator? What was she going to do? Apply to the Palm Springs Police Department as a trainee or put out a shingle and become a private eye?

I mean, it was such a crazy notion.

And yet oddly compelling.

She had always fantasized during her acting days of starring in a series where she was the detective and not just the secretary. She had considered herself far more adept at deductive reasoning than Angie Dickinson in *Police Woman* or the rotating lineup of women in *Charlie's Angels*. Still, how would anyone, starting with herself, even begin to take her seriously as a licensed professional detective?

"Well, why not?" Violet asked.

"Because I'm too old, for one thing," Poppy said.

"No you're not. Sixty is the new forty," Violet said encouragingly. "And Jessica Fletcher was in her fifties."

"Jessica Fletcher is a fictional character," Poppy argued.

"I'm sorry, but you're never too old to write," Violet said.

"Write?" Poppy asked, confused.

"Mystery novels. You're never too old to write mystery novels," Violet said.

"Oh, I thought . . ." Poppy let her voice trail off, suddenly embarrassed.

"What did you think she was talking about?" Iris asked.

"I thought you were suggesting that I try my hand at actual detective work," Poppy said softly.

Iris and Violet looked at one another and burst into roars of laughter.

"You mean literally solve crimes out in the field, not in front of your computer?" Iris managed to get out between guffaws. "Oh, honey, that's a good one!"

Poppy chose to laugh along with her girlfriends.

She couldn't blame them.

It was an absurd and wacky idea.

And yet, as her two best friends finally calmed down from all the hilarity and summarily dismissed the idea before moving on to the topic of where the three of them should have lunch, Poppy just couldn't seem to shake it.

In fact, after salads at Spencer's, Poppy drove straight home and began to research on her laptop how one actually became a private investigator in the state of California.

She told herself she was just Googling it for fun.

But by the time she crawled into bed that night, having filled out the preliminary application on-line, she knew on some deep level, a serious plan had just been set in motion.

Chapter 8

When he opened the door of his cabin on Big Bear Mountain, Poppy swore she was staring into the face of the ruggedly handsome Sam Elliott, with his bushy mustache, silver hair, lanky build, and laid-back, laconic charm. She had met the actor when she landed a small role in a 1981 TV miniseries called *Murder in Texas*, based on a true story about a plastic surgeon (a sexy, shaggy-haired Sam, in his midthirties at the time) who murdered his wife (the iconic Farrah Fawcett) in order to marry his mistress (played by Sam's real-life spouse, Katharine Ross). The lovable sheriff Andy Taylor himself, Andy Griffith, played Farrah's father, who was determined to prove his scheming son-in-law had offed his beloved daughter, and his performance garnered Griffith his only Emmy nomination in a long, storied career. Anyway, Poppy had a tiny role, barely seen in the final cut, but she'd been struck by Sam's winning personality during the four days she spent on the set.

And here he stood now, right in front of her.

But she knew this was not the real Sam Elliott.

This was another Sam from her past, one who simply bore a striking resemblance.

This was Sam Emerson, the ex-lawyer and private eye who had worked as a producer for three seasons on her TV show *Jack Colt, PI.*

Sam stepped back, mouth agape, as he looked Poppy up and down. "My God, Poppy. You haven't aged a bit."

"I'm sorry to hear you have cataracts, Sam," Poppy laughed as she threw out her arms and the two embraced.

"Damn. How long has it been?"

"Gosh, must be going on thirty years now."

"I was so surprised when I got your message on Facebook," Sam said, leaning back to take her in some more, his arms still clasped around her. "I can't stand the whole social media thing, but my grandkids insist I stay connected to the world. Personally, I'd be happy just dealing with the bears and squirrels and raccoons and the rest of the wildlife I live with up here."

Poppy leaned back as she smiled at him. He gazed into her eyes. His bright green eyes were hypnotic. She felt a wee bit awkward once she realized she was still in his embrace, his hands dangerously close to resting on her butt. He must have sensed her discomfort, because he suddenly released his grip and waved her into the cabin.

The interior of the cabin was rustic but tidy, with only a few hints of civilization, including a laptop computer and a small TV and DVD player. There was a loft with an unmade bed, the kitchen was tiny but serviceable, and there was a massive fireplace with a stack of burnt wood, crackling with the last embers of a fire that was quickly dying out.

Poppy had been to Big Bear only once, when she had a girls' weekend with Iris and Violet. They had rented a cabin and had intended to go skiing, but they'd wound up reading dime-store romance novels, drinking wine, and spending most of their time lounging and gossiping in the hot tub on the wooden deck, even as a snowstorm raged around them.

After she contacted Sam and he invited her up to see him, she'd dreaded the long hour-and-a-half drive straight up a mountain from Palm Springs. But she was on a mission and was not to be deterred. Sam didn't even bother to ask why she had written him out of the blue, and by the look on his face now, he simply didn't care. He was just happy to see her.

"Can I offer you a drink? It may look like I don't have much up here, but I'm never without a fully stocked bar," he said.

"Maybe a glass of wine," Poppy said.

"Red or white?"

"Whatever you have."

Sam opened a bottle of pinot noir, poured two glasses, and led her onto the porch, with its breathtaking view of the lake, which was just bouncing back after a long drought, and the seemingly endless surrounding forest.

They sat down in rocking chairs and spent the first twenty minutes talking about everyone connected to *Jack Colt, PI*—the cast, the crew, the memorable guest stars, those who had passed away, the ones who were still working in Hollywood, and all the people who had fallen off the map, living quieter lives as far away from the crushing glare of show business as they possibly could, which, of course, included Sam himself.

Sam told her that he had made enough money writing scripts for TV to buy his cabin and that he had a modest income from his Writers Guild pension to pay his bills. He saw no need to travel the world at this point, having seen most of it during his younger years. He was perfectly content hunting and fishing and skiing up here in the mountains.

"What about you?" he asked. "You still married to . . . what's-his-name?"

"Chester."

"Yeah, Chester. Sweet guy, as I remember. How is he?"

"Dead."

Sam rocked back in his chair. "Oh, I'm sorry."

There was a brief lull in the conversation as he took a sip of his wine, and all they could hear were the birds and the crickets ardently making their presence known in the surrounding nature.

Poppy took a deep breath and explained everything she had gone through the past two months.

She could see on Sam's face that he was more curious to hear about why she had come all the way up here to see him.

Was she looking to rekindle something that was long in the past?

Yes, it was true he and Poppy had dined together many times during the run of the show and, on several occasions, after too much wine, had stumbled into bed together.

Oh no.

Poppy suddenly panicked, afraid she was giving the wrong impression. Here they were, drinking wine together, which had precipitated their hookups four decades ago.

She quickly set her wineglass down on the wooden coffee table between them, which he had probably carved and built himself.

"I should probably explain why I came all the way up here . . . ," Poppy said after clearing her throat.

Sam leaned back in his chair again, a peaceful look on his face, his eyes twinkling, as if he was sending the message that if she really wanted to go back there, he was game.

"I need to get a job in order to support myself, so I've decided to become a private investigator."

She could tell Sam had not expected to hear this. She waited for him to break out laughing, like Iris and Violet did when she first proposed the idea, but he didn't. He nodded, thought about it, and then said, "I think you'd be very good at it."

Poppy wanted to jump in his lap and kiss him.

Which he probably would not have minded.

But she resisted the urge.

Still, this was the first person who had anything encouraging to say about her decision. Not that she had shared the idea with many people. Outside of Iris and Violet and her lawyer, Edwin Pierce, everyone in her life was basically in the dark, including her daughter, Heather, who was too wrapped up in her new romance with the irritating wannabe actor to care all that much what her mother was up to.

"I passed the exam with flying colors, and I borrowed the money from my friends to pay for the license. The only thing left to do on my to-do list is find someone who will vouch for my practical experience."

"What kind of practical experience are we talking about?"

"I have to have three years of paid investigative work if I don't have a law degree or an associate's degree in criminal justice or police science."

"I'm guessing after Hollywood, you didn't have a second career studying criminal law."

"No. And I don't have the luxury of going back to school. But I do have three years of paid investigative work."

"You have experience working for a PI?"

"Well, you were technically still a private investigator when you wrote on *Jack Colt*, right?"

"Yes. What are you getting at?"

"Well, the show lasted three seasons, so that's three years, and I was paid. . . ."

"As an actress playing the secretary of a fake private eye. I wouldn't count that as real, practical experience."

"Yes, but you were a real one, and I helped you solve many cases."

"Those were pretend cases I dreamed up for scripts!"

"Many of which were based on actual crimes you personally investigated. There is a case to be made that during your time as a writer on the show, you were still solving cases as a fully licensed investigator, and so . . ."

Poppy reached into her bag and produced a piece of paper. She carefully set it down on the wooden coffee table, along with a ballpoint pen.

"What's that?"

"It's a form I need to submit to the licensing board, stating that I was under your employ for three years, assisting you in your investigative work."

Sam stared at the piece of paper and shook his head, smiling.

"You're really serious about this, aren't you?"

"It's my only option at this point, and I can't do it without your help."

Sam didn't move at first. She could tell he was mulling over the ramifications of signing the paper. He glanced over at Poppy, who sat still, holding her breath, waiting for him to decide if he was going to help her out or not.

Then, after winking at her, he leaned forward, picked up the pen, and scribbled his signature.

Poppy let out a huge sigh of relief.

"Oh, Sam, thank you. You have no idea how much this means to me."

"Anything for you, Poppy. Now, how about some more wine?"

"I better not. I have to drive down that long, curvy mountain road, and it's almost dark."

"You can't leave yet. If you're going to be a private investigator, you're going to have to show me you can shoot."

"A gun?"

Sam stood up. "Come on. I got a sexy Smith & Wesson in my cabinet with your name on it."

"No! Honestly, Sam, I couldn't! I hate guns! I

could never actually shoot anything, especially a live animal or a person! I could never live with myself!"

"You never know. You may have to in your new line of work."

"Forget it, Sam. I just don't have it in me."

"You'd be surprised. Now relax. I'm not suggesting we go out back and shoot a squirrel out of the trees. I have some empty beer cans I can line up on the woodpile for you to aim at."

Sam took her by the arm and guided her back into the cabin. She had never thought about actually using a firearm. Taking some pictures with her phone of a cheating spouse was more her speed.

But remarkably, despite her apprehension, within twenty minutes she was out in the woods, with Sam standing so close behind her she could feel his hot breath on the back of her neck, his arms wrapped around her as he guided her aim. She had one eye closed, both hands wrapped around the pistol, her finger on the trigger. Sam gently released his grip and stepped back and whispered, "Anytime you're ready!"

She fired her first shot. The bullet hit the beer can, sending it hurtling into the air. She shot again and again and again, taking out all four beer cans, adrenaline coursing through her veins like when she bowled three strikes in a row with the girls last week.

"You're a natural!" Sam laughed.

She couldn't believe she had such an accurate aim.

By the time she said good-bye to Sam and drove back down the mountain, she was already planning to download an application for a permit and make an appointment at the local firing range.

Not that she expected to ever need a gun.

But having one in her new job might be smart safety insurance.

And it didn't hurt that Sam was turned on when she got all Annie Oakley on him.

Chapter 9

Poppy slipped out of her clothes and stuffed them in the wicker clothes hamper basket in her walk-in closet. She pulled her favorite Eileen West Moonlight Sonata nightgown off a wooden top hanger and shimmied into it before stepping into her cushiony spa thong slippers.

And then she stood there, staring at the rack of clothing on the left-hand side of the closet, which had belonged to Chester. Four business suits, twelve button-up, short-sleeved shirts, nine dress shirts in various colors, six pairs of casual slacks draped over hangers. On the floor some polished fancy shoes; a cruddy pair of sneakers for puttering around in the backyard; two sets of deck shoes, one gray and one tan; and two different pairs of leather sandals. Pretty much Chester's entire wardrobe, besides a drawer full of underwear and a shelf stacked with five different brands of khaki shorts and ten T-shirts.

She stepped forward, closer to her husband's

hanging shirts, until her nose practically touched the fabric on a light purple golf shirt.

She breathed in deeply.

There it was.

Her husband's distinctive scent.

She yanked one of the shirts off its hanger and brought it up to her face and closed her eyes. It was as if Chester was there in the closet with her at that moment, standing right in front of her, calming her with his puppy dog eyes and warm, reassuring smile.

Poppy knew she would have to clear out Chester's clothing at some point, but she had kept putting it off, waiting until the escrow on the house closed and she was forced to move. In the meantime, she just honestly wasn't ready yet to part with the last of her husband's belongings.

Shortly after Chester's funeral, Poppy had run into a woman she often golfed with at the club. The woman had sadly lost her husband late the previous year. Her frank advice to Poppy was, "Don't waste too much time. You should pack up his things and donate them to Goodwill as soon as possible. What's the point in leaving constant reminders in front of you? It just allows the grief to linger."

She insisted it was best to move on as quickly as possible and go on living the rest of your life.

Despite her good intentions, Poppy found that advice cruel and unfeeling.

She and Chester had been married for almost twenty years.

Perhaps the whole "Stay calm and carry on" theory worked for her friend, but Poppy couldn't just erase all evidence of Chester's existence. Not yet. They had shared too much. And she wasn't prepared to let him go so soon, especially given how suddenly he had been taken away from her.

Poppy padded out of the closet and over to Chester's side of the bed, where she plopped down on the plush comforter and stared at the half-read book on the nightstand. It was a James Patterson novel. One of his heart-stomping, page-turning serial killer thrillers. Although Poppy read her detective novels on her iPad, Chester had insisted on holding a real book, with the creased paperback cover and dog-eared pages. She flipped through the book to page 263, where Chester had left off and wedged a custom bookmark that said FELL ASLEEP HERE into the binding.

Poppy giggled.

She desperately missed Chester's silly sense of humor.

It depressed her to think he would never know how the book ended, although, as with most of Patterson's stories, the beleaguered detective would win the day and the depraved killer would almost certainly be vanquished. And when Poppy had pointed that out to Chester, he would always answer with one of his typical trademark clichés, such as "It's not about what's at the end, but how you get there."

Poppy opened the drawer of the nightstand.

She fingered Chester's passport, the pages stamped with the destinations of their travels together. France, Italy, Spain, Greece, Germany, Austria, Brazil, Argentina, Peru, Mexico, and just last year, Australia and New Zealand.

Chester loved to travel.

And there were so many more countries and cultures he had wanted to see and experience. It broke her heart that he was never going to make it to Prague or Budapest, both cities on the top of his list.

Underneath the passport was a birthday card from Poppy that he had kept from a couple of years ago. He treasured the sentiment she had written to him, that every day she got to spend with him was like a birthday of her own, a celebration with the best present in the world . . . him. Poppy remembered meaning every word when she wrote it.

It was not like they hadn't fought every so often or had their issues and individual idiosyncrasies. They both had sometimes needed a break from each other. Poppy's twice annual vacations with the girls, usually cruises to Mexico or the Bahamas and once even to Alaska, were key to the success of her marriage.

But by the end of the week, no matter where in the world she was, she would start missing Chester terribly and would be anxious to get home to him. And when she finally arrived back in Palm Springs and walked through the door of their home, he would always put on a good show, pretending he had enjoyed an amazingly relaxed week free of her henpecking. It was obvious, however, that he had been lost without her.

Once, when Violet asked Poppy to meet some friends at the club for drinks, one of the ladies had asked Poppy what the secret to her long-lasting happy marriage to Chester was. Poppy had jokingly replied, "Low expectations."

The line had got a huge laugh at the bar.

And on some level, there might have been a grain of truth to it.

But she hadn't really meant it.

She couldn't help but love the guy, which made the recent revelations about him so tough to handle.

She had thought she knew her husband better than anyone.

He was predictable and comfortable, not the type to suddenly surprise you. No, in her mind, he was a creature of habit, incapable of living some kind of double life behind her back.

But that was exactly what he did.

And it had totally blindsided her.

She picked up a cuff link she had given him last Christmas.

His initials, CH, were engraved on the front.

She pawed around for the other one but couldn't find it.

Maybe he had lost it and hadn't dared tell her.

She had always scolded him about his forgetfulness.

She couldn't remember a time they left the house when he didn't forget his wallet or keys.

Poppy could feel the tears welling up in her eyes. She tried to fight them back but failed and soon found herself bent over, wailing, barely able to catch her breath.

After a few minutes, exhausted from crying, she sat upright and looked up to heaven.

"Chester, how could you?"

She half expected him to answer, but of course, he didn't.

Then, after a few moments, she pulled the comforter down, crawled in between the sheets, and cried herself to sleep.

Chapter 10

When Poppy arrived at Iris's house on a quiet palm tree–lined residential street in the Smoke Tree section of South Palm Springs, she found taped to the front door a yellow Post-it note that read IN THE GARAGE. Poppy circled around the house and knocked on the side door to the garage.

She heard Iris shout, "Come in!"

When Poppy entered, she suddenly stopped in her tracks. There were no storage boxes or golf clubs or trash cans lining the walls. No grease spot on the floor where Iris parked her 2008 Chevy. The entire garage looked like an office, with three tabletop desks and swivel chairs set up on one side, along with laptop computers and filing cabinets. In the middle was a sitting area with a couch and chairs and a large flat-screen TV hanging on the wall. There was even a kitchenette in the back, complete with a Sub-Zero refrigerator, a long marble counter, and cupboards painted a soothing canary yellow. An air-conditioning unit hummed in the one window providing light.

Iris and Violet stood off to the side expectantly, with excited looks on their faces, as Poppy slowly closed the door behind her to keep the cool air inside and the oppressive ninety-nine-degree heat outside.

"Well, what do you think?" Violet squealed.

"It looks lovely," Poppy said, looking around. "Are you two starting some kind of business?"

Violet nodded and opened her mouth to blurt out the answer, but as usual, Iris beat her to the punch. "Yes, with you."

That was when Poppy noticed the sign hanging above one of the desks. On it was stenciled THE DESERT FLOWERS DETECTIVE AGENCY. Just below the name were three flower prints of an iris, a violet and, of course, a poppy.

"You want to be a part of my detective agency?" Poppy asked, stunned.

"Yes!" Violet exclaimed. "Isn't that wonderful?"

"Clearly, it is not," Iris spit out, insulted by Poppy's muted reaction. "She obviously hates the idea!"

"No, it's not that! I think what you've done here is remarkable and sweet, and I couldn't ask for more supportive friends. . . ."

"Brace yourself for a *but*, Violet, because here it comes . . ." Iris scoffed.

"But . . ." Poppy whispered.

"There it is!" Iris said, nodding.

"But you can't imagine how difficult it was to obtain a private investigator's license. Filling out hundreds of forms, studying for the exam, not to mention the years of practical experience you must have in order to even be considered . . ."

"So only one flower on the sign has an actual investigator's license. Big deal. That doesn't mean we can't gain practical experience on the job, working for you . . . who, as of this week, is a licensed detective," Iris said.

Poppy couldn't argue with Iris's logic.

In fact, she rarely could.

"Before I was a principal, I was a high school English teacher," Violet said proudly.

"How does that experience translate to detective work?" Poppy asked gently.

"Do you know how many stories and excuses I heard from my students? I became quite good at being able to tell who was lying and who was telling the truth."

"She's basically an expert on human behavior, which can be an asset in any kind of investigation. Plus, she has a master's in education, so it goes without saying she knows how to do extensive research," Iris said.

"And what about you?" Poppy asked, suddenly amused.

"I worked as a bookkeeper in my uncle's law firm in Munich during my summers while I was attending college, so I can help run the financial side of the business," Iris boasted, chest out. "And we all know I am always at the top of anyone's list who throws a party."

"Yes. You'll get no argument from me on that, but how . . . ?"

"I can charm people, get them to open up, tell me what's really going on. I have seen things and done things in my lifetime that no one else has ever experienced, and I will use that to draw people in so I get the information I want," Iris said, amazed that Poppy hadn't recognized this unique and valuable skill of hers long before now.

Iris put an arm around Violet. "You've got book smarts and street smarts. That's not a bad combination for a business like this."

"You two have really thought this through," Poppy said, still reticent but certainly intrigued with the idea of forming a team, especially with her two best friends.

"It's a no-brainer, Poppy," Iris said. "So hire us already so we can get to work."

"That's the problem. I have nothing to hire you with yet. I have no cases, and I certainly have no start-up money. I spent my last dime paying the fee for my license, and I still had to borrow most of it from you two."

"Not to worry! We will work for free," Violet offered.

"At least in the beginning!" Iris quickly interjected. "And then as you start to take on clients and collect your retainer fees, we can discuss splitting a percentage of the gross. Of course, as the licensed investigator, you will get most of the money, because, after all, this is your operation, not ours."

"You're the queen. We're just the worker bees!" Violet said.

Iris shot her an annoyed look. "I wouldn't go that far, Violet."

Poppy glanced at the three flowers on the sign.

Iris. Violet. Poppy.

In that order.

"We put all three of us on the sign only because the flowers looked so pretty next to each other, right, Violet?"

"Right. And also, you said it would save us money replacing the sign down the road, once we got our own investigator's licenses."

Iris glared at Violet.

"And you don't mind me working out of your garage?" Poppy asked, looking around, impressed by the detail they had put into the office.

"Of course not! It was my idea!" Iris replied. "You can't meet with clients at your place, wherever that may be. The last thing you need is for them to know where you live. And once we are . . . I mean, you are successful, then we can talk about you paying a monthly rental fee for this office space."

Suddenly, it appeared as if Iris had been thinking about this crazy plan for a while. Ever since Poppy first confided to them that she might be serious about this whole private-eye scheme.

The idea of her two best friends being on call to back her up, being around so she could bounce theories off them, and helping her with the legwork sounded infinitely reassuring. Both Iris and Violet were a calming influence, she trusted them and, hell, they always had fun together. And three of them working a case was definitely better than one. Not to mention that old saying "There's safety in numbers."

Poppy's hesitation about involving the two of them in this new endeavor slowly began to melt away, and with a grin on her face, she walked over to the largest desk and sat down. "Okay, then let's get to work."

"That's my desk," Iris said quietly.

Violet threw her an exasperated look. "Iris . . ."

Iris shot back, "I thought she'd want the one

nearest to the window. It's fine! I'll move my things to that one!"

Poppy was flushed with an enthusiasm she hadn't felt since long before Chester died as Iris gathered up her pens and knickknacks and framed photographs of herself with famous people and carried them over to the smaller desk by the window.

The Desert Flowers Detective Agency was officially open for business.

And three weeks later, they still had not received one inquiring call or e-mail that might lead to an honest-to-goodness case.

Chapter 11

Poppy had never seen Heather so furious, not even when she was sixteen and Poppy caught her smoking pot and immediately grounded her, which forced Heather to miss the big homecoming dance at her high school, where she was crowned homecoming queen in absentia after a landslide victory. Heather accused her mother of cruelly robbing her of an adolescent memory that she would have cherished for the rest of her life. Thanks to her mother's unnecessarily harsh sentencing for such a tiny infraction, now she would never get to experience the thrill of accepting her crown to the adulating applause of her peers. If Heather had inherited one trait from her mother, it was her flair for overdramatizing.

But that little dustup almost fifteen years ago was nothing compared to what was unfolding at Poppy's house today.

Heather had shown up at the door, waving a *Pennysaver* she had picked up at the supermarket while shopping for dinner. Inside, while scouring the rag for coupons, she had come across a small corner ad touting a new private investigation firm, the Desert Flowers Detective Agency, which had recently opened its doors in Palm Springs. She might have brushed right past it if the e-mail address hadn't caught her eye. It belonged to her mother, as did the accompanying phone number.

When she called Poppy on her cell phone from the parking lot, fearing her mother's contact information might have somehow been hacked, her mother confirmed the news, albeit reluctantly, that she had opened up shop as a local private eye. After hearing a brief scream and a scuffle, Poppy asked her daughter if she was still on the line. Heather claimed her mother's bombshell announcement had nearly killed her as she had carelessly stepped off the curb and in front of a car, almost getting run over.

Poppy sighed, knowing her daughter was probably slightly exaggerating, and steeled herself for the inevitable showdown that was soon to come.

In fact, it kicked off twenty minutes later, which was the length of time it took for Heather to jump behind the wheel of her own car and race over to her mother's house.

And now, standing in the living room, her face wild with fury, Heather had not taken a breath since her mother had opened the door and ushered her in the house, because she had not stopped yelling.

"I don't know what could have possessed you to believe you were remotely qualified to do something like this! Mother, this is not some TV show where a highly paid writer feeds you clever lines or tells you where to look for clues. This is a real, serious line of work, one that takes a lot of brainpower and deductive reasoning and a degree of physical strength."

Poppy tried to ignore the fact that her daughter was basically saying she was borderline stupid, lacked any kind of logical thought process, and was hopelessly out of shape.

Poppy bit her lip and forced herself to stand there silently and take it.

She should at least give Heather the opportunity to release all her pent-up anger before diving in and stating her case.

"Honestly, I'm worried about you. Every therapist I've ever been to has told me never to make any major life decision for at least two years after the death of a spouse or loved one. Chester's been gone only a couple of months! Have you gone off the deep end? Are you so consumed with grief that you're experiencing some sort of psychotic break?"

Poppy waited a few moments to make absolutely sure that it wasn't a rhetorical question and that Heather was actually waiting for her to answer before she responded. "Actually, I've never felt more focused and alive in my whole life."

Heather slumped, like a punctured tire fast losing air. "Oh, Mother . . ."

"I'm not in this alone. Iris and Violet are helping. . . ."

"I suspected it was Iris and Violet who put you up to this crazy idea. Sometimes they're not exactly the best influence. . . ."

Best influence?

Poppy didn't appreciate the role reversal her daughter was engaging in, treating her like some wayward, impossibly impetuous teenager.

"I've done nothing wrong."

"Then why did you hide it from me?"

"I didn't hide anything. . . ."

"We talk at least two times a week. Not once did you mention you were training and studying to be a private detective! I probably would have remembered if you had casually brought it up in conversation!"

"Okay, I didn't tell you, because I expected this reaction, and I was afraid it might scare me off from seeing it through."

"Why, Mother? What's really going on here? You must have some reason you're doing this! What is it?"

Poppy hesitated, reading her daughter, knowing she was never going to stop until she knew the whole unvarnished truth.

"Does it have anything to do with Chester's debts?"

She had told Heather about her stepfather's financial crisis shortly after their dinner at Las Casuelas.

Chester's gambling problem.

A mountain of debt that was going to have to be paid back.

But she couldn't bring herself to let Heather know just how dire the situation was, and so she'd omitted key information, that she was on the verge of bankruptcy, that she was going to lose the house any day now, and that Heather's inheritance had been obliterated.

She'd thought doling out the bad news in increments would somehow soften the blow.

But then she began studying for her PI license, and Heather was preoccupied with her egotist boyfriend, so they hardly saw each other, and then as time wore on, it became more difficult to tell her, and so she left it on the back burner.

"I'm broke," Poppy whispered.

"Oh, Mother, don't be such a drama queen!"

"I'm dead serious, Heather. In fact, when I knew you were coming over, I ran outside and took the FOR SALE sign off the front yard and hid it in the garage."

This finally got Heather's attention.

"You what . . . ?"

"Chester didn't just rack up a few gambling debts. He completely wiped us out."

Heather's eyes grew wide and round as she processed this news. Her bottom lip quivered slightly, and by the time she used her index finger to draw away a few stray strands of hair from in front of her face, her complexion was a ghostly white.

"I don't understand. . . ."

"There's nothing left."

"But the trust fund he set up for me when you two married, that's still there, right? I mean, he couldn't have . . ."

"He cleaned it out."

Heather stumbled over to the couch and sat down. She wrapped her arms across her chest and rocked back and forth as a flood of tears streamed down her face.

"I can't believe he would do such a thing. . . ."

Poppy trailed after her daughter and sat down next to her, then put a comforting arm around her and kissed her cheek. "It's going to be all right. We'll both be fine."

She knew once Heather had time to think about

everything, she would get angry at her for conceal-
ing the whole truth for so long, but until then, she
would try to be a rock of support for her daughter.

After ten minutes of feeling sorry for herself and
worrying about her own future, Heather turned
her attention to her mother, who had also been so
severely wronged.

"Where are you going to live?"

Poppy shrugged. "I'm sure I'll find something."

"You can come live with me."

"Your apartment is too small for the both of us.
I can stay with Iris or Violet, at least until I can afford to get my own place."

"But you're my mother. It's my responsibility to
take care of you in your old age . . . ," Heather
said, choking on the words, consumed with guilt.

"Okay, first of all, you need to retract that last
statement about old age, because I will not have
you talking to me that way," Poppy said, only half
joking.

"I'm sorry, but it's not fair. You shouldn't have
to worry about money in your golden years. . . ."

"Golden years? Again, not a term that is going
to boost my morale!"

"You're right! You're still young enough to start
over," Heather said, choosing a path of measured
optimism.

"That's right!"

"But a private detective? Oh, Mother . . ."

That was her girl.

Take the path of optimism and then veer right
to Negativity Road.

"Do you really think you're going to make ends
meet that way? I mean, even Jessica Fletcher had
her mystery novels to fall back on."

"Why don't you let me worry about making it work, okay? You concentrate on your own life. Your job, your boy-friend . . ."

That boyfriend.

Matt Cameron.

Poppy's greatest fear was that the self-possessed, long-winded, good-looking cad Heather had so recklessly fallen head over heels with would flee the scene once it became known that she would no longer be an heiress to a small but comfortable fortune someday, after both her parents finally passed.

And Poppy once again would have to be there to pick up the pieces.

Was she being fair to her daughter's budding romance?

Probably not.

Was she convinced she was right?

Absolutely, without a doubt.

Chapter 12

Poppy stared at the twelve-year-old boy standing in front of her. He kept wiping his nose with his finger and blinking his watery eyes. His spindly, skinny legs were like sticks protruding from his oversize cargo shorts, fastened tight around his waist with a scuffed brown belt. A chocolate-stained orange T-shirt was draped over his tiny bony frame, and on the front of it was printed if history repeats itself, i'm getting a dinosaur! He was suffering from a cold and clearly wanted to be anywhere else, and he hung closely to Violet, who beamed as she introduced him to Poppy and Iris.

"I just cannot believe you have never met my grandson Wyatt, but he rarely visits from LA. He's so busy with school and his friends, and no matter how much I whine and plead, I get to see him only once or twice a year!"

"Stop it, Maw-Maw . . ." the boy murmured into her side.

"He's a bit shy," Violet explained.

"Maw-Maw?" Iris asked with a decidedly raised eyebrow.

"That's what he's called me ever since he was a baby. Isn't it cute?"

Poppy flashed a look at Iris, warning her to keep her opinion to herself, and for once, Iris surprisingly obeyed and kept mum.

"Well, it's nice to meet you, Wyatt," Poppy said, stepping forward and extending her hand.

She instantly regretted it when Wyatt begrudgingly shook her hand and she noticed his fingernails were caked with dirt and his hands were covered in gooey snot. Wyatt suddenly sneezed and didn't bother using his free hand to cover his mouth.

Poppy ducked to avoid the kid's saliva shower and quickly withdrew her hand, then slowly backed away. "I'm sure Wyatt is a lovely boy and gets very good grades, but I'm still confused about why you think he is what we need to jump-start our business."

"I am an expert in all the latest wiretapping and hacking techniques," Wyatt boasted, straight-faced and businesslike.

And then he sneezed again, startling Iris, who struggled not to order him out of her garage before he spread his nasty germs to all of them.

Violet fished in the pocket of her white shorts and pulled out a small package of Kleenex. She yanked one out of the plastic opening and handed it to her grandson.

"He's very tech savvy," Violet said, beaming with pride.

"Well, we're a very low-tech operation, and I'm

not sure when we would need someone to hack into someone's computer," Poppy said, locking eyes with Violet, who ignored her pleas to stop this well-rehearsed sales pitch.

"Let's say you're hired by some old lady to find out if her husband's cheating," Wyatt said, irritated that he had to make a case for his mad skills. "With just a few strokes of the keys on my laptop, I can have all his texts and e-mails and every app on his smartphone up on this screen for you to look at in minutes. You can find out who he is secretly talking to without ever leaving this office."

"Okay, that sounds impressive," Poppy agreed. "But it also sounds illegal."

"Every private investigation firm needs a surveillance division if it's going to be taken seriously," Wyatt said. "I just do what the U.S. government and all the Internet and phone corporations already do to us every day . . . monitor our communications."

"So you're twelve?" Iris asked, not quite believing it.

Wyatt nodded. "You also have no online presence. Maw-Maw showed me the sad ad you put in the supermarket *Pennysaver*. That's not going to draw any clients willing to put up real money to hire you."

"What do you suggest?" Iris wanted to know, suddenly intrigued.

"I already designed you a Web site and opened Desert Flowers Facebook and Twitter accounts," Wyatt said.

"You did what?" Poppy gasped. "Now everyone is going to know what I'm up to!"

"That's the whole point, Poppy," Violet said excitedly. "We need to raise our profile and get our name out there."

"Wait until you see the site I designed. It's totally awesome and interactive." Wyatt smiled. "Normally, you would pay something like five thousand bucks for a site like this."

"We can't pay you even close to that," Poppy said.

"No worries." Wyatt shrugged, just like his grandmother. "You can give me a cut, like you will with Maw-Maw and Aunt Iris, once your billing system is up and running."

"I'm not your aunt." Iris glowered at him.

"Yeah, but it's okay if I call you that, right?"

"No," Iris said flatly. "You can call me Ms. Becker."

Wyatt nodded, chastised. He obviously wasn't intimidated by much, but Iris was an exception. The kid turned back to Poppy, and after another brief sneezing fit and blowing his nose into the wadded-up Kleenex, he continued.

"Your Facebook and Twitter accounts went live this morning. I posted a few articles about some of the cases the agency has recently solved, and you already have ten inquiries from potential clients."

"But we haven't solved any cases!" Poppy cried.

"Fake news doesn't work just for the Russians," Wyatt said matter-of-factly.

"Mark my words, this kid is going to be working for the NSA someday," Iris said, shaking her head.

"I don't feel right about any of this!" Poppy said before whipping around and staring down Wyatt. "I want you to shut it all down until we've had a chance to thoroughly discuss this."

Violet gulped. "That may be a problem."

"Why?" Poppy moaned.

."We have a consultation with a client scheduled in five minutes."

"What?"

"I wanted to surprise you," Violet said sheepishly, only now considering the downside to her actions. "His name is—"

"Call him right now and cancel before he gets here!"

"Mrs. Harmon, I'm confused. Maw-Maw said you wanted to make money as a private investigator to help dig yourself out of debt," Wyatt said.

"You told him all that?" Poppy said, spinning on her heel to confront Violet.

Violet shrugged, guilty as charged.

Poppy turned back to the kid. "Yes, Wyatt, I do," she sighed. "But this is all happening so fast, and I've never actually investigated a real case before, and I basically lied about my practical experience, and now this whole thing feels like a really bad, misguided idea. Maybe Heather was right."

There was a knock at the side door of the garage.

"That's him," Violet said. "What do I tell him?"

"Tell him there's been a mistake, and send him away," Poppy pleaded.

"No," Iris said. "This is my house, and I can invite in whomever I please."

"Iris!"

"We might as well hear what he has to say. If it sounds too difficult or if he is some kind of nut job, we will just send him away," Violet said.

Iris bounded over to the door and swung it open.

A wiry, skittish young man with dark glasses and a high forehead, dressed in a formless red T-shirt and khaki shorts that rested below the band of his Hanes underwear, stood there. He was short, about a foot smaller than Iris, and stared up at her commanding figure.

"Is this the Desert Flowers Detective Agency?"

"Yes. I am Iris Becker, and that is Poppy Harmon and Violet Hogan, and the kid is our tech supervisor, Wyatt something or other," Iris said.

"Wait, you three are the Desert Flowers?" the young man asked, eyes widening.

"Yes. Are you deaf? Iris Becker, Poppy Harmon, and Violet Hogan. Now get in here. The open door is sucking out all the cool air," she commanded.

"Is this some kind of joke?" he asked, frowning.

"Do I look like I joke?" Iris asked, towering over him and glaring down at his incredulous face. "Now, how can we help you?"

"Forget it! You three old bags should be sued for false advertising on your Web site!" the man yelled before turning around and storming off, stopping only once to hike up his shorts, which had shimmied all the way down to his knees.

"What was that all about?" Poppy asked.

"And who is he calling an old bag?" Iris spit out.

"I may have exaggerated a few things on the Web site to get some people in the door," Wyatt said.

"Show me that Web site right now, young man," Poppy demanded.

Wyatt once again shrugged just like his grandmother Violet and flipped open his laptop as he set it down on Poppy's desk. Once he typed in his password, he brought up the home page for the Desert Flowers Detective Agency Web site.

Poppy stumbled back with a start. Three young, gorgeous girls with California tans—and wearing teeny, tiny string bikinis, one pink, one yellow, and one kelly green; sporting matching right-shoulder tattoos; and identifying themselves in cursive script as Poppy, Iris, and Violet—smiled and waved in a picture underneath the company logo and contact information.

"Dear God, what have you done?" Poppy whispered.

"Hey, sex sells!" Wyatt exclaimed, staring happily at his handiwork.

Iris turned to Violet. "Did you know about this?"

"No! I swear!" Violet shouted. "Wyatt, sweetheart, that young man is right. This is false advertising."

"This is going to get people to show up here, and maybe nine out of ten will turn around and leave because they were expecting hot babes to take care of their needs. . . ."

"That sounds dirty for a twelve-year-old," Iris said.

"But trust me, there will be one who will stick around and lay out what he wants you to investigate, and it only takes one to get things going."

The kid made sense.

But it was an utterly humiliating way to conduct business, and Poppy's ego was not willing to endure it, especially after years of playing an object of male desire in a string of television shows and movies.

"Shut it down," Poppy said. "Now."

"Fine," Wyatt huffed, clicking keys on his computer.

Violet hugged her grandson from behind. "I'm very proud of you for being so enterprising, dear, but you just went about it the wrong way."

"Whatever," Wyatt scowled.

"Before you shut it down, print me out that list of inquiries from potential clients," Iris said.

"Why?" Poppy asked.

"I'm going to call everyone left on that list and explain to them what happened, and if they want to see a real photo of us, I'll show them the one of us on vacation last year, bodysurfing in Maui, so they get a clear picture of who to expect, and if any of them still want to sit down with us, I'm setting up an appointment."

"Iris, no, I couldn't . . ." Poppy objected.

"Stop being a negative Nellie, Poppy," Iris barked. "This whole private-eye scheme was your idea. If we want to make it work, we're going to have to get creative. The kid is right. It only takes one."

Poppy wanted to argue.

But deep down she knew they were right.

The point for a new business was finding customers.

And maybe that was going to take a little creativity.

Chapter 13

When Poppy read in *The Guide*, a magazine chronicling Palm Springs life, months ago that Oscar-winning actress and popular 1970s sit-com star Shirley Fox was bringing her cabaret act to the Purple Room on East Palm Canyon Drive, she had immediately gone online and purchased two tickets for her and Chester. Chester was a huge fan, and Poppy had thought dinner and a show starring one of his favorite performers from the past would be a nice birthday gift. She had forgotten all about the tickets until she happened to be driving past the Purple Room and saw Shirley's name and the show dates on the marquee.

Instead of wasting the tickets, Poppy had invited Heather to join her. She hadn't seen much of her daughter, since she had been so focused on obtaining her investigator's license. Plus, she knew Heather's feelings about the whole enterprise, so she hadn't felt much like receiving another lecture from her strongly opinionated daughter.

Still, she'd felt guilty for not spending more time

with Heather, so she'd called her a few days before
and invited her to join her for the show. Heather
barely knew who Shirley Fox was, except for a
vague memory of catching a few episodes of her
family sitcom late at night on Nickelodeon when
she was a teenager.

Heather insisted on picking her mother up instead of meeting at the venue, and Poppy feared
she wanted to lay into her one more time about
her reckless decision to become a private eye, but
mercifully, Heather didn't bring it up and instead
prattled on about how happy she was dating her
perfectly wonderful actor boyfriend, Matt.

Poppy smiled evenly, nodded, trying her hardest to be supportive, but she still couldn't shake
the feeling that this Matt character was an untrust-
worthy lout who was going to somehow take advantage of her blind-with-love daughter and leave
her heartbroken in the end. Of course, she had no
concrete proof of Matt's motives, but she herself
had dated enough men in her lifetime to harbor a
natural suspicion. Especially when it came to actors.

When Poppy and Heather arrived at the Purple
Room and were waiting to be seated at the hostess
station, Poppy marveled at a framed poster of
Shirley Fox, still gorgeous at seventy-five years old,
her ample bosom nearly popping out of a skintight
black ruffled gown, her platinum blond hair swept
up, and her face, though caked with makeup, still
vibrant and alive. Her hand was raised, and her
crooked finger beckoned her audience to come
inside and be entertained.

Poppy couldn't help but feel a slight pang of jeal-
ousy. Shirley was still going strong after all these

years. Granted, she didn't have much of a choice. She had weathered a stormy life, despite her storied career, with many ups and downs, loves found and lost, fortunes earned and squandered away by disreputable business managers and greedy ex-husbands. In fact, her bad choices in men were the primary reason she was still on the road, hustling to earn a paycheck by playing cabaret rooms like this one all over the country. But despite the fact that she still had to work, Shirley was beholden to no one now and was lucky enough to be making a decent living.

Perhaps if Poppy had persevered like that, not married the first man who promised to take care of her, whispering in her ear that she would never want for anything in life ever again, if she hadn't fallen for that fantasy hook, line, and sinker, she might not be in the dire situation she found herself in now.

The hostess led Poppy and Heather to a table for four, set down three menus, and told them to enjoy the show.

Poppy glanced at Heather, confused. "I didn't know we were going to have to share a table with two more people. That's odd," Poppy said.

"We're not," Heather said, scooping up a menu and rifling through it, purposely not making eye contact with her mother. "There's only one more joining us. I called and ordered a ticket for Matt."

"Oh," Poppy said, disappointed.

So much for some quality time with her daughter.

"He loves Shirley Fox!"

"I'm surprised he even knows who she is. He

wasn't even born when her TV show was on the air."

"He is a movie buff and a huge fan of her films from the late fifties and sixties, when she was an up-and-coming musical star."

"I see," Poppy said.

"Are you mad at me for inviting him?"

"No, of course not," Poppy lied, then swallowed hard before she finally spit out, "He's your boyfriend."

Poppy looked over her menu to see the hostess leading Matt toward them. There was a handsome older gentleman, close to Poppy's age, trailing behind them.

"There he is," Poppy said, feigning enthusiasm.

After all, she was an actress and could feign many moods and emotions.

"Hi, baby," Matt crowed, then bent down to plant a long, wet kiss on Heather's lips before springing back up and touching the hostess underneath her right elbow. "We're going to need another chair."

Poppy and Heather turned to look at the older gentleman with slicked-back gray hair and a welcoming face with just enough lines to make him distinguished. He was nicely dressed in a polo shirt and slacks.

"This is Buddy Rhodes," Matt said, slapping him on the back. "We're doing a show together here in Palm Springs. I hope you don't mind me inviting him to join us."

"No, not at all," Poppy lied.

"No," Heather echoed, lying just like her mother.

The hostess returned with a fourth chair, and the two men sat down. Matt instinctively reached over and placed his hand over Heather's and squeezed it. She smiled and winked at him, although she was still a bit discombobulated by the stranger who had joined them.

Buddy turned to Poppy. "Matt and I bonded over our love of Shirley Fox, so you can imagine how I jumped at the chance to come tonight when he told me she was in town performing."

"Luckily, they had a cancellation," Matt said, patting Buddy on the back.

"Well, it's nice to meet you, Buddy," Poppy said.

"Oh, we've met before," he said with a sly smile.

"We have?"

"About thirty years ago. On the set of *Jack Colt*. I had a bit part playing a surfer dude in the two-hour season premiere set in Hawaii, when you and Jack fly to Honolulu to find his missing Vietnam war buddy."

"I played a surfer early in my career, too, Buddy!" Matt felt the need to add.

Poppy studied Buddy closely. "I'm sorry. I don't remember."

"Well, like I said, it was a bit part. And you had all the big-name guest stars swarming around you, demanding your attention. I remember staring at you from afar as I waxed my surfboard between takes, thinking you were the most exquisite woman I had ever laid eyes on, and now seeing you after all these years, I can't say I've changed my mind."

He was laying it on pretty thick.

And Poppy, unsurprisingly, didn't seem to mind.

There certainly was no harm in receiving an admiring man's compliments.

Heather, however, appeared rankled and annoyed by the whole situation, and when the two men picked up their menus to peruse the dinner choices, she leaned over and whispered in her mother's ear, "I swear I knew nothing about this."

"It's okay," Poppy said with a reassuring smile.

"I could use a drink," Buddy said, scanning the room for the waitress.

Heather used the distraction to rip her hand out from underneath Matt's and whisper angrily, "How could you think this was a good idea? Chester has been gone only a few months."

"I don't know what you're talking about. Buddy's just a friend of mine. There's no matchmaking going on here," Matt said. But the grin on his face clearly betrayed his true intentions. He definitely had orchestrated a fix-up and was proud of it.

Matt turned away from Heather and focused on Poppy, who sat frozen in place, suddenly uncomfortable at the idea of being on a date.

"Buddy and I are starring in a murder mystery at the Palm Springs Playhouse. I play the dogged detective caught in a snowstorm at a country estate, and Buddy here is the family patriarch, who may have drowned his wife in the bathtub, although the house is full of other suspects."

"Sounds very Agatha Christie," Poppy said.

"My favorite author," Buddy said, piping in. "Pure genius. I've read every novel, play, and short story she ever put out."

"I just play a detective onstage. Poppy here is one in real life!" Matt exclaimed.

"You don't say," Buddy said, curious, although as an actor, he probably knew already and was just pretending to have found out this little fact in the moment. "How interesting. I would love to hear more about it."

"There's not much to tell. I haven't really gotten started," Poppy said, desperate to end this particular discussion and talk about something else.

Heather felt exactly the same way. "The crab cakes look good, but I wonder if there are any specials."

Matt wasn't having it. "I think it's incredible that someone like Poppy, who has had such a fascinating life, first as an actress and then as a wife and mother, could at this point, later in life, start over and take on a challenge like this, don't you, Buddy?"

Buddy nodded vigorously. "Remarkable. What made you decide to do this?"

"I'm broke," Poppy said without the slightest pause.

She wanted to get that fact out in the open immediately.

Buddy was clearly still a struggling actor in his midsixties.

Which meant, he probably didn't have a penny to his name.

And she was acutely aware that most older men, when in the presence of a potential love match, saw one of two things.

A nurse or a purse.

And she wasn't interested in playing either role for any man.

There was an awkward pause.

"My husband, Chester, who just died, left me financially strapped, so I had to do something to pay my bills, and outside of applying to be a Walmart greeter, this was the only thing I was remotely qualified to pursue."

Much to Poppy's chagrin, Buddy did not seem deterred.

He grabbed her hand and lifted it up to his lips, then gave it a gentle kiss. Then he set her hand back down on the table, released his firm grip, and, with eyes sparkling, stared at Poppy and smiled. "What a woman."

Heather rolled her eyes and glared at Matt.

Matt caught her angry look, and for a moment, he slumped down in his chair, dismayed, before recovering. "This is fun!"

The waitress finally appeared and jotted down their drink order before scooting off toward the bar.

It was an agonizingly long evening, the low point being Buddy sending his steak back three times because it was undercooked, and Matt haranguing Poppy until she finally agreed to come see him and Buddy in their show.

But finally, after the plates were cleared and the lights dimmed, Shirley Fox took to the stage and made everything better with her angelic and melodious voice, no longer in its prime, but still strong and packing a wallop.

And to her enormous relief, Poppy could finally lean back in her chair and enjoy herself.

Except for the two times Buddy Rhodes tried to play footsie with her under the table.

Chapter 14

After saying good night outside the Purple Room and watching Matt and Buddy stroll off together arm in arm, joking and ribbing each other, toward Matt's decade-old red Prius, which was covered in dents and scrapes, Heather remained unusually tight-lipped, until she and Poppy were in her car, seat belts clicked into place and the engine started.

"I'm so sorry about tonight," Heather said, turning around and staring out the rear window as she slowly backed out of her parking space.

"You don't have to apologize. You didn't know."

"Matt shouldn't have done that without checking with me."

Poppy smiled and gently touched her daughter's arm. "Seriously, I had a nice time. Shirley was in top form, and Buddy, well, he had a certain charm, I have to admit."

"I'm not blind, Mother. I know Matt can be oblivious sometimes and a bit overbearing, but he's a sweet man at heart, and his intentions are good."

Poppy was still not fully convinced that this was the case, but she decided to keep her mouth shut in the interest of détente.

"He's like a beagle with a tennis ball, so enthusiastic and playful, and frankly, I could use some of that energy right now given my recent past relationships."

"The last one, the hipster musician, he was pretty dour," Poppy said quietly.

"All those songs he wrote about suicide and the pointlessness of life? There were so many red flags! Why can't I ever see the red flags right in front of me?"

Poppy could hardly argue with her daughter on that point.

Heather sighed. "But Matt's different, I think. He makes me laugh, and at this moment, having made so many bad choices with men, losing Chester so suddenly, well, his cheerful excitement is infectious, and it's like some much-needed medicine."

Heather gripped the wheel, kept her eyes fixed on the road, waiting patiently for a response from her mother.

"Heather, I love you, and I support you. If you want to be with Matt, that's fine by me."

"Thank you, Mother," Heather said, turning off East Palm Canyon and heading up the winding road where Poppy's house was located, near the top.

They drove in silence until Heather pulled her car over in front of the house.

"How long have you got?" she asked.

"The bank is holding the short sale in a few weeks. I've held it off as long as I can, but I've run out of delaying tactics. Once they have a buyer, I'll have about six more weeks to clear out."

Heather nodded, fighting not to cry.

Poppy noticed and touched her daughter's arm again.

"I'll be all right. I'm going to stay with Iris until I can find an apartment."

"But what about all your things?"

"I'll take anything sentimental, but the rest is just stuff. I've been in touch with a few consignment houses."

"Oh, Mother, this is awful!" Heather couldn't hold it back any longer, and with a flood of tears, she dropped her head down on the steering wheel.

Poppy lightly stroked the back of her daughter's hair as she sobbed.

"Sweetheart, life can be very unpredictable. Chester's heart attack, his gambling addiction, the lost fortune, I didn't see any of it coming. But I'm healthy and alive, and I have you, and I have my close friends, so I'm just going to count my blessings and roll with it."

"But this is supposed to be your golden years. . . ."

"You really need to stop saying that."

"I know, but you should be traveling and enjoying life, and now, because of Chester, you're going to have to start working again, and that's so unfair."

"I've had a lot of time to think about this. Yes, it was a shock, and yes, for the first month I just felt sorry for myself, but maybe I can look at this as a new kind of challenge, to have a purpose. Who knows? Maybe working will be my salvation."

"But you haven't worked since the nineteen eighties, and this silly idea you have of being a detective—" Heather stopped herself. She knew she had gone too far.

There was a long uncomfortable silence.

Heather spoke first. "I saw the Web site."

Poppy's heart sank.

Heather turned to face her mother. "Pretending to be three gorgeous twentysomething models? What were you thinking?"

"That wasn't my idea! Violet's grandson—"

"Wyatt? You had a twelve-year-old design your company Web site?"

"Other than that misleading photo, I thought he did a bang-up job."

"I just think . . ." Heather paused. Poppy could see the words churning around in her daughter's mind as she tried not to say them in a mean way. "I just think this . . . project . . . might be counterproductive to your current situation."

Poppy heard her phone buzzing inside her purse. She reached inside and pulled it out.

It was a text from Iris.

Called every damn name on the list. No one wanted to meet after I told them we were not the girls on the Web site.

It was punctuated with a frowny face.

Iris made no secret of hating emojis, and yet she could never resist using them in her texts and Facebook messages.

"You're right," Poppy decided as she clicked her phone off and dropped it back inside her purse.

"Really?"

"Yes. I'll just forget the whole thing."

"I think it's best," Heather said, relieved, as she leaned over and pecked her mother on the cheek. "Good night."

"Good night, dear. Thank you for a lovely evening," Poppy said as she got out of the car and stood on the curb, waiting while Heather pulled away. She waved with a bright smile, which faded the instant the car was finally out of sight, and then she turned and took in the sight of her beautiful mid-century home, one she would be abandoning in a matter of weeks.

It depressed her.

She tried to silently give herself a pep talk as she rummaged for her keys and then quietly entered her eerily still house. She would find a job. Something would come up. It had to, or she would be in real trouble.

It was sad.

She honestly had thought she had found the answer.

She hadn't held a real job since she was an actress.

And she was ballsy enough to believe that she could not only excel at a new career but also run her own business.

But after all the hard work and preparation she had put into becoming a private detective, it just wasn't meant to be.

Chapter 15

"Stay where you are, Atticus!" Detective Yorn yelled at the top of his lungs, pointing a gun at a young, skinny, odd-looking man with a bulbous nose and thick glasses, who stood over a dead body, his hands drenched in blood. "It was you! You killed them all!"

"No!" Atticus cried, shaking his head. "I came in here and saw Pearl lying on the floor! I bent down to see if she was okay, and that's when I got her blood on my hands!"

"You heinous fiend! It had to be you! Everyone else is dead! We're the only two left. I know I didn't kill anyone, so it had to be you!"

"Please, Detective, I didn't harm anyone! You have to believe me!" Atticus pleaded as he stepped forward.

"Stay where you are!" Detective Yorn warned.

But Atticus was wild with grief over the loss of his beloved girlfriend Pearl, his mind cloudy, and he kept advancing on the detective, who, fearing for his life, pulled the trigger.

There was a loud pop, and Atticus clutched his chest as blood seeped through his fingers, and then, with his mouth open in a cry of silent pain, he collapsed to the floor.

Detective Yorn, in a state of shock, dropped the gun, and it clattered to the floor.

He stared at Atticus's still body, which was now facedown next to Pearl, whose own youthful, lovely pale face was turned out, her dead eyes staring out into space.

Detective Yorn brought a shaky hand to his mouth.

The horror of the brutal murders at this snowbound estate was finally over.

He had successfully vanquished the deranged killer.

Suddenly, a loud snorting sound cut through the stillness.

Heather nudged Poppy and frantically pointed to Iris, who was sitting in the seat on the other side of Poppy, her head back, mouth open, snoring loudly.

The entire audience in the darkened theater at the Palm Springs Playhouse could hear her sawing logs during the performance.

Poppy quickly turned and shook Iris's arm in a frantic attempt to wake her.

Iris's eyes snapped open, and as she was suddenly roused out of her slumber, she said in a booming voice, "Is this thing over yet? I am bored out of my mind!"

There was a loud sigh from an irritated woman sitting in the row behind them.

Her husband, who sat next to her, shot forward and hissed at Iris, "Shhh!"

Iris casually looked around to find the source of the commotion that was upsetting everyone in the vicinity, in a failed attempt to pretend that it was not, in fact, her.

Detective Yorn, who was being played by Heather's boyfriend, Matt Cameron, walked over to the two bodies lying on the floor, leaned down, and stroked Pearl's long, blond hair. "How could you do it, Atticus? Your own fiancée, her entire family!"

Heather leaned into her mother and whispered in her ear, "He's really quite good, isn't he?"

Poppy couldn't disagree, as much as she wanted to, because Matt was indeed a fine actor. From the moment he took the stage, he electrified the audience with his intense, sexy, commanding portrayal of Detective Dale Yorn, a young, up-and-coming British inspector with Scotland Yard who was called to the scene of a murder at an estate in the English countryside. The wife of the wealthy landowner, Sir Roger Green, had been found drowned in the bathtub by a hysterical maid. Then, when a raging snowstorm trapped the entire family, including family members who had been visiting for a family reunion, alongside our intrepid detective, more bodies began piling up, one by one, until only two people were left, Detective Yorn and Atticus, the troubled fiancé of Sir Roger Green's only daughter, Pearl. Pearl was the sixth victim, following her mother, Claire, who drowned in the bathtub; her older brother Charles, who was stabbed to death; her grandmother Maggie, poisoned with strychnine in her tea; her loyal maid Tessa, who died by strangulation; and of course, her father, Sir Roger

Green himself, who was bludgeoned and left to die outside in the freezing snow.

Most of the other actors struggled through the performance with underwhelming line readings and, especially in the case of the actress playing Pearl, a striking lack of stage presence. Now that she was playing dead, she was actually at her most convincing. As for Buddy Rhodes, who was floundering in the role of Sir Roger Green, he was the worst of all. His line readings were over the top, when he could actually remember his lines, and he played too much to the audience. When Atticus ran in from outside to inform the last three survivors that he had stumbled across the family patriarch's dead body in the snow, the audience undoubtedly resisted the urge to burst out in applause.

But Matt, he was the obvious exception, and Poppy found herself waiting for him to come back on the stage when he was not in the scene. At the very least, though she still had not warmed up to him as a person, she had to respect his raw talent as an actor.

She totally believed him as a detective.

"So many questions you must have, Detective," a voice said out of nowhere.

Matt, aka Detective Yorn, snapped to attention. "Who said that?"

Buddy walked back onstage, a gun in his hand, a menacing look on his face, or at least Buddy's idea of what menacing should look like. He was overdoing it so much, all he was missing was a twirling mustache.

"Sir Green, you're alive!" Matt cried.

The shocking plot turn elicited a number of gasps from the audience.

Iris audibly groaned. "Oh, come on! I thought we had finally gotten rid of him! You're telling me he did not die, after all?"

Violet, who was sitting to Iris's left, elbowed her in the rib cage.

Iris pushed her away.

Then Poppy glared at Iris, signaling her to stop talking.

"Yes, my boy, I convinced that poor sap Atticus that you were the killer, and that it would behoove us to pretend that I had been beaten with a snow shovel and left out in the cold, where I died of frostbite, a simple ruse that would allow me to secretly prove you were responsible for the murders while I was no longer in your crosshairs. . . ."

"And when Atticus and I were the only ones left standing, I would reasonably conclude that Atticus had to be the killer. . . ."

Matt stared down at Atticus's prone body. "Dear God, I killed an innocent man!"

Matt's eyes brimmed with tears, and Poppy found herself choking up, moved by the wretched pain he was conveying.

There was a hush over the audience as they watched, riveted.

"Why? What possible reason could you have to slaughter your own wife and children?"

"To put them out of their misery from being in this lousy play," Iris whispered to Poppy, who shot daggers at her to keep quiet.

"You see . . ." Buddy said, turning to the audience, almost winking at them.

There was a long awkward pause.

Matt tried again. "Why, Sir Roger? Why did you do it?"

"You see . . ." Buddy's mouth hung open as he waited for the words to come out, but they didn't. Sweat formed on his brow. His eyes were full of panic. He had forgotten his next line.

"Because they disappointed you?" Matt offered.

"Yes! All of them! My whore of a wife was sleeping with the stable boy. My moneygrubbing, greedy son and daughter were conspiring behind my back to have me declared mentally incompetent so they could take control of my affairs and estate. . . ."

"And the poor maid and your daughter's fiancé . . . ?"

Buddy stared at Matt, his mind a blank.

Iris chuckled.

The show was getting worse by the minute, careening off the rails in spectacular fashion, and for the first time since the curtain opened, Iris was starting to be entertained.

"Wrong place, wrong time?" Matt asked, trying to prod a discombobulated Buddy.

"Yes!"

Another excruciating silence as Buddy tried to remember what came next. He kept glancing back at the pretty, petite stage manager, who was holding the script and was whispering frantically from the wings, "And now it's your turn!"

Buddy cupped a hand to his ear, looking off stage. "What?"

"And now it's your turn!" the stage manager whispered louder.

Buddy still couldn't hear what she was saying. "Huh?"

"And now it's your turn!" several voices from the audience shouted.

Buddy finally heard the line and whipped around, raised the gun, and pointed it at Matt's chest.

"And now it's your turn!"

He pulled the trigger.

Another pop.

Matt, his face full of surprise, dropped to his knees, but before succumbing to his bullet wound, he got off one last shot, hitting Sir Roger Green.

And then he toppled over, dead.

The only one left standing on the stage was Buddy, who missed his cue and reacted to being shot about ten seconds too late. Finally realizing it was his turn to die, he flopped forward in one of the least convincing death scenes ever witnessed.

And then, mercifully, the curtain closed.

The audience applauded warmly, if not enthusiastically.

And as the actors bounded back onstage to take their bows, there was a sustained polite cheering. That is, until Matt appeared, looking humble and appreciative. The audience jumped to their feet, bestowing upon him a thunderous ovation. Poppy found herself eagerly jumping up, too, clapping her hands energetically, wildly impressed.

Heather and Violet followed suit.

Only Iris remained in her seat, foraging through her purse for a breath mint.

The cast joined hands for one final bow and then stepped back, the curtain fell in front of them, and the lights came up in the theater.

Iris was already marching up the row toward the exit. "I'm starving! Can we go eat now?"

"Wait! I told Matt we would stick around and say hello after the show," Heather said.

"Of course," Poppy said. "You go find him, and we'll meet you in the lobby."

Poppy's mind raced as she and Violet moved with the crowd out of the theater.

She hadn't expected Matt to be such a damn good actor, and so believable, even nailing the British accent.

But it was his wholehearted commitment to the role of a detective that impressed her most.

Watching him perform was revelatory.

His charm and wit, so expertly utilized to get the suspects to open up and talk to him. His keen sense of observation when it came to identifying clues and interpreting human behavior. The personality quirks he effortlessly used to throw his adversaries off guard.

Even though the play was an obvious rip-off of one of Agatha Christie's classics, *And Then There Were None*, Poppy was thoroughly convinced even the author herself would have been inspired by Matt's original and engaging take on a tried-and-true classic detective character.

And then the idea hit her like a freight train.

No, it was such a crazy thought.

It would probably never work.

She decided to ignore it.

Unfortunately, the harder she tried to get it out of her mind, the louder it got.

By the time the crowd had thinned out and only a few patrons were left loitering in the lobby with her, Iris, and Violet as they waited for Heather and Matt to arrive, she couldn't contain it any longer.

"I think we should hire Heather's boyfriend, Matt, to be a part of our detective agency."

"What? I thought we decided not to do the whole Desert Flowers Agency thing," Violet said, confused.

"We did. But only because nobody wants to hire three women in their sixties to do the kind of work they associate with younger people. But you saw Matt. I absolutely believed him as a detective. I can totally see people trusting him and wanting to hire him."

"But he is not a detective, Poppy," Iris scoffed. "He was just playing one onstage."

"Yes, but nobody has to know that. Do you honestly believe that anyone could resist hiring such a handsome, charming, debonair detective like the one we watched tonight?"

Iris and Violet exchanged uneasy looks, not sure if Poppy was just joking or was actually serious.

"But you said he's nothing like that," Violet said.

"Well, yes, he's kind of obnoxious, and we'd have to keep his real personality under wraps, but if he managed to stay in character just long enough to keep the clients happy, the three of us could go about actually solving the cases."

In Poppy's mind, the concept made perfect sense.

Iris and Violet were having a harder time buying it.

"Wouldn't we be lying to our clients?" Violet asked.

"Not if he's an official member of the agency," Poppy said.

"You mean he gets the same split as me and Violet?" Iris asked warily.

"We can work all that out later, but let me put it this way. Chester always said, 'You have to spend money to make money.' "

"Chester left you penniless," Iris reminded her.

"Okay, maybe that's not the best example, but I have a good feeling about this," Poppy said, turning to see Heather leading Matt into the lobby.

The few theatergoers who were left—they were mostly younger and female—raced up to him to get a selfie.

And Poppy became even more convinced she was onto something.

Chapter 16

Matt's handsome face nearly jumped off the computer screen. He smiled from ear to ear, his perfect white teeth flashing, blue eyes sparkling, and his impressive jawline reminding anyone of a certain age of Dudley Do-Right. This was his head shot, one he had been blindly submitting to casting directors in Hollywood through the small-time talent agent who had agreed to take him on as a client.

Poppy had enlisted Violet's grandson, diminutive tech whiz Wyatt, to slap the photo on the home page of the Desert Flowers Web site, with the promise to take the kid up on his offer to employ his services down the road for any surveillance a case might require.

When Poppy called a meeting with her two Desert Flowers cofounders at their office garage at Iris's house, both Iris and Violet remained skeptical about her idea to incorporate Matt into their business model, but Poppy was adamant this was the right call, and quite possibly their only avenue to future success as private detectives.

"I have to admit, he does add a little pizzazz to the Web site," Iris said, unable to take her eyes off Matt's gorgeous mug.

"He's dreamy," Violet sighed. "If I was ten years younger . . ."

"Ten?" Iris scoffed. "Try thirty."

Violet shot Iris a hurt look, then chose to ignore the dig and turned to Poppy. "Does he even know about this yet?"

"No, but he will. I asked him to come over here and told him only that I had a business proposition to discuss with him. He should be here any minute," Poppy said.

"Are you sure this is going to work?" Violet asked, her eyes still locked on Matt's smiling photo on the screen.

"It already has," Poppy said, breaking into a wide grin. "Five minutes after Wyatt made the update, we received an e-mail from a potential client."

"Who?" Iris asked.

"A man named Jayden Emery. He asked for a meeting, so I scheduled one for later today, after we've had a chance to talk to Matt," Poppy said.

"But what if Matt doesn't agree to any of this?" Violet asked, worried.

"He will. I'm feeling lucky," Poppy said, brimming with confidence.

"I'm sure that's what Chester said at the craps table right before he lost your house!" Iris said.

"That was unnecessarily bitchy, Iris," Poppy said, glaring at her.

"You're right. I take it back. But this is all happening so fast. I wish we could take some time to think about it some more."

"I'm sorry, but I don't have the luxury of time. If we are going to make a go of this, we have to do it now, before I fall further into debt."

There was a knock at the door, but before Iris could make a move to answer it, the door flew open, and Matt poked his head inside.

"Knock, knock!" Matt said, flashing that intoxicating killer smile.

Violet's knees nearly buckled, but she managed to keep her balance.

"Hi, Mom!" Matt crowed as he bounded over to Poppy for a hug.

Poppy let him squeeze her tightly for a few seconds before gently pushing him away. "Please don't call me that."

"Mom? I guess I'm getting a little ahead of myself. Okay, Mrs. Harmon it is."

"That makes me sound too matronly. Poppy is fine."

"Okay, Pop."

"Poppy. Please add the *y*. Pop makes me sound like the owner of a soda shop."

"Got it! Poppy!" Matt said, winking at her.

"Matt, you remember my friends Iris and Violet? You met them at your show the other night."

"Of course! I hope you ladies enjoyed the performance."

"Actually, I thought it was—" Iris said.

Violet pushed her aside and quickly cut her off. "Wonderful. So suspenseful and scary, and you were absolutely perfect in the lead role."

Matt turned away bashfully. "Awww, you're just saying that."

"No, you were so believable as a smart, sexy, hard-boiled detective who is . . . sexy . . . and possesses such impressive intuitive skills . . . and is so sexy . . ." Violet gushed.

"Sexy! We get it! You can stop saying sexy!" Iris sighed.

Matt slipped an arm around Violet's waist and pulled her closer to him, loving every minute of her free-flowing and gushing compliments. "Well, it's nice to know I have a fan."

Violet erupted in a fit of giggles and nearly melted in his embrace.

"Actually, your role as a detective was what we wanted to talk to you about, Matt!" Poppy said.

"Oh?" Matt asked, intrigued.

Poppy could tell he was under the impression they might have a lead on a paid acting gig, and she quickly dispelled that notion and launched into a long explanation about her desperate circumstances and her unusual decision to become a professional crime solver.

Matt listened with rapt attention.

He had been aware of Poppy's new career but ignorant of how she had gotten to her momentous decision. Heather, who had been so against the plan, had clearly chosen to keep him in the dark about her mother's and, if truth be told, her reduced circumstances.

When Poppy finished her story, they all stood silently as Matt processed the mountain of information. He was very still, almost like a statue. And then, after nearly a minute, he became animated again and flew across the room, arms wide open. "Wow! What a story!"

Poppy tried to duck, but she wasn't fast enough,

and Matt managed to grab her in another big bear hug.

"Not a lot of women your age have the balls to do something so out-of-the-box crazy!" he laughed, squeezing Poppy so tight, she had to catch her breath when he finally let go.

The ladies weren't sure at first how to take his reaction.

Was he insulting them?

But Matt didn't miss a beat. "I think it's awesome!"

"Thank you," Poppy said, relieved.

He looked around the office. "So is this your secret headquarters?"

"That is so cute," Violet chortled, staring at Matt, goggle-eyed. "Isn't that cute?"

"You are embarrassing yourself, Violet," Iris barked.

Matt's eyes settled on the computer screen with his head shot. "What's that?"

He walked over to get a closer look.

Poppy's heart leapt in her throat. Her plan had been to ease softly into his possible role in the endeavor, but now he was gawking at his own face on the company Web site.

"Matt, let me explain. . . ." Poppy raced over and almost threw herself between Matt and the computer.

But he was already one step ahead of her.

"Did you use my face without my permission because you thought people searching online for a detective to hire would take one look at me and feel comfortable hiring your agency?"

Poppy was taken aback by his sudden and smart deduction.

There was no sugarcoating it.

It was time to put all her cards on the table.

"Yes."

Matt let this roll around in his mind a bit.

His face gave nothing away.

Was he angry?

Poppy worried she had just plowed ahead without thinking and had made a huge mistake and might now be in real, honest-to-goodness trouble.

She held her breath.

Iris and Violet exchanged concerned looks.

"Genius!" Matt finally hollered. "What a mind-blowing, totally inspired idea! I love it!"

Poppy exhaled as Matt did a little enthusiastic dance that was as odd as when Tom Cruise jumped up and down on Oprah's couch to profess his undying love for Katie Holmes.

"I am truly flattered, honored, really, to be even a small part of your clever little operation!" He hustled back over to stare at himself on the computer screen. "I can see it! I'm the spitting image of the cool, laid-back private eye you see on TV! It is going to be so much fun working together!"

Poppy's heart skipped a beat.

Working together?

That wasn't what she had in mind.

And at that moment, she had no idea just how involved Matt Cameron, the new face of the Desert Flowers Detective Agency, planned to be.

Chapter 17

"Shirley Fox?" Poppy blurted out, taken aback.

"Yes, she's my employer," Jayden Emery said.

He was young, in his midtwenties, thin but nicely muscled, African American, and—based on how many times he couldn't resist glancing over at Matt with a wolfish smile—clearly gay.

"What exactly do you do for Ms. Fox?" Poppy asked.

"I'm her personal assistant," Jayden said before turning back to Matt. "I'm sorry. Who is this?"

"Poppy is my secretary. Iris over there is my bookkeeper, and Violet primarily does my research," Matt said proudly, flashing a charming grin.

Iris grunted, and Violet gave Jayden a friendly wave.

"Man, you must be pretty successful to hire all this help," Jayden said, impressed.

"I've been very fortunate to have solved a number of high-profile cases. The publicity has allowed me to expand my client base outside the Coachella Valley."

Poppy feared Matt's con job was too good and might inspire Jayden to actually look him up online, where he would find no such stories of any high-profile cases for the Desert Flowers Detective Agency.

"Now, how can I help you?" Matt said, casually strolling over closer to Jayden and sitting down opposite him, hypnotizing him with his piercing blue eyes. Matt knew he was catnip to most women and gay men and was not above using his charm and sex appeal to seduce anyone, including a potential client.

Poppy sat back at her desk, watching him, engrossed in his inspired acting performance, which seemed to be working at the moment.

"Ms. Fox has recently been a victim of a crime. Someone broke into her home in the Palm Leaf Retirement Village while she was at the Purple Room, performing her cabaret act."

Matt leaned forward in his chair, listening intently to Jayden, who was so dazzled and aroused by the handsome "detective" and his mesmerizing eyes, he could barely concentrate on telling his story.

Jayden cleared his throat and shifted in his seat, trying his hardest to remain professional. "Apparently, there has been a rash of burglaries in the Palm Leaf lately."

"It's a gated community, correct?" Poppy asked.

"Yes," Jayden said, not even bothering to look over at her, which would require him to tear his eyes away from Matt.

"So there is a strong possibility it's an inside job," Poppy theorized.

"I suppose so," Jayden sighed, annoyed that the secretary was interrupting his intimate private conversation with Matt.

Matt sensed Jayden's discomfort and turned to Poppy. "Poppy, would you be a dear and take notes, please?"

Poppy sat there grimacing, but she knew Matt was bossing her around in order to win over the client, so she simply nodded and picked up a notepad and pen and began scribbling the highlights of their conversation that had transpired so far. She noticed Iris suppressing a laugh across the room.

"What do the police say?" Matt asked.

"Not much. They've gone through the motions, of course, interviewed a few people, mostly just the maintenance staff on the grounds, but so far have come up with nothing. They really don't appear to be all that interested, maybe because most of the victims are old and retired. Who knows?"

"So Shirley has decided to take matters into her own hands to help her fellow Palm Leaf residents?" Matt asked, winking at Jayden.

Jayden demurred, with a bashful smile, before continuing. "No, she's not that magnanimous. The thief made off with a cache of her priceless jewelry, which, unfortunately, was not insured."

"Ouch," Matt said.

"She's beside herself. And so she gave me the green light to find some outside help."

Matt reached over and flirtatiously touched Jayden on the knee. "Well, don't you worry, Jayden. I'll make sure your boss gets her jewelry back."

"And the good news is Shirley Fox is rich and can afford our fee!" Iris cried out, unable to contain her excitement.

Matt shot her an irked look. "That's our beloved Iris, so concerned with our bookkeeping. But we can discuss all that later. Right now, I want you to go back to your boss and tell her to relax, because the Desert Flowers Detective Agency is on the case."

Jayden stood up and extended his hand. "I don't know how to thank you, Matt."

Matt leapt to his feet and seized him in one of his signature bear hugs. "Come here. I'm a hugger!"

Jayden practically swooned, his eyes threatening to flutter up inside his head. When Matt finally released him, Poppy thought Jayden was going to topple over and fall flat on his butt, but he maintained his balance with an assist from Matt, who kept a firm grip on the young man's elbow until he was steady enough.

"Is it me, or is it hot in here?" Jayden asked, flushed, as he waved a hand in front of his face.

"It's you," Iris said, rolling her eyes.

"Ladies," Jayden said, finally acknowledging the three other people in the room, before turning to leave. He stopped at the door and spun back around. "By the way, I'm curious. Why do you call your agency the Desert Flowers?"

Poppy froze, unsure how to answer.

After all, why would a big-time private eye name his agency after his secretary, his bookkeeper, and his researcher?

Without missing a beat, Matt said, as if he were James Bond in a tux and were drinking a martini, shaken, not stirred, "That's me. I'm Flowers. Matt Flowers."

Poppy had to give him credit.

He certainly was fast on his feet.

And their fictional private detective character was officially born.

Chapter 18

When Poppy arrived at Heather's apartment building in downtown Palm Springs, she had the sickening feeling all was not well. Heather's voice, though measured, had betrayed a seething anger when she called her mother and requested she pop by for a visit. There was no question about what she wanted to discuss. Although Poppy, Iris, and Violet had tried to gently coax Matt into keeping quiet about his involvement in their detective agency, Matt was all about being up front and honest and sharing everything with the woman he was dating. In most instances, Poppy would have wholeheartedly agreed, except when it came to her high-strung, sometimes emotionally volatile daughter.

Poppy grabbed the railing and hauled herself up the stairs to the second level of the apartment building, where Heather lived in the last apartment, which faced north and overlooked the sprawling Spa Resort Casino. She knocked on the door three times, dreading what was to come, and when Heather opened the door, her worst fear was confirmed. Heather's steely-eyed stare and stiff demeanor said it all.

"Please come in, Mother," Heather said, stepping aside and allowing her to enter.

The apartment, though clean, was packed with knickknacks and stacks of boxes filled with books, classic record albums, and bundles of photographs. Poppy feared her daughter might soon be featured in one of those depressing hoarder shows on cable. It was also stifling hot, and Poppy felt beads of sweat forming on her brow.

"I'm sorry. The air conditioner is on the fritz," Heather said. "They're not coming to fix it until tomorrow."

Poppy spied Matt sitting at the small kitchen table, dabbing his face with an ugly green towel, his bright orange button-up, short-sleeved shirt open just enough for her to see his dark chest hair, which was wet and matted. He was melting from the heat and kept chugging from a liter of bottled spring water. He offered a limp smile, knowing what was to come and feeling guilty about it.

Poppy nodded, acknowledging him, but then turned to face the firing squad.

Heather cleared her throat, tucked her mousy brown hair behind her ears, and glared at her mother. "I suppose you already know why I asked you to come."

"Yes," Poppy said.

"And what do you have to say for yourself?"

"Heather, you don't have to talk to me like you're the mother and I'm the daughter."

"Well, lately I've been having a hard time figuring out which one of us is which," Heather scolded.

"Honey, that's not fair . . ." Matt interjected.

"Stay out of this, Matt," Heather said. "This has nothing to do with you."

"This has everything to do with me," Matt argued. "I'm the whole reason you dragged your poor mother over here in this hundred-and-ten-degree heat wave."

"Heather, I didn't exactly force Matt to become a part of my detective agency," Poppy said.

"Do you hear yourself? Your detective agency? Do you even realize how ridiculous that sounds?"

Poppy felt the sting of her daughter's words.

But it only strengthened her resolve.

"It's bad enough you've involved your dearest friends, Iris and Violet, in this screwball scheme of yours, but now you have to rope in my boyfriend, too?"

"She didn't rope me in, sweetheart," Matt said, standing up. "I'm a big boy, and I can make my own decisions."

Heather ignored him. "Please, Mother, I'm begging you. Stop this now, before it gets any more out of hand."

"Heather, if I give up on this, then what? I fall further into debt and have no money to pay for even my basic needs, and then I'll be forced to live off the kindness of my friends or you, and I just couldn't handle that. At least this screwball scheme, as you call it, has a small chance of working."

"And what if it doesn't?"

"Then I'll try to get a hostess gig at a restaurant or train to be a cashier or—I don't know—try my hand at out-call massage. Who knows? But please don't shut me down until I've at least given it a decent shot."

"All right, Mother. If you feel that strongly about

it, I'll stop badgering you, but you're going to have to do it without Matt. I don't want him mixed up in any of this madness."

"I understand." Poppy nodded solemnly.

Matt stepped forward. "Sorry, babe. There is no way in hell I'm missing out on this."

Heather twisted around, aghast. "What?"

"This is the acting challenge of a lifetime! Playing a richly layered, complex hero, not on the stage or in a movie or on television, but in real life! How often does an opportunity like that come around for an actor?"

"Matt, I'm asking you, as your girlfriend, not to do this," Heather said, her tone strained.

"That's so not cool," Matt said. "A good girlfriend is supposed to be supportive of my goals. She's not supposed to stand in the way of them."

Heather's mouth dropped open. "Are you saying that if I don't allow you to do this, you'll break up with me?"

"I'm saying you shouldn't be allowing anything. You should just let me do what makes me happy."

"And this . . . working with my mother, of all people, is going to make you happy?"

Matt grinned at Poppy, who stood off to the side, supremely uncomfortable with having to be present to bear witness to this lovers' quarrel.

"Well, you said you wanted us to bond. How can we not when we're going to be working so closely together?"

"Just to be clear, Matt, you're not required to actually work on cases with me. You're just the face of the agency and . . ." Poppy interjected.

"Sure. We'll talk about all that later," Matt said, brushing her off.

"Well," Heather said weakly, eyes downcast. "I guess I don't have a choice. I hope it's everything you want it to be."

Matt slapped a hand over his heart and blew a kiss to Heather before bounding over and swallowing her up in a bear hug.

Poppy watched the two of them.

There was something about this out-of-work actor.

Maybe he might be good for Heather.

Loosen her up a bit.

Perhaps they could even have a bright future together.

Poppy chuckled and thought to herself, *No, Poppy, don't get ahead of yourself. Always remember one thing. He's an actor.*

Chapter 19

Poppy tossed and turned on the upper bunk as Iris snored loudly below her on the bottom bunk. She snatched one of the pillows embroidered with characters from *Toy Story* from underneath her head and pressed it over her exposed ear. It didn't help much. She could still hear Iris grunting and snorting.

Frustrated, Poppy gingerly climbed down the fire engine–red stepladder, lifting up the hem of her baby blue nightgown so she would not trip, until her bare feet touched the cold floor. She then bent down to gently shake Iris's shoulder. Iris mumbled something and turned over on her side. Mercifully, the snoring stopped.

Poppy sighed with relief and began her climb back up the tiny ladder, but by the time her foot touched the second rung, Iris was back to snuffling and wheezing, this time even louder than before.

Poppy gave up, crawled back up into the small, lumpy single-size bed, and laid her head down on the pillow to endure the relentless snoring. She stared at a poster tacked to the wall of the boy band One Direction; all the baby-faced members were smiling at her seductively. She closed her eyes and tried to tune out Iris, but it proved impossible, and when she popped her eyes back open, there were those young, bright-eyed boys smiling and staring at her, which felt downright creepy.

It was official.

She was never going to get any sleep tonight.

Moving temporarily into Iris's friend Betty's house in the Palm Leaf Retirement Village while Betty was visiting friends in Florida for a month had seemed like an ingenious idea when Poppy first thought of it. Why not set up headquarters in the same gated community that had been targeted in a series of burglaries? It was the perfect cover. Three friends of Betty's innocently offering to house-sit while she was away. No one would be suspicious of their motives for suddenly showing up at all the social mixers or for striking up casual conversations with the other residents who were out for a morning stroll. They were just three Golden Girls anxious to take advantage of the property's three swimming pools and expansive golf course and cheap happy hour cocktails. No one would ever suspect they were three private investigators poking around for clues. And Betty's house was perfectly located only two streets over from Shirley Fox's far more palatial home.

However, when they'd arrived with their bags and let themselves in with the key Betty had sent overnight via Federal Express to Iris, the house turned out to be much smaller than they had anticipated. There were only three beds to choose from, and after two coin tosses, the first one eliminating Iris and then the second one knocking out Poppy, Violet was the lucky winner and briskly moved her bags into the master bedroom. That left the small guest room, decorated for when Betty's grandchildren came to visit from Arizona, for Poppy and Iris.

Another coin toss determined who would have to sleep on the top bunk, and Iris won. Poppy was feeling about as lucky as her late husband, Chester, had at the Spa Resort Casino.

"Pedro, you're being fresh . . . ," Iris moaned in her sleep. "I am warning you. . . . I'm not a dog. Stop petting me. . . . No, I don't like it. . . . Well, maybe just a little . . ."

Great.

Iris was now talking in her sleep.

Poppy knew she was dreaming about the famed Spanish film director Pedro Almodóvar, whose colorful and moving films were modern classics. Iris often bragged about her summer in Madrid during 1989, when she became a part of his social circle and even had a tiny walk-on role in his bondage-inspired *Tie Me Up! Tie Me Down!* Poppy and Violet had expected to see Iris decked out in leather and brandishing a whip when they saw the film, but fortunately, Iris's role was as a passerby in the background, one who wore a skintight multicolored designer dress and walked a white poodle on a glittery faux diamond–studded leash.

"Pedro, you scoundrel, you . . . You're supposed to be gay!"

Poppy had heard enough.

She was not about to relive Iris's wild exploits from the past.

She hoisted herself up and climbed back down the ladder and padded out of the room. Upon entering the hallway, she heard someone rummaging around in the dining room.

Her heart nearly stopped.

This was their first night in the neighborhood.

Was Betty's house already being ransacked by the thief?

Poppy squinted to see in the dark. Farther down the hall, past the living room, the moonlight reflected off the shimmering pool in the backyard and illuminated most of the area around the kitchen. She could hear the thief going through drawers. Poppy passed the small bathroom adjacent to the guest room and spotted a plunger stored behind the toilet. She reached in, wrapped her fingers around it, slowly pulled it out, and raised it up over her head. It was the only weapon she could find.

Then, taking a deep breath and mustering her courage, she bolted forward and around the corner, ready to bludgeon the thief with the plunger and hopefully scare him off!

Violet, who was sitting on a stool next to the kitchen counter, let out a yelp and dropped a knife, which clattered to the floor. In front of her was a plate of vegetables and a plastic container of garlic hummus.

"Violet, what are you doing up so late? You scared the life out of me!"

"What? Look who's talking, Poppy! You just nearly gave me a heart attack!"

"I'm sorry. I heard noises and thought—"

"I couldn't sleep!"

"Can you hear Iris snoring all the way over on the other side of the house?"

"No. I've shared enough hotel rooms with Iris where I've managed to block out her constant night groans and moaning and gibberish. I meditate and get to a very Zen place, and suddenly I don't hear it anymore."

"You'll have to teach me how to do that sometime."

"Actually, it was all the Disney characters staring at me in the dark that was keeping me awake. Betty apparently is a Disney fanatic. She has a whole glass case of porcelain cartoon characters in her bedroom. I couldn't handle all seven of those dwarves staring at me like that. I half expected to wake up and find them crawling all over me. It completely freaked me out."

"Well, it's not much better in the guest room. I've got a boy band watching me."

"Which one?"

"One Direction."

"Oh, I saw them on *The Today Show* once. They're adorable. I'd much rather have them staring at me than those seven little horny old men."

Poppy laughed and took a seat on a raised stool next to the kitchen counter.

"Here. Have some veggies and hummus," Violet offered, shoving the plate closer to Poppy.

Poppy shook her head. "I'd rather have something bad for me. Did you see anything laced with sugar in the fridge?"

"Some leftover chocolate pudding on the bottom shelf."

"Perfect."

Poppy slid off the stool, opened the fridge, and grabbed a mixing bowl that was covered in plastic wrap. She then searched the drawers for a large wooden spoon and found one among a collection of baking spatulas and metal whisks.

"There are some dessert bowls in the left cupboard."

"I don't mind eating out of the bowl, because once I start, I won't stop until it's all gone, anyway, and there will be less dishes to wash."

"Did you finally text Matt back?"

"Yes."

"What did he want?"

"He wanted to come over and sleep on the couch. He didn't want us investigating the case without him."

"That's so sweet of him."

"No it's not. I made it clear that his role is simply bringing in business and glad-handing the clients, not working with us in any real capacity as a detective."

"Did he agree?"

"No. He doesn't listen. Finally, I said if people saw a grown man staying here with us, it would raise eyebrows, and it's vital that we keep a low profile, for the good of the case. He seemed to buy that one. But I'm worried he's going to be a problem, always wanting to do more."

Poppy sat back down on her stool and dug into her chocolate pudding.

"So what's the plan in the morning? Just wander around, trying to find people to talk to and ask questions about the burglaries?" Violet asked.

"Yes, but we can't be so direct. We're going to have to ease into it. A lot of people get nervous talking to police or detectives, which is why we're in the perfect position to find out if anyone here knows anything. No one is going to mistake us for the cops. . . ."

"Just gossipy old biddies," Violet laughed.

Poppy frowned. "Gossips would have been just fine, Violet. There was no need to go that extra step and add old biddies."

"Got it. Sorry."

But she was right.

They were women of a certain age, perfectly positioned to ferret out information. And Poppy knew in her gut that someone here at the Palm Leaf Retirement Village had to be in possession of some kind of information that would hopefully break the case wide open.

If they could maintain their Golden Girls cover.

And, of course, keep Matt a safe distance away from them.

Chapter 20

"I don't understand," Jayden said, sipping a Chinese-print cup of Earl Grey tea before setting it down on a matching saucer. "Why isn't Matt here?"

There was an awkward silence as Jayden studied their faces, waiting for a response. He was resplendent in a tight-fitting, white, short-sleeved shirt and white pants and sneakers, a stark contrast to his beautiful chocolate-brown skin. He looked as if he could have easily slipped into the role of the Teen Angel in a local production of *Grease*.

Poppy brushed past the question. "I called the police department and spoke to a detective who has been assigned to investigate the break-ins. I told him I was a concerned new resident at the Palm Leaf and wanted an update on the case. He said he's been stymied by the fact that there has not been any sign of forced entry at any of the targeted homes. It's as if the thief had a key and let himself or herself right in through the front door."

Violet appeared on the patio with a coffee cake

topped with a gooey white frosting and gently set it down on the raised glass table where Poppy sat with Jayden and Iris on three leather-cushioned high stools. She then scurried back inside for plates, forks, and knives as Jayden eyed the cake hungrily.

"I suggest now that we are on the inside, we focus on all the victims, starting with Shirley," Poppy said, sipping her tea. "I'd like you to come up with a list of everyone who has access to Shirley's house, including any gardeners, pool boys, or handymen she might have hired in recent months."

"Okay," Jayden said warily. "So you three have set up house here in the Palm Leaf in order to be closer to where the break-ins took place, figuring you might see something the police missed?"

"That's the plan," Poppy said with a reassuring smile.

"So what's Matt doing?" Jayden asked, eyes narrowing.

Mercifully, Violet reappeared with her dishes and utensils and slammed a turquoise porcelain plate down in front of Jayden and handed him a fork and knife. "Dig in! Doesn't it look delicious? I wish I could say I made it myself, but truth be told, I picked it up at Trader Joe's."

Jayden picked up a knife and cut into the coffee cake. "Yummy! To hell with my diet, at least for today."

Poppy waited for Jayden to take a few bites of the coffee cake. Iris quickly followed suit and scrunched up her face after her first tiny bite. Jayden, however, closed his eyes and moaned, a little bit of frosting finding a home on his upper lip.

Violet picked up a napkin and dabbed at it. "Just got a little something there, dear."

She retracted the napkin, and the frosting was gone.

"Thank you," Jayden said, stabbing at another piece of cake with his fork.

"I think it's dry," Iris huffed, pushing her half-eaten piece away from her and back in Violet's direction.

Violet's perpetual smile faded a bit as she glowered at Iris, who didn't seem to care or notice, as she was guzzling her tea to wash away the offensive taste of the coffee cake.

Poppy slid off her stool and reached into her Fendi Peekaboo satchel bag, her last splurge at Neiman Marcus before the shocking discovery that she was basically penniless, and pulled out her MacBook Air. She set it down on the glass table and popped it open. As it fired up, she turned to Jayden, who was now cutting his second piece of coffee cake.

"Now, how about we start with you giving me some names?"

Jayden looked at her, mouth open, fork half raised to his mouth, with a hunk of dry coffee cake on it. "I would feel more comfortable if Matt was here. I mean, after all, I did hire him, not his three assistants."

"I see," Poppy said through gritted teeth. She pulled out her phone and began texting. "He's out in the field now, but let me see if I can get him to drop whatever he's doing and come right over."

"I would appreciate that," Jayden said with a tight smile.

Matt replied to Poppy's text instantly.

He was at Heather's apartment.

And based on how fast he agreed to rush over to the Palm Leaf Retirement Village and join them, Poppy figured he was looking for any excuse to get out of there.

Jayden had polished off the entire coffee cake by the time they heard Matt ringing the doorbell. Violet shuffled off to let him in, and Poppy noticed Jayden frantically wiping coffee cake crumbs off his pristine white shirt and checking himself out in the reflection from his iPhone to make certain he was presentable.

This kid was completely smitten.

His face brightened when Matt blew out onto the patio, shook his hand, holding his grip longer than necessary, and complimented Jayden's lovely designer shirt, noting the contrast to the client's gorgeous smooth skin. Jayden practically melted on the spot.

Matt bounded around the table and hugged his three assistants one at a time. He got to Iris last, and she predictably squirmed uncomfortably in his grasp, but he didn't seem to notice or care.

Finally, Matt sat down on the stool vacated by Violet, who had gone to fetch him some tea, and fixated on Jayden, who stared at him longingly, just grateful to be back in this master detective's rarified presence.

"So have my girls been taking good care of you?" Matt asked with a wink.

"Oh, yes, but I'm glad you're here so we can finally talk about the case," Jayden said, smiling apologetically at Poppy, whom he knew he had insulted, before returning his undivided attention back to Matt.

"Where are we?" Matt asked, playing the assured, focused, no-nonsense film noir private-eye role to the hilt.

"We were discussing who had access to Shirley's house," Poppy said.

"That's a start," Matt said, placing a hand over Jayden's. "Can you help us with that, Jayden?"

"Of course!" Jayden said, shivering from Matt's touch. "The gardener, the pool man, and the handyman all work for the property and have been there for years. The management company and the HOA trust them implicitly, so I would be surprised if they had anything to do with the burglaries."

"Did you get all that, Poppy?" Matt asked.

Poppy, caught by surprise, began fiercely typing on her laptop. She hadn't expected she would be assigned the role of secretary yet again, but the reality was, it was the role she was most famous for on television. "Yes, Mr. Flowers."

Matt removed his hand from Jayden's and jumped off the stool, then paced back and forth around the patio, his mind racing.

Poppy, Iris, and Violet all followed him with their eyes, fascinated by his fully committed performance.

"What about Shirley's family?" Matt inquired, then stopped momentarily to scoop a bit of frosting off the side of Iris's plate with his left index finger and stick it in his mouth. "Oh, that's good. Did you make it, Violet?"

"Trader Joe's," she said, shaking her head, embarrassed.

"There's Shirley's deadbeat son Lucas. He's certainly worth looking at," Jayden said, piping in.

"You obviously don't have a high opinion of him," Matt said.

"God, no! He's a lazy parasite who wastes his life surfing in LA, when he's not doing drugs and sponging off his mother. Shirley leased a small studio for him in Venice, but then he got busted for dealing meth. Shirley hired a high-priced lawyer to get him off, and after that he ran to Palm Springs to have Mommy take care of him."

"When was that?" Iris asked.

Jayden didn't hear her.

He was too busy staring at Matt's handsome face.

Matt glanced at Iris, who was fuming at being ignored, and then quickly asked, "When was that?"

"A few months ago. Right before the burglaries started."

"Anybody else you can think of in Shirley's orbit who might be a credible suspect?" Matt asked.

"Well, there's Shirley's husband, Dash."

"Dash?" Iris snickered.

"What's he like?" Matt asked.

"He's a good-for-nothing hanger-on, in my unvarnished opinion," Jayden said, scowling. "Shirley has always had a taste for handsome, younger men. . . ."

"How much younger . . . ?" Poppy asked.

"Dash just celebrated his thirtieth birthday last month," Jayden said with a resting bitch face.

"That young?" Violet shrieked before catching herself. She quickly gathered up the dessert plates and scooted inside the house, shaking her head in disbelief as she went.

"Dash is a self-described 'entrepreneur,' but I've

never even seen a hint of any business deals, so basically, he does pretty much nothing. And he's only about five years older than Shirley's son."

"How did they meet?" Poppy asked.

Jayden didn't answer.

He was distracted by something.

Matt cleared his throat. "How did they meet?"

"Oh, at one of her cabaret shows in Phoenix. He conned his way backstage after her act and told everybody he was writing a review for a local arts rag and it was going to be a rave. He was vague about which publication, and we never actually saw the review, but by then it was too late. He had wormed his way into her heart, and Shirley was smitten. They were married about five months later."

"And are they happy?" Poppy asked.

"I'm sorry," Jayden said, fixated on Matt. "I didn't notice before, but . . . your eyes are such a stunning blue . . . like a shimmering ocean. They literally take my breath away. . . ."

"Thank you. That's very kind of you to say," Matt said, nonplussed. He was obviously used to receiving adoring compliments about his good looks. "Are they happy, Shirley and Dash, I mean?"

Jayden shrugged. "I suppose so. He's having a ball spending all the money she makes from her tours and acting residuals."

"And what about Shirley?" Matt asked.

"Blinded by love, as usual," Jayden said sadly. "And like all her past marriages, sooner or later she's going to wake up and realize she's been taken for a ride . . . one more time."

"Can you ask Jayden how Lucas and Dash feel about each other?" Iris barked, giving up any hope of getting a direct answer from the client without Matt's help.

"They despise one another," Jayden huffed, annoyed at Iris's rudeness, but finally acknowledging someone else besides Matt on the patio. "They have a lot in common. They're both despicable human beings, and they see each other as a threat to their first-class seat on the Shirley Fox gravy train."

"So both could be suspects, at least for the break-in at Shirley's house," Matt surmised, tapping a finger on the glass table.

"Dash was with Shirley while she was performing at the Purple Room on the night of the burglary at her house. He has an airtight alibi. I was there, too, and didn't see him slip out at any point. He was at a table in the back during the show, drinking and flirting with a waitress the whole time. It couldn't have been him."

"Unless he hired someone to steal her jewelry and had a key made for him so he didn't have to bust his way in," Poppy said.

Matt gasped. "That's good, Poppy!"

"Thank you, Mr. Flowers," Poppy sighed.

"And Lucas? Where was he that night?" Matt asked.

"His alibi is a lot shakier. He said he went to a movie by himself, some superhero blockbuster, but he has nobody to back up his story and couldn't even remember the details of the movie's plot when the police questioned him. He claimed he fell asleep and missed most of it."

"Anyone else who could be a suspect?" Matt asked.

Jayden shook his head. "Not that I can think of at the moment."

Matt placed a comforting hand on Jayden's shoulder. "Well, don't you worry, Jayden. I'm not going to rest until I retrieve Shirley's valuables."

"I have the utmost confidence in you, Mr. Flowers. I feel as if I'm in good hands."

Jayden slid off the leather stool and straightened his shirt with his hands, meticulously checking for wrinkles. He extended a hand to Matt, who brushed it aside and grabbed Jayden in a hug.

"I'm a hugger," Matt said.

"Yes . . . I . . . remember now. . . ."

Matt released Jayden, who struggled to remain upright. He lowered a hand to cover the sudden bulge in the front of his white pants.

Poppy wasn't sure how to take this new reality, that Matt Cameron, aka Matt Flowers, was going to be a permanent fixture in her new endeavor.

But she had to give him some much-deserved credit.

Through sheer charm and personality, he had thoroughly questioned the client, and now they had some solid leads in the case.

Chapter 21

Matt's Prius sat across the street from Shirley Fox's house in the Palm Leaf Retirement Village. Inside, Poppy sipped a Starbucks latte and kept careful watch over the comings and goings, while Matt, behind the wheel, furiously typed on his phone.

"Matt, this is a stakeout. You're supposed to be keeping an eye out for any suspicious activity."

"I will, I promise. I just want to tweet about it."

"Tweet about what?"

"Our stakeout," Matt said, distracted, still typing.

Poppy snatched the phone out of his hand and gasped at the sight of a whole Twitter account created for his newly minted Matt Flowers, Private Eye character.

"You can't be telling people what we're doing while investigating a case!"

"Why not?"

"First of all, it's totally unprofessional. And second, it alerts any bad guys whom we might be following as to exactly where we are and what we're up to at all times."

Matt thought about this for a second, then grabbed his phone out of Poppy's grasp and continued typing.

"Did you hear what I said?" Poppy hollered, setting down her Starbucks latte in the cup holder.

"Yes, but look at how many followers I have already. That could translate into a lot of new business for the agency."

"Well, if you don't focus on old business, like the Shirley Fox case, there won't ever be any new business, because nobody will want to hire a detective who can't solve a case!"

Matt begrudgingly put down his phone and sighed. He picked up Poppy's coffee and took a swig.

"That is my latte, Matt," Poppy said. "You didn't want any coffee, because you're off caffeine, remember?"

"Oh, right," Matt said sheepishly, handing her back the paper cup. He suddenly sat up in his seat and pointed at the house. "Look!"

A grungy-looking young man with stringy blond hair and dressed in brightly colored cargo shorts and a neon yellow tank top had ambled out of the house, carrying a gym bag. He hopped in a silver Mercedes convertible parked in the driveway, which Poppy assumed belonged to his mother, Shirley, backed out, and peeled away.

"Go, Matt, go! Before you lose him!" Poppy barked.

Matt sprang into action, turned the key in the ignition, and fired up the Prius. He tried doing a U-turn to reverse direction, but unfortunately, he cut his turn too wide and was forced to do a three-point, losing precious seconds.

Poppy sighed, wishing she was the one in the driver's seat.

Matt slammed down on the gas pedal and made up some time, and after a few guesses about street turns, Poppy spotted the Mercedes just a few cars ahead of them. Lucas drove west, and Matt swerved in and out of traffic to keep up, nearly sideswiping a diminutive grandmother—whose head barely made it over the steering wheel—who was tooling along in an oversize Chevy sedan.

As they entered Cathedral City, Lucas turned sharply onto Perez, drove past a sea of auto dealers, and ended up in a dusty, remote industrial park. He pulled over next to a pawnshop, climbed out of the Mercedes with the gym bag, and strolled inside.

Matt pulled in behind the Mercedes, keeping his eyes on the pawnshop, and slammed into the back of the Mercedes.

Poppy was jolted back in her seat. "Be careful!"

"Sorry," Matt said, still staring at the pawnshop, completely unconcerned that he had just rear-ended their client's car. "You think he's in there right now pawning his mother's jewelry?"

"Possibly," Poppy said. "He may have staged the break-in at his mother's house to make it look like the work of the thief behind those other burglaries in order to throw suspicion off himself."

"We should get in there and stop him!" Matt shouted, struggling to free himself from the seat belt but only further entangling himself.

"Wait. I think we should hang back until we know exactly what's going on!"

Matt's fingers finally found the button that released the belt, and after the strap slapped him in the face, he managed to throw open the driver's side door and leap out.

"But we can catch him in the act right now!"

He bounded across the street, and a truck, with its horn blasting, nearly mowed him down as he ran across the dividing line.

Poppy jumped out of the Prius and chased Matt across the street. By the time she rushed inside the shop and paused to catch her breath, Matt was already confronting a wide-eyed Lucas and a confused pawnshop owner, a small Asian man with a pronounced paunch and a cigarette dangling from his mouth.

"I don't know what the hell you are talking about, man," Lucas drawled in a disaffected, flat Southern California accent.

"I demand you open that bag right now and show me exactly what you plan on selling to this gentleman!"

The pawnshop owner's eyes widened, astonished, hardly used to being called a gentleman.

"And who are you?" Lucas asked.

"Matt Flowers, private eye," Matt announced proudly.

Poppy rolled her eyes.

It was already clear undercover assignments might not be Matt's strong suit. He loved bragging about his new title too much.

"Get lost, loser," Lucas said, shaking his head.

"What's in the bag, Lucas?" Matt demanded.

Lucas glared at Matt. "How do you know my name?"

"Never mind that. Tell me what's in the bag."

"That's none of your business!" Lucas spit out, turning his back on him to resume his conversation with the owner.

Matt tapped him on the shoulder. "I'm not through talking with you, mister," Matt said.

Lucas turned back around, eyes blazing. "Yeah? Well, I'm through talking with you!"

Lucas grabbed Matt by the fingers that were clamped down on his shoulder and twisted them back. Matt howled in pain and dropped to his knees, allowing Lucas to bend down and get an arm around his throat. He squeezed as hard as he could, choking him out, as Matt wheezed and coughed, trying to catch his breath.

Poppy sprang into action, swinging her beloved and ridiculously expensive Fendi Peekaboo satchel bag over her head a few times before swatting a surprised Lucas in the head. He was momentarily stunned but didn't let up on his hold. Matt desperately tried to pry Lucas's strong arm away from his neck with his fingers but had little success. Poppy attacked Lucas again, this time pounding him on the head over and over as beads and buttons flew off the bag, clattering to the floor everywhere. The pawnshop owner watched the scene unfolding in his shop with utter disbelief, smoke swirling off the end of his lit cigarette.

Finally, Lucas released his grip on Matt, who dropped to the floor, and covered his head with his hands.

"Stop! Please, lady. I'm in pain here. Stop!" he wailed.

Poppy finally stopped hitting him and glanced wistfully at what was left of her last prized possession, her now destroyed Fendi bag. She tossed it on the floor and knelt down beside Matt, who was lying facedown, trying to breathe normally again.

"Are you okay?" Poppy asked.

Matt tried to answer, but all he got out were a few wheezes and gasps, so instead he just nodded.

Poppy stood back up, stepped over a moaning Lucas, who was curled up in a ball next to the pawnshop counter, gingerly touching his head to check for blood, and opened the bag of items he had brought to the shop.

The owner instinctively stepped back, unwilling to confront this badass of an old lady who had so dramatically stormed into his shop and had viciously beaten up one of his customers.

Poppy sifted through everything in the bag. There were autographed photos of Shirley Fox with a variety of screen legends. A few props from her 1970s TV show. A small stack of dresses that were labeled with the titles of a few bad horror movies Shirley had appeared in when her career was on the decline.

There was no jewelry.

"Who the hell are you?" Lucas barked, still rubbing his head.

"We are investigating the theft of your mother's jewelry," Matt said, catching his breath.

Poppy sighed and rolled her eyes.

The man just couldn't keep his mouth shut.

"Does your mother know you're selling her belongings?" Poppy asked.

Lucas nodded, refusing to make eye contact with Poppy. "Yes, she knows! She wanted to donate it all to Goodwill, but I asked if I could have it . . . for sentimental reasons."

"So sentimental you wasted no time racing over

here to pawn it off and make a quick buck," Poppy said.

Lucas stared at the floor, embarrassed, still gently rubbing his head.

"For drug money, I bet," Matt whispered in a hoarse, raspy voice.

"Call her if you don't believe me," Lucas said, seething.

Matt gripped the counter and tried to climb to his feet, but he nearly lost his balance halfway up. Poppy dashed over to his side and grabbed him by the elbow, then helped to lift him until he was finally upright.

"Thank you, Poppy," Matt said, brushing himself off, trying valiantly to hide his humiliation over having totally lost control over the situation. "You better believe we'll be speaking to your mother."

Matt stared Lucas down for almost a full thirty seconds before stalking out of the pawnshop.

"Have a nice day," Poppy said, smiling at the pawnshop owner, who stood frozen in place, the cigarette still hanging off his bottom lip. And then she shot out the door.

As Matt drove Poppy back to Betty's house, he apologized profusely for screwing up the stakeout and assured her that from here on in, he would follow Poppy's orders to the letter. He was grateful just to be a part of the operation and would no longer put himself front and center, or cause a scene that could potentially harm or compromise their investigations.

Poppy wanted to believe him.

She really did.

But just two hours later, when Poppy called Shirley

Fox's personal assistant and their client contact, Jayden Emery, with an update, he excitedly told her that he had already heard from Matt about his brave heroics, breathlessly recounting how the vile, despicable Lucas Fox had gotten the upper hand on Matt's devoted secretary, Poppy, nearly crushing her windpipe in a violent choke hold, and how Matt had awesomely intervened by rushing to Poppy's rescue, karate chopping the muscle-bound baddie, and freeing his motherly helper from Lucas's drug-fueled savagery.

She had to hand it to Matt.

When it came to adjusting optics, he had no peer.

Chapter 22

Shirley Fox belted out "I'm Still Here," the Stephen Sondheim–penned, crowd-pleasing anthem from his 1971 hit Broadway musical Follies. It was the perfect song for Shirley, who was herself a battle-scarred survivor. Through the song, she flipped through a mental scrapbook of her life, all the good, the bad, and the ugly, and by the end she came out the other side stronger and triumphant. Shirley Fox had experienced the heady highs and devastating lows of a decades-long show business career and was still here to tell us about it.

Even the normally unimpressed Iris sat riveted to Shirley's big, brassy voice, which may have been a little weary from age, and was definitely tinged with undeniable cynicism from the harsh blows in her life, but was still powerful and unencumbered by the frailties of her advancing years. When she reached the final notes, Violet couldn't contain herself any longer and leapt to her feet, applauding wildly, leading the rest of the crowd that made up the audience at the Purple Room to follow suit and jump up from their chairs, clapping enthusiastically. Iris begrudgingly joined everyone else, unable to deny that the broad deserved every ovation she received.

Poppy noticed only one man in the house who refrained from standing. He sat alone at a corner table down front, hunched over and brooding, stirring a cocktail with his right index finger. She instantly recognized him as Farley Mead, Shirley Fox's boozy ex-husband, a singer himself in the Neil Diamond mold.

Farley had a couple of hits in the seventies, one that served as the theme song for a Clint Eastwood Western and was nominated for an Academy Award. Farley was asked to perform it at the Oscars ceremony, but his nerves got the best of him, and he completely blanked on the lyrics in front of tens of millions of viewers around the world. That Western was the closest the poor guy ever got to a movie career, which had always been his lifelong dream. The only problem was, he couldn't act. That was evidenced by his cameo appearance in the film as a wisecracking barkeep in the saloon town in which Clint arrives to clean up a gang of roughriders. At the Oscars, the song lost out to a James Bond theme, and Farley's career never recovered. After that, Farley descended into a morass of alcohol and prescription painkillers, never to be heard from again. Rumor had it he had moved to the desert, but Poppy had never crossed paths with him.

Until now.

Poppy checked her watch. There was only about

ten minutes left in the show. Then, as she had previously discussed with Jayden, they would be escorted backstage to have a sit-down with Shirley
and ask her questions about the burglary and who
in her circle she might consider a possible suspect,
if indeed it was an inside job. Otherwise, they had
a much wider net to cast, but Poppy remained convinced that whoever was responsible for the rash
of break-ins was already inside the Palm Leaf Retirement Village community.

Shirley smiled modestly at the adoring crowd
and then, feigning embarrassment over such an
over-the-top ovation, gestured for them to take
their seats, which they did once the raucous applause had finally begun to die down.

"Thank you so much," Shirley whispered breathlessly into the microphone. "Sometimes I can't believe I am still here."

"Neither do I!" a man's voice bellowed.

Shirley shielded her eyes from the harsh stage
lights and peered out into the darkened room to
find the person who had yelled at her.

The yelling had come from a corner table.

Her ex-husband, Farley Mead.

"Still singing for your supper and shaking it for
tip money!" Farley shouted and then laughed bit-
terly.

Shirley's face soured. "Is that you, Farley?"

"In the flesh, baby!" Farley said, struggling to his
feet.

Iris audibly gasped.

Poppy whipped her head around. "Iris, what's
the matter?"

Iris's face had turned a ghostly white as she

stared at Farley, who fought to keep from swaying side to side and was forced to grip the edge of the table to keep himself steady on his feet.

"How many Johnnie Walkers is that, Farley?" Shirley asked calmly, although her face betrayed a hint of agitation and discomfort.

Nervous titters from the crowd.

"I lost count at five," Farley slurred, playing along. "You should have stayed married to me, sweetheart. I wouldn't have made you keep working."

"If I were still married to you, I'd be doing three shows a night just to pay your bar bill," Shirley said loudly into the microphone.

The audience erupted into boisterous laughter.

"Ladies and gentlemen, my ex-husband, Farley Mead, is here tonight. . . ."

A smattering of applause as Farley stood and took a theatrical bow.

Most of the clapping came from a gaggle of middle-aged women who undoubtedly spent their teenage years pining for the suave crooner with the brooding good looks. Judging by his bloodshot eyes; leathery, sun-damaged skin; receding hairline; and the big gut hanging over his belt, those days were definitely far in the past.

"Sit down, Farley. I'd actually like to dedicate this next song to my current husband. . . ."

"What are you going to sing? 'Thank God for Kids'?" Farley chuckled. "Remember that little country ditty by the Oak Ridge Boys?"

Shirley stood frozen on the stage, not sure what to do.

Poppy could see Shirley's hand shaking slightly as she gripped the microphone and took a deep breath.

The rotund piano player, who was stuffed in a purple shirt and black vest, ignored Farley's heckling and began banging out a few notes. Shirley tried regaining control of her show by launching into a moving rendition of "I Will Always Love You," written by Dolly Parton but made a number one pop hit by the late Whitney Houston, on *The Bodyguard* movie soundtrack. Shirley's voice cracked slightly after the first few notes, and Poppy feared she just might bolt from the stage in tears, but she managed to hold it together and power her way through the song.

"She sure as hell ain't singing that about me!" Farley shouted above the music, guffawing.

"Sit down!" a man yelled from the back.

Suddenly, from out of nowhere, a young man, lean and fit, impossibly handsome, with smooth olive skin offset by a perfectly pressed white linen suit, appeared behind Farley and grabbed him roughly by the shoulders.

"Hey! What the—!"

Before Farley could protest any further, the young man, his face filled with grim determination, hustled Farley away from his table, banging the back of Iris's chair in the process as they brushed past, causing Iris to spill her cocktail all over the table. The young man kicked open a side door and ejected Farley Mead outside to face the last rays of the hot desert sun before it disappeared behind the grand mountains surrounding the Coachella Valley.

The young man slammed the door shut as several grateful patrons offered supportive applause.

Shirley, ever the trouper, kept going, as if Farley Mead had never crashed her cabaret act and tried to embarrass her, giving the song everything she had left in order to make her audience forget the ugly scene they had just witnessed.

The young man turned to face the woman standing alone on the stage, singing her heart out, and blew her a loving kiss.

Poppy knew that the young man who had so valiantly come to her rescue was the same man she was at this moment singing to, the man, according to the lyrics, whom she would always love, her much younger husband, Dash.

Violet reached out and touched Iris's arm. "What's the matter? You look like you're going to be sick!"

Iris shook her head, in a state of shock.

"Do you need some water?" Poppy whispered.

"I'm not sick," Iris said in her normal voice, causing a disgruntled woman at the next table to shush her.

Iris didn't pay heed to the woman's request.

She continued talking at her usual volume. "I know him."

"Who? The young man who bumped into you?" Violet whispered.

"No. The other one."

"Farley Mead?" Poppy asked.

Iris nodded. "Back in nineteen-seventy-eight. He was touring Europe, and I was living in Munich, working as an exotic dancer at a very exclusive men's club."

The woman at the next table was now not so anxious for Iris to shut up. She casually leaned forward, curious to know more.

"We met when he came to see me dance after

his concert, and, well, we unexpectedly hit it off, and we ended up spending the weekend together at his hotel. . . ."

"Doing what?" Violet asked, eyes wide.

"Playing chess, Violet," Iris said, irritated. "What do you think? Sex! Having sex!"

Now everyone at the surrounding tables was more interested in hearing Iris's story than listening to Shirley Fox sing a love ballad to her boyish husband.

According to Jayden, Shirley was scheduled to finish her cabaret act at 9:30 p.m. sharp, but once she got through "I Will Always Love You," she thanked everyone for coming and quickly fled the stage. It was only 9:20 p.m. She obviously had been shaken up by her ex-husband's rude heckling.

As the audience filed out of the Purple Room, Poppy, Iris, and Violet remained seated at their table, waiting for Jayden to arrive and usher them backstage. After twenty minutes, as the waitstaff finished cleaning all the tables and the hostess kept glancing over at them, hoping they would leave, Poppy finally stood up.

"I'm going to see when we can talk to her," she said.

She made a beeline for the curtain leading backstage, but before she had a chance to push her way through, Jayden appeared, blocking her path.

"Where's Matt?" Jayden asked in a chilly tone.

"He had to fly to San Francisco on another case," Poppy lied. "Big client in the tech industry, messy divorce case."

Actually, he was across town, performing the last show of his play, probably ad-libbing at the mo-

ment to cover for Buddy Rhodes, who was undoubtedly forgetting his lines.

"Well, I certainly hope he considers Shirley a
priority," Jayden sniffed.

"Of course. He'll be back tonight and focused
one hundred percent on retrieving Shirley's valuables. Is now a good time for us to question
Shirley?"

"Without Matt?"

"Yes. I plan on taking extensive notes, which he
will review later."

"I'm afraid tonight isn't going to work out," Jayden said, glancing back at Shirley's dressing room.
The door was closed, and Poppy swore she heard
faint crying.

"It won't take long," Poppy pressed.

"Shirley is very tired," Jayden growled.

He was done talking to a lowly assistant.

"How about tomorrow morning?"

"Have Matt call me," Jayden said. "I'd rather
deal with him directly."

"Of course," Poppy said, her insides burning up.

"I hope you enjoyed the show," Jayden said with
a fake smile.

He stood his ground, not budging, waiting patiently until Poppy finally realized she was never
going to get anywhere near Shirley's dressing
room. She finally turned around and headed toward the exit, Iris and Violet falling in behind her.

Poppy knew poor Shirley had been devastated
by her lousy ex-husband's surprise appearance,
which had ruined her show.

They were just going to have to find some way
to study the residents of the Palm Leaf without
Shirley's help.

How could they get everyone in the community in one room?

That was an easy one.

Poppy knew exactly what would draw a community full of retirees.

A party with an open bar.

Chapter 23

There was nothing like a fully stocked bar to loosen people up and get them talking freely. And luckily, Betty's bar was the centerpiece of her living room. Iris served as bartender, and Violet flitted about the room with a plate of crab-stuffed mushrooms, offering them to the early birds who had already arrived. Meanwhile, Poppy played hostess as more guests arrived in a steady stream through the front door. She was surprised so many residents of the Palm Leaf were showing up, as she had hastily pulled the party together.

Matt, excited to be posing as Poppy's nephew visiting from out of town, held court for about a half dozen swooning and fluttery old ladies congregated around him as he entertained them with made-up stories about his "nephew" character's exciting world travels.

As Poppy introduced herself to all the arrivals, she made a mental note of their names and what streets they lived on and any other pertinent information they provided. She didn't have to worry about loosening any lips about the spate of break-ins, because it was the only topic anyone was remotely interested in talking about.

There were many theories among the locals, but the majority of Palm Leaf residents were convinced the thief was a deadbeat son or grandson of a current resident, one who was into drugs or other illegal activities. No one under fifty-five was allowed to buy a home and live in the Palm Leaf, but the rules permitted owners' family members, no matter their age, to come for extended stays. Shirley Fox wasn't the only one in the retirement village who was allowing her lazy, out-of-work, troublesome kid to crash at her pad.

The house was soon packed to capacity, and there was very little room to move around by the time Shirley Fox and her husband, Dash, blew through the front door, making a fashionably late grand entrance.

Poppy wasted no time in making a beeline for her.

"Ms. Fox, I am so happy you could make it," Poppy cooed, extending her hand. "I'm Poppy Harmon."

Shirley shook it and smiled demurely. "Of course I know who you are. I used to watch your TV show *Jack Colt, PI* all the time back in the day."

"I'm flattered."

"I had a giant crush on the sexy star Rod Harper. Whatever happened to him?"

Dash flinched and squeezed his wife's arm, not in a loving manner, but more of a jealous, controlling one.

"He's still working in TV. We talk occasionally," Poppy said.

"Well, you were quite good in that show."

"Thank you."

"Do you still act?"

"God, no! I fled town in my thirties, got married, and never looked back," Poppy said. "I just didn't have the energy, not like you. I saw your show the other night. It was wonderful. I so admire how you're still going strong."

"She's like the Energizer Bunny," Dash joked.

Suddenly, Matt appeared at Poppy's side and flashed a smile at Shirley. "Hi, I'm Matt, Poppy's nephew from Boston."

Poppy had overheard Matt telling a guest five minutes earlier that he was her nephew from Chicago. She worried he wasn't going to be able to keep his backstory straight and would get tripped up when someone pressed him.

"You don't have to pretend with me. I know exactly who you really are, Mr. Flowers," Shirley whispered conspiratorially, with a flirtatious wink. "My assistant, Jayden, showed me your picture. He speaks very highly of you."

"What are you talking about?" Dash asked.

Shirley glanced around to make sure no other guests were within earshot, and then leaned into Dash and whispered, "Mr. Flowers is a private detective. I've hired him to recover my stolen jewelry."

"You what?" Dash growled, going pale. "Why didn't you tell me?"

"I don't have to get your approval on every decision I make, Dash," Shirley seethed.

Dash's nostrils flared, but with Poppy and Matt staring at him, he quickly recovered and plastered a polite smile on his face. "I know that, dear."

Shirley couldn't take her eyes off Matt.

"Very smart, posing as the nephew of our hostess," Shirley said with a smile.

Dash glared at Matt and then quickly turned his attention to Poppy. "Are you a detective, too?"

"No, she's my secretary," Matt said, beaming.

"Oh . . ." Shirley exclaimed. "I didn't know you worked for Mr. Flowers. I was under the impression you didn't have to work. . . ."

Shirley regretted her words the instant they spilled out of her mouth.

Poppy shifted uncomfortably. "Yes. Unfortunately, at this stage of my life, I suddenly find myself in reduced circumstances."

Embarrassed, Shirley looked away and scanned the room to see who else was there. She spotted someone, and her face darkened.

"What is she doing here?" Shirley hissed.

"Who?" Poppy asked, following her gaze.

"Olivia Hammersmith. I thought she was out of town."

Olivia Hammersmith was one of Shirley's peers, an iconic actress who had starred in a string of romantic comedies in the 1960s and 1970s, in which she always played the same character, the blond ditz, in the vein of Doris Day or Goldie Hawn, only less funny and charming. When the movie parts dried up after a slew of box-office bombs, and once the novelty of her one-note performances finally wore off, she spent the next ten years out of work, before reinventing herself in the 1990s as a daytime soap opera maven, the proud, strong matriarch of a scandal-plagued family in Houston. She became such a staple, so identified with her lovable mother role, that even today the producers brought her back for small guest appearances on all the holiday-themed episodes, when the whole family gathered together.

"I need a drink, Dash," Shirley said, scowling.

"That's Iris behind the bar. She'll make you whatever you want," Poppy said.

"Thank you," Shirley said as Dash guided her away, a firm hand on the small of her back.

Matt touched Poppy's arm. "I'm sorry. I didn't mean to upset you with my comment about you being a secretary."

"There's nothing to be sorry about. This whole thing was my idea," Poppy said.

"I don't like the husband. I caught him checking out several of the female guests. He strikes me as a real player, and I suspect he has a taste for more mature women."

"Or he has a taste for their money. He claims to be some kind of entrepreneur. Maybe that's his business model. Romancing hapless widows in order to clean them out of their savings."

Matt chuckled. "If he is the local gigolo, that would probably give him access to a lot of homes in here."

Poppy stared at Matt, impressed. He was actually thinking about the case. "Yes, but he's married to Shirley, and she's loaded, so why would he need to steal from other women?"

"They don't look too happy together. Maybe he's secretly storing up his reserves so he can eventually leave her and not have to worry about fighting for alimony."

"That's a really good theory, Matt," Poppy said, smiling. "You're really getting the knack of this detective role you're playing."

"I know, right? I am a really, really good actor!" Matt boasted. "I'm going to go chat up those ladies over there and see what they know." He gave Poppy a quick peck on the cheek. "Later, Aunt Poppy."

She watched him glide over to the ladies, who stopped their conversation in mid-sentence upon his arrival, and all of them ogled the handsome young man as he introduced himself. He charmingly waved off their handshakes in favor of kissing the backs of their hands.

Over at the bar, Iris handed Shirley a cocktail, and before she could take a sip, she spotted Olivia Hammersmith approaching from across the room. Using Dash as a shield, Shirley scurried off in the opposite direction to avoid any contact.

Violet scuttled up next to Poppy. "I just served the last mushroom. Should I take the shrimp puffs out of the oven? They should be done by now."

"Sounds like a plan," Poppy said, still staring at Shirley and Dash, who were now off in a corner by themselves, quietly arguing.

"Did you see Olivia Hammersmith? I didn't know she lived in the Palm Leaf."

"Yes, and apparently, she and Shirley Fox are not on the best of terms."

"Oh, I know. I spoke to her a few minutes ago, when she circled around for another crab-stuffed mushroom. It's much worse than you think. She and Shirley despise each other. Their feud makes Bette and Joan's look like a children's tea party."

"Why? What did she say?"

"Well, back in the nineteen seventies, Shirley's husband at the time, Farley Mead, was cast in a film with Olivia, you know, one of her frothy romantic comedies, which I loved watching!"

"I didn't know Farley ever starred in a movie."

"He didn't. He got fired before the production even started because, according to Olivia, and I quote, he sucked in the rehearsals. But that didn't stop her from sleeping with him. Shirley found out and never forgave her. She also spread it all over town that Olivia was a backstabbing whore. Again, her words, not mine! I'm a retired school principal. I don't use words like that."

"How did I not hear about the famous Shirley Fox–Olivia Hammersmith feud? I used to be so clued in to all the juicy Hollywood scandals."

"Olivia's been waiting years to exact her revenge on Shirley for bad-mouthing her, and now she has the perfect opportunity," Violet sputtered breathlessly. "She got a book deal with a major publisher in New York, and she's writing a tell-all memoir, and it's going to be chock-full of stories about Shirley sleeping her way to the top!"

"How devastating," Poppy sympathized.

"I know! I can't wait to read it!"

"I wonder if Shirley even knows about it."

"If she doesn't, she will soon. Olivia's been prattling on to everybody about it ever since she got here."

A bitter archrival about to expose her deepest, darkest secrets. Married to a lecherous, scheming gigolo. A drunk ex-husband stalking her at her own cabaret act. And a fortune in jewelry swiped from her home. Shirley Fox was having a really bad year.

Almost as bad as Poppy's.

Chapter 24

Over by the bar Poppy spied Iris serving a wheel-chair-bound woman in her mideighties, with long, white hair and a flower-print dress. Her wheelchair was being pushed by a bespectacled man in a loud red Hawaiian shirt like the one Tom Selleck wore in his *Magnum, P.I.* series and in white shorts that showed off skinny, hairy legs and knobby knees. He was rather short, or at least he appeared to be, since he had bad posture and was slouched over as he gripped the handles of the wheelchair. He sported longish, shaggy blond hair, and his face was red from too much desert sun.

They had just arrived.

Poppy casually strolled over to join them.

"Thank you for coming. I'm one of the hosts, Poppy Harmon," Poppy said, extending a hand.

The woman took Poppy's hand and shook it. "Esther Hamilton, and this is my son Sammy."

The man nodded but refused to shake Poppy's hand.

"Don't mind him. Sammy's a germaphobe," Esther said, eyeing her son disapprovingly. "We live just a few blocks over from you."

Iris handed Esther a drink. "Here is your cosmopolitan. What about you, Sonny?"

"Sammy," he whispered.

"He doesn't drink," Esther said, almost disappointed. "He's always been such a straitlaced boy."

Boy?

He was at least in his midforties.

Definitely a mama's boy, in Poppy's opinion.

"I'll have a diet cola, please," Sammy muttered.

Iris eyed him warily and then flicked open a soda can and poured some soda in a plastic cup.

"You have a lovely home," Esther said, looking around.

"Oh, we don't own it. We're just renting it for the season. Betty is an old friend, and she was so kind to let us move in while she's away. She encouraged us to throw a party and get to know the neighbors."

"How lovely," Esther said. "Quite a turnout."

"Yes, and everyone seems so nice," Poppy said.

"Yeah, well, don't get used to it. This place is packed with vipers," Esther said.

"Mother, don't start," Sammy begged.

"It's true. They're nice to your face, but then, the minute you leave the room, they're trash-talking you. And don't get me started on that one," Esther said, pointing across the room.

"Who?" Iris asked.

"Over there. The big star!" She was pointing at Shirley Fox. "What a piece of work. She blows in here like she's the queen of England, and has everyone buzzing, and then she has the gall to flaunt her husband, who, let's face it, is young enough to be her grandson! So disgusting!"

"Mother, please . . ."

"I just speak the truth, Sammy. And I don't want you anywhere near her. The last thing I need is you getting mixed up with that cradle robber!"

Poppy and Iris had to suppress smiles.

The odds of Shirley setting her sights on the nerdy germaphobe Sammy when she had the attention of the far more striking and muscled Dash were a bit far-fetched, to say the least.

"Sammy has a weak spot for actresses. He's watching TV all the time, too much, if you ask me. I'm always saying, 'For the love of God, kid, read a book for once or go outside and get some sun!' "

"I did that this morning, and look, now I'm as red as a tomato. Thank you, Mother," Sammy said, scowling.

"Poppy was an actress once," Iris said.

Poppy shot her an annoyed look.

"Really?" Sammy asked, eyes as wide as saucers. "Have I seen you in anything? You look kind of familiar!"

"Remember *Jack Colt, PI*?" Iris asked.

"Iris . . ." Poppy scolded.

Sammy gasped. "Now I know who you are! Of course! I watched *Jack Colt* every week when I was a kid! It's so nice to meet you!"

Sammy grabbed Poppy's hand and pumped it excitedly.

So much for his germaphobia.

"Leave her alone, Sammy," Esther ordered.

Sammy stared, goggle-eyed, at Poppy, dazzled to be in the presence of a real, live TV star, granted one who hadn't been on the cover of *TV Guide* in thirty years. "Can I get a selfie with you?"

"Sure . . ." Poppy said, embarrassed.

"Mother, give me your phone," Sammy said, snapping his fingers, impatient.

Esther shook her head, annoyed, and fished through a bag she had next to her in the wheelchair. She pulled out a phone and handed it to Sammy, who in turn gave it to Iris.

"Do you mind?"

Iris snatched the phone and quickly took a few photos of Poppy and Sammy smiling. Suddenly, they were alerted to a loud commotion over by the front door. They all turned to see Lucas, Shirley Fox's son, in torn jean shorts and no shirt, forcing his way inside the house as Dash tried to push him back out.

"Now is not the time, Lucas!" Dash warned.

"Out of my way, Romeo. I'm here to see my mother!"

Shirley Fox's face went white as all the guests fell silent.

Lucas was drunk and bleary-eyed and in a violent, dark mood. He looked around at all the gawking faces. "Sorry, folks. I hate crashing your fancy party, but I have some business to discuss with dear old Mom!"

Shirley hustled up to her son and pushed Dash out of the way. "What do you want, Lucas?"

"Just a couple hundred today, Mom. I'm sorry I had to come here, but you weren't answering my calls."

Shirley yanked a checkbook and pen out of her purse and frantically began scribbling.

"Actually, five hundred would get me through

the month," Lucas said, realizing he was in a power position now that his mother was desperate to get rid of him.

Shirley never looked up. She just tore the check off the pad and shoved it at him.

Lucas accepted it with a smile. "Thanks, Mom. You're the best."

"Just leave, Lucas," she whispered.

Dash grabbed his arm to escort him out, but Lucas shook it off. He turned to go but spotted Poppy standing frozen in place by the bar, next to her newfound fan, Sammy.

Poppy quickly turned away to hide her face and murmured to Iris, "Where's Matt?"

"I sent him out for more ice," Iris said, confused.

That was one silver lining.

At least Lucas wouldn't spot Matt Flowers, private eye, at the party.

"Well, well, well, look who it is. The big, bad detective lady with the killer purse! I should sue you for assault, you know. I still got the bruises to prove it!"

"What's he talking about?" Esther asked, curious.

"She's a private detective! That's what I'm talking about! She's working for my mother to find her stolen jewelry!"

"No I'm not," Poppy said weakly. "I just work for one part-time, as his secretary. . . ."

"Just like in *Jack Colt*! Art imitates life! How cool is that?" Sammy exclaimed.

"So that's why you threw this party? So you could gather as many of the residents as you could in one room and investigate us as possible suspects?" Esther asked pointedly.

"No, like I said, I'm just the secretary. I don't do any of the real investigating. . . ."

"Sure looked like you were when I ran into you and your boss at the pawnshop . . ."

"Enough, Lucas. You got your money. Now just leave!" Shirley said to her son.

He didn't budge.

"Do not test me, or that will be the last check I write out to you ever again, I swear," Shirley whispered.

Lucas finally relented, threw one last threatening look toward Poppy, and then stalked out the door.

All the guests in the house were staring at Poppy with expressions of shock, confusion, and outright suspicion.

Violet scampered up to Poppy. "Would now be a good time to serve the bruschetta with peach salsa and melted Brie?"

"Yes, Violet," Poppy said, her face reddening to the point where it now matched the sunburned complexion of her new number one fan, Sammy Hamilton, who still stood next to her, with a goofy smile and adoring eyes.

Chapter 25

"You must see the view of the mountains from the bedroom," cooed Candace, the perky, blond, suntanned real estate agent, as she led Poppy from the rather drab, empty, surprisingly small living room space and through a door to the bedroom. Candace eagerly yanked open the curtains and gestured to a tall four-story apartment building.

"I'm sorry. Where is the mountain?" Poppy asked after walking over and peering out the window.

"Just to the right," Candace said, an encouraging smile firmly planted on her face.

Poppy had to crane her neck in order to see the "breathtaking mountain view," as promised in the ad. She could just make out a piece of it between the apartment building directly in front of her and the mini mall next door.

"Lovely," she lied.

Candace knew her sales pitch was faltering, and fumbled with some papers in her hands. "Let's check out the kitchen, shall we?"

As they left the bedroom, Poppy's heart sank. She hated this apartment for so many reasons, but it was within her price range, and she could afford the down payment with the advance she had received from the Shirley Fox case. Her beloved house had already been sold, and she had been staying with Iris until they all moved into Betty's house to work on the case. However, with any luck, the case would be solved quickly, and she didn't want to have to move back in with Iris. She abhorred the idea of encroaching on her friend's privacy any more than she already had, and she was anxious to finally settle in somewhere she could call home.

The kitchen was even less impressive.

Tiny stove.

Tiny refrigerator.

Narrow counter.

One small drawer for utensils and very little cupboard space.

Poppy had learned to cook after retiring from acting and considered herself a gourmet, especially after bingeing on all those Food Network competition shows and ticking off in her mind just what ingredients she would use to win the first-place prize. Working in this kitchen would be downright depressing after the expansive, U-shaped, luxury custom white kitchen with a dark island and a built-in wine rack she had treasured in her last home with Chester.

Poppy told herself all that was in the past and she was living a new reality now and simply had to make the best of it. Still, her eyes welled up with tears, but she forced a smile and turned to an expectant Candace.

"It's very nice, but I'll have to think about it."

"Don't wait too long. These units are being snapped up like crazy!"

That was a tough buy, to be sure, but Poppy nodded politely and said, "I won't."

Outside, she climbed into the shiny blue used Toyota Yaris she had bought after trading in her Mercedes, and called Violet.

"Hi, Poppy! How did you like the apartment?"

"I'd rather not talk about it," Poppy said.

"What did she say?" she heard Iris ask in the background.

"She didn't like it," Violet confirmed.

"I hate to say I told you so, but I could tell from the photos it was not for you," Iris said after grabbing the phone.

Iris never, ever hated saying, "I told you so."

"I'm going to keep looking," Poppy said.

"Good. You are welcome to stay as long as you want at my house after we move out of Betty's," Iris said. "Normally, houseguests who overstay their welcome get on my last nerve, but not you. I actually enjoy your company. I was totally surprised. I was certain I was going to resent you after a few days."

"Thank you . . . I think. Now, how's it going with you two?" Poppy said, anxious to change the subject.

"Violet's drinking too much. It's barely noon," Iris said.

Violet took the phone back. "Don't listen to her. I am undercover and just trying to fit in with the rest of the Palm Leaf crowd. Everyone's having a Bloody Mary!"

"She's already slurring her words," Iris said.

"I am not slurring my words!" Violet cried. She slurred the word *slurring*.

For a self-proclaimed teetotaler, Violet sure was adapting to the cocktail-hour life in the Palm Leaf faster than either Poppy or Iris.

Poppy had assigned Iris and Violet to have lunch at the Palm Leaf Country Club, where most of the residents hung out for lunch or a drink after their daily golf game, hoping they might socialize some more with the home owners and possibly suss out additional valuable information related to the break-ins that the two women could use in their investigation. Better them than her, since Lucas had pretty much blown her cover at the party.

"So have you heard anything useful yet?" Poppy asked.

There was an awkward pause on the other end of the phone.

"Iris, Violet, are you still there?"

"Yes, we're here," Iris said solemnly. "To be honest, Poppy, the only topic of conversation anyone here is interested in is you working as a secretary for a private detective."

"Let me guess. They're gloating over the fact that the once semi-famous actress and former happy housewife to a wealthy businessman is now desperately trying to make ends meet with menial office work?"

"No, it's not like that!" Violet said in the background.

"Yes, it is, Violet. Don't lie. Poppy deserves to know the truth," Iris barked.

"Well, it's not like I'm surprised. It's natural for people to gossip about someone's dramatic fall from grace," Poppy said, resigned.

Violet grabbed the phone from Iris and wailed, "People can be so mean!"

"Listen, why don't you two hang out there and talk to as many people as you can until it thins out."

"What are you going to do?" Violet asked.

"I'm going to go back to Betty's house and do a little online research about everyone we befriended at the party. Maybe something suspicious or revealing might pop up."

"How are you going to do that?" Violet asked.

"I'm going to start with Facebook. People tend to overshare on social media, so there's no telling what clues we can mine there."

"That is such a smart idea! Oh, Poppy, I always knew in my heart you were cut out for this line of work," Violet cried.

Poppy heard Iris yelling in the background. "Stop sucking up, Violet. It makes you look utterly foolish!"

"Keep up the good work, girls," Poppy said, then ended the call.

When Poppy pulled into the driveway of Betty's house fifteen minutes later, she was overcome with a sense of foreboding.

She had no real reason to feel afraid.

The house looked exactly as she had left it earlier that morning.

Poppy fumbled in her pocket for the key and let herself inside.

The air conditioner was humming.

Nothing appeared out of place.

Until she noticed the sliding glass door leading to the patio was open a crack.

Iris and Violet had been up and gone since dawn.

She had been the last one to leave that morning, and she was absolutely certain she had locked that door before she left.

Upon closer inspection, Poppy's stomach did a flip-flop. The flimsy lock was lying outside, on the cement patio. It was bent and busted, as if it had been pried off the door with bolt cutters.

She glanced around the living room area, kitchen, and patio. Nothing else appeared disturbed or out of place.

She carefully and deliberately made her way into the guest room with the bunk beds, where she stayed with Iris. Beds made. Toys put away. Again, nothing out of the ordinary. She crossed the hall and went into the master suite, where Violet slept. Same story. Bed made. All of Betty's collectible Disney figurines positioned exactly as they were before.

Suddenly, she heard a tapping noise coming from the master bath. She slowly turned around. The door was open halfway, and there was a figure dressed in black and wearing a ski mask scrawling something on the mirror with Violet's Rouge Dior lipstick.

Poppy impulsively screamed.

Startled, the intruder dropped the lipstick on the basin and spun around.

Their eyes locked.

Before Poppy could make a run for it, the masked intruder flew out of the bathroom, grabbed her violently by the arms, and hurled her to the floor before bolting out of the room and out the front door.

After lying on the floor a few seconds to catch her breath and recover from the shock, Poppy slowly crawled to her feet but was too shaken to give chase.

Besides, the intruder appeared far stronger and fitter.

There was very little chance she would be able to catch up to him, let alone overpower him.

She walked over to the bathroom door that was ajar and just stared at what the intruder had hastily scribbled on the bathroom mirror in Violet's lipstick.

Drop the case or die!

Chapter 26

"So can you describe the man you caught in your bathroom?" Detective Lamar Jordan asked, his penetrating brown eyes fixed on a nervous Poppy, who was still rattled by her unexpected encounter with the Palm Leaf burglar.

"He was wearing a ski mask, so I didn't see his face," Poppy answered.

They stood in the master bedroom, and Detective Jordan, a strikingly handsome African American man who was over six feet tall, with a deep, melodic, soothing voice, glanced at the mirror in the bathroom. "Why do you suppose the intruder wrote that on the mirror? Drop the case or die? Do you have any idea what that means?"

Poppy cleared her throat and murmured, "Yes. I'm a private investigator."

"I beg your pardon?" Detective Jordan said with a raised eyebrow.

One of the young uniformed officers who had accompanied the plainclothes detective stopped in his tracks as he was passing by, looking for clues, and stared at Poppy, his mouth agape, convinced he hadn't heard right.

"I'm a private detective," Poppy said, this time louder.

The officer snickered and, after a sharp, disapproving look from Detective Jordan, scurried out of the bedroom to join his partner, who was poking around the living room.

"I see," Detective Jordan said, obviously suppressing a smile.

"Does that surprise you?"

"No, ma'am. Just trying to get down all the information," he said, yanking a notepad and pen from his coat pocket and jotting down notes from their conversation. "Are you licensed?" he asked.

"Yes," she replied firmly. "With the state of California."

"Okay. Got it," he said, keeping his eyes glued to his pad and writing furiously. "What kind of case does the intruder want you to stop investigating?"

"We've been hired to recover some stolen jewelry from a client," Poppy said.

"We?"

"Yes. My partners, Iris Becker and Violet Hogan, and I."

"And what is the name of your agency?"

"The Desert Flowers Detective Agency."

He looked up from his pad and smiled. "That's cute."

"What?"

"You're all named after flowers. The Desert Flowers. It's adorable."

"If you think so."

Poppy had made the strategic decision to leave out Matt's role in their operation, mostly because she didn't want to give this smug, patronizing detective any more reason to think she was a joke.

He was already amused by the fact that she fancied herself a detective on par with him, and that irritated her.

"And all three of you live here?"

"No. We're house-sitting for a friend who is out of town."

"And who would that be?"

"Betty Mason."

"I was expecting her name to be Rose," Detective Jordan chuckled.

"Why is that?"

"Another flower."

"Funny," Poppy said with a straight face.

"I'm sorry. That was rude."

Poppy didn't dispute his snap assessment.

"So I assume you moved in here temporarily to be closer to where the rash of break-ins occurred?"

"Yes. The police have basically been, shall we say, lagging in their efforts to solve the case, so our client enlisted us to see if we might be more effectual," Poppy said pointedly.

"I'm sure they're doing the best they can," Detective Jordan said defensively. "They have a lot on their plate."

"And I suppose a few stolen watches in a sleepy, retirement community isn't what they consider a top priority."

"That's not true," Detective Jordan said, now stone-faced.

Poppy shrugged, thoroughly unconvinced.

"Who's your client?" he asked.

"That's privileged information."

"No it's not. You're not a lawyer, and we're not in court. You can tell me who hired you."

"I'd rather not."

"Why not?"

"Because I think it's best I respect her privacy."

"So it's a woman," Detective Jordan said, scribbling on his pad.

Poppy wanted to kick herself for being so stupid. She still had a lot to learn about being a cagey private eye.

The officer who had been scouting the living room ambled in and nodded politely to Poppy.

"Find anything?" Detective Jordan asked.

The officer shook his head. "We're still dusting for fingerprints."

"You won't find any belonging to the man who broke in here. He was wearing gloves," Poppy said.

"Okay, well, I think we're about done here. Here is my card, if you remember anything else," Detective Jordan said, pressing his business card in the palm of her hand.

"Thank you, Detective," Poppy said.

Suddenly, they heard the front door of the house burst open and Matt's booming voice. "Poppy! Poppy! Where are you?"

"In here," Poppy said, suddenly regretting not telling the detective everything about the Desert Flowers Detective Agency.

Matt bounded in the room, wearing a bright purple Izod pullover shirt, white shorts, sneakers, and bearing a tennis racket. "I rushed over as soon as Iris called me! I was playing a few sets with Buddy. Are you all right?"

"I'm fine, Matt. You didn't have to come," Poppy said, suddenly sweating.

"Are you her son?" Detective Jordan asked.

"No, her boss," Matt said, extending a hand. "Matt Flowers."

"As in the Desert Flowers Detective Agency?"

"Yes! Wow! You've heard of us?"

Detective Jordan eyed Poppy warily. "Poppy was just telling me all about it."

"Actually, I'm Mr. Flowers's secretary," Poppy muttered.

"I see," Detective Jordan said with a sympathetic look.

It was better that he believe Poppy was just a sad, pathetic, insecure woman who found it necessary to make up stories in order to project a more successful, empowering image of herself than Poppy explain to the detective the real, far more complicated situation.

It also made her more determined than ever to prove to the police and to herself that she was entirely capable of solving this case.

"I won't take up any more of your time," Detective Jordan said, offering Poppy a compassionate smile before walking out.

Matt suddenly threw his arms around her. "Oh, Poppy, I was so worried about you!"

"I'm fine," Poppy said, wriggling free from his grasp.

"I should've been here working on the case with you instead of playing tennis!"

"Really, you're doing great. Just focus on being the face of the agency."

Her words fell on deaf ears.

She could tell he was totally invested in being an equal partner with the rest of them, inserting himself into all the action.

"I should call Heather," Matt said, reaching in his back pocket for his cell phone.

"No!" Poppy cried, grabbing his arm.

"But she'll want to know. . . ."

"Yes, because it will further bolster her case that I should give up on this whole private detective scheme."

"Poppy, she's your daughter. . . ."

"Yes, and I love her dearly, but, Matt, listen to me. Heather is so against this already. If she finds out I was attacked, it will just make things much worse. She'll be hounding me and you even more than she already is, and I can't have her continually distracting us from our first case."

"I don't know. . . ." Matt hesitated.

"You have to promise me you will not say a word to her. Otherwise, this whole thing goes away, and I can tell you're having a lot of fun doing this."

A smile creeped across Matt's handsome face.

"Do you swear?" Poppy implored.

After a few tense moments, during which Matt rolled the whole matter over in his mind, he finally raised his little finger. "Pinkie swear?"

"My God, sometimes you act like a five-year-old."

"I like to think I'm just young at heart," he said, hugging her again.

Poppy sighed with relief, feeling as if she had plugged a possible leak for now. But Matt was a blabbermouth, and she worried it was only a matter of time before he slipped and Heather found out that their big case had suddenly taken a dangerous turn.

Chapter 27

Poppy was impressed when she arrived at the Desert Flowers Detective Agency garage office to discover that Violet had set up a mini command center with her grandson Wyatt. The kid wore a gray T-shirt with the Captain America shield emblazoned on the front of it, and was glued to a desktop computer, working feverishly, as Violet busily laid out a row of printed documents on her desk. A pizza box with only two pepperoni slices left in it was lying on the counter in the kitchen area, alongside several empty soda cans. It appeared as if they had been working hard for quite some time.

Violet looked up and peered over her thin, gold reading glasses when she heard Poppy enter. "Oh, good. You're here."

"What's all this?" Poppy asked.

"Wyatt and I have been doing a little research on Shirley Fox's ex-husband, Farley Mead. According to public records we found online, Farley is suing her for back alimony. I printed out all the court documents for you to look over."

"I didn't even know we had a printer."

"We didn't. I had to buy one at Office Depot. I put it on the company card."

"We have a company card?"

"Yes. We needed one for business expenses, so I applied for one at the bank. It just arrived in the mail. Now, I've read over the lawsuit, and it looks like Farley is claiming that Shirley had some previously undisclosed income from a real estate deal she had gotten involved in when they were still married and that the property has appreciated in value—quite considerably, I might add—and so he's going after half of the equity, which he claims he is entitled to according to California law."

"Is he?"

"I'm not sure. She went into escrow on the property when they were still officially married, but she delayed signing the papers until the day after their divorce was final. Her lawyers are, of course, arguing that the case is without merit, since she didn't technically acquire the property until after the divorce. The whole lawsuit whiffs of desperation."

"Farley has money problems?"

"Boy, is that an understatement! Wyatt was able to hack into his bank portfolio, and let's just say it's a pretty bleak picture. He's drowning in debt!"

"Like, way more than your husband, Aunt Poppy!" Wyatt said, piping in, before picking up a piece of chewed-up pizza crust that lay on the desk, next to the computer, and gnawing at it.

"I'm sorry. Can we go back? Wyatt did what?"

"I know it sounds difficult to bypass all those security firewalls and such, but I watched him do it, and he made it look so easy," Violet said with a bright smile. "I'm so proud of him."

"You do realize that's illegal!" Poppy cried.

"It's only illegal if you get caught," Wyatt said.

"Eat your pizza, dear," Violet said quickly. "Grandma will handle this."

"Violet, you can't ask your grandson to hack into a major corporation's Web site. We could all go to prison!"

"It was his idea!" Violet argued.

"It wasn't like it was Bank of America or something! It was just one of those dinky local banks. Their security system sucked big-time. Trust me, they'll never know," Wyatt offered.

Violet crossed to the refrigerator and plucked out a bottle of water and carried it over to Wyatt. "Drink this, dear. Too much soda isn't good for you."

"Neither is breaking the law!" Poppy shrieked.

Violet nodded submissively. "You're right, Poppy. I'm sorry. Wyatt, apologize to your aunt Poppy and promise to never do it again."

"Yeah, okay, sorry. I promise I won't do it again, Aunt Poppy."

Poppy didn't believe a word the kid was saying.

To begin with, she wasn't even his real aunt.

"Looking at Farley's finances got me thinking. What if he was afraid his lawsuit was going to get thrown out of court, and then where would he be? Maybe he stole Shirley's jewelry so he could hock it for the cash to help him get out of debt!"

"What about the other burglaries?" Poppy asked.

Violet shrugged. "I don't know."

"Maybe he did those, too," Wyatt offered excitedly. "You know, to make it look like they were all random so he wouldn't look suspicious."

"You're such a smart boy, Wyatt. Why are you getting Cs in school?" Violet asked.

"Because I'm bored out of my mind, and I hate all my teachers! They're know-nothing idiots!" Wyatt yelled. "Can we order more pizza?"

"Of course, dear," Violet said before turning back to Poppy. "He is such a valuable asset to our detective agency, don't you think?"

"So what are we supposed to do with this information?" Poppy asked.

"We have that covered. Wyatt and I had a brainstorming session over pizza, and we think one of us should get close to him and press him into opening up, and maybe he'll slip and say something useful or incriminating."

"One of us, meaning Iris," Poppy said.

"Of course! She already has a history with him. By the way, where on earth is she?" Violet said, glancing at the clock on the wall. "I called her twenty minutes ago and told her we needed her over here immediately because Wyatt used her e-mail address to contact Farley and set up a Skype call so she can ask him out on a date."

"You what?"

"It's already three minutes to four."

As if on cue, the door flew open and Iris marched inside. "What is so damn important I had to cut my card game with the girls short and race over here?"

"We are working on a case, Iris. You need to make yourself available at all times," Violet scolded.

Iris's face reddened, but she refrained from comment.

Suddenly, the face of Farley Mead appeared on the computer screen, next to the Skype icon, and a ringtone indicated an incoming call.

"That's him," Violet said. "Iris, we need you to go out to dinner with Farley Mead."

"What are you talking about?"

"It's for the Shirley Fox case. We'll explain everything later," Poppy said, deciding on the spot that Violet and Wyatt's scheme actually wasn't half bad.

"I most certainly will not!"

"But it's your duty as an operative for the Desert Flowers Detective Agency to investigate a suspect by any means necessary!" Violet cried.

"I did not sign up for this! I will not be a prostitute!"

"No one is asking you to have sex with him!" Poppy said.

"Wyatt, cover your ears," Violet ordered, flashing Poppy a hard look.

"Please, Grandma, I know all about sex! I'm twelve!" Wyatt said, rolling his eyes.

"They grow up so fast nowadays," Violet said, shaking her head.

Poppy grabbed Iris by the shoulders and hustled her over in front of the tiny camera above the desktop computer screen. "You wanted to be a private detective. Now's your chance to prove how good you are. This is a simple undercover assignment. You can do this, Iris. Just invite him out to dinner for tomorrow night."

Iris sighed, glared at all of them, and then straightened her blouse and cleared her throat. Poppy and Violet scooted out of sight of the camera, and Wyatt clicked a button on the keyboard and then ducked out of the frame.

"Iris? Is that you?" Farley asked.

All that they could see was a giant cleft chin.

"Sit back a little, Farley. You're too close to the camera!" Iris said, sighing.

He adjusted himself, and now his large nose and wide nostrils were all they could make out.

"Is that better?" he asked.

"No!" Iris roared. "Go farther back! You're still too close!"

Farley moved back, but now only half his face could be seen.

"Move right, Farley! I can see only half of you."

He moved left and was now completely gone.

"Your other right, you stupid—"

"Be nice, Iris!" Poppy hissed under her breath from the other side of the room.

Farley finally entered the frame, and they could now see his entire face.

"Sorry. I'm just not used to using this Skip thing."

"It's Skype!" Iris said, correcting him and shaking her head.

"I have to tell you, the last thing I expected to get today was an e-mail from the lovely Iris Becker. Hearing from you brought back a lot of colorful memories from that summer in Munich. . . ."

"Yes, that was a long time ago," Iris said.

"Remember the night backstage after my show, in my dressing room, when you did that sexy little striptease to . . . ?"

"Shut up, Farley!" Iris screeched.

"Oh, come on. It's just the two of us here. . . ."

"I don't remember that!"

"Don't be shy, you little minx! You certainly weren't that night, as I recall. . . ."

Violet clapped her hands over Wyatt's ears.

"You did it to 'Yes Sir, I Can Boogie,' by Baccara. That was your favorite song at the time. . . ."

The blood was draining from Iris's face, but she recovered quickly and barked, "Have dinner with me tomorrow night, Farley! We can reminisce about all those wild nights!"

"I'd love to!" he crowed.

"I will e-mail you tomorrow with a time and place," Iris said.

"I look forward to seeing your lovely face again after all these years," Farley said with a seductive smile, or at least his attempt at one. "There's just one thing."

"What?" Iris moaned.

"I have a friend staying with me while he's in town, doing a play. Maybe we could make it a double date if you have a friend? He's a great guy. Name's Buddy Rhodes."

Matt's bloviating and aggravating costar who couldn't remember his lines!

No! Not him!

Anybody but him!

"As a matter of fact," Iris said, a satisfied smile creeping on her face, "my friend Poppy just dropped by as we were talking."

Iris reached over, seized Poppy by the collar, and yanked her in front of the camera.

Poppy gave Farley a feeble wave.

"Pretty lady," Farley said, leering. "Are you free to join us for dinner, Poppy?"

"I suppose so, yes," Poppy said, defeated.

"Great! See you gals tomorrow! Now, how do you turn this off—"

Wyatt, who was on his knees, reached up and clicked a button, cutting him off prematurely.

Poppy buried her face in her hands. "Not Buddy Rhodes."

"You wanted to be a private detective, Poppy. Now's your chance. It's a simple undercover assignment," Iris said, thoroughly enjoying herself.

Chapter 28

"Looks like we hit the jackpot tonight, hey, Buddy?" Farley Mead said, elbowing Buddy Rhodes, who was sitting next to him, and leering at Poppy and Iris as they were escorted to the table by a rail-thin blond host in his early sixties, who was wearing a snappy blue dress shirt and crisp tan slacks, his eyes pried wide open and his inflexible cheeks impossibly tight from an obvious face-lift. He gave the ladies a Joker-like smile as he gestured to the two gentlemen waiting for them.

"Ladies, enjoy your dinner," he said, which, in Poppy's mind, was downright unimaginable, given the presence of their two lecherous dining companions.

Poppy had to admit, she was happy to be having dinner at Copley's, a Palm Springs staple, with its gorgeous outdoor patio next to a charming little abode purportedly once owned by Cary Grant. Its movie-star pedigree got names on the reservation list, but the imaginative menu got them coming back.

Buddy sprang from his seat and pulled out a chair for Poppy, who smiled and whispered, "Thank you," before sitting down.

When Farley attempted to do the same, Iris waved him away, refusing to allow him any opportunity to be gentlemanly.

"I can sit all by myself, thank you very much," she barked.

Farley gazed lovingly at her, not the least bit deterred. "You both look lovely this evening," Farley marveled. "Don't they, Buddy?"

"I'll say," Buddy agreed before placing a paw on Poppy's hand, which was reaching for a menu. "I was surprised you agreed to be my date tonight. When Matt first introduced us, I got the impression you weren't all that interested in me."

"Well," Poppy said, sighing, "I've decided to take more chances in life, be more spontaneous, see where life leads me, be less rigid."

Buddy winked at Farley. "We love women who aren't so rigid, don't we, Farley?"

Farley cackled. "I'll say."

Iris rolled her eyes, visibly disgusted. "I need a drink."

"I've already ordered us a bottle of pinot noir," Farley said.

"I always start with a vodka cocktail first, and then I move on to wine with dinner. That's how I like to do things, and I am not going to change my habits for you," Iris scoffed.

"Very well," Farley said, waving over the waiter. "You haven't changed a bit, Iris. Still outspoken and refreshingly honest."

A tall, gangly waiter scooted over expectantly.

"I need a vodka as soon as you can get it to me," Iris said.

Noticing that Buddy was holding Poppy's hand, Farley quickly made a play to grab Iris's hand, but she slapped it away.

Iris turned to the waiter. "Make it a double."

The waiter scurried off.

Chastised for the moment, Farley kept his hands to himself and smiled. "What a coincidence that you two ladies are friends and that Buddy and I are pals, too. We go way back, late seventies, am I right, Buddy?"

"Oh, yeah, we met up in Vegas in nineteen seventy-eight, I believe, when we were both there trying to score a guest spot on *Charlie's Angels*. The show was there shooting a big two-hour episode with Dean Martin, and frankly, neither of us were interested in actually getting parts. We just wanted to score with one of the Angels."

"Did you?" Poppy asked, attempting to at least appear engaged in the conversation.

"Nah, never got near them," Buddy said. "Farley had a better shot than me. He was a famous crooner. I was just an unknown bit player. But we bonded trying. Been friends ever since."

"I got close, though. I was the second choice to play a lounge singer who turns out to be a bad guy, but in the end, they went with Dick Sergeant, you know, the second Darrin on *Bewitched*," Farley said.

"Do you two honestly think this passes as interesting conversation?" Iris asked.

Poppy kicked her under the table.

Iris flinched and shot Poppy a look, but she finally got the hint and stopped with the insults.

Neither man appeared offended.

"We can always talk about our summer in Munich if you prefer, Iris," Farley teased.

"I'd rather go back to hearing about you trying to get inside Cheryl Ladd's pants," Iris barked.

The next thirty minutes were devoted to Farley and Buddy's wild days tearing up the town together in Hollywood during the drug-fueled 1980s, chasing after the hot TV actresses at the time, like Michelle Pfeiffer and Kim Basinger, long before they ever became über-famous film stars.

Never once did they inquire about their dates or their interests or any stories they might want to share.

It was as if Poppy and Iris weren't even there.

These two drinking buddies were too busy enjoying each other's company to be bothered with paying any attention to their dates for the evening. Which was fine by Poppy, because when she did interject something or ask a question, suddenly Buddy would focus on her and try to play footsie with her under the table. It was far preferable that he just forgot she was even present at the table.

After polishing off a bottle of pinot noir before their appetizers, Hawaiian ahi tacos and pan-seared jumbo scallops, Farley and Buddy quickly moved on to hard liquor, downing one scotch on the rocks after the other, their voices getting louder with each war story about bedding—or trying to—one Hollywood starlet after another.

Iris didn't even try to suppress a yawn.

But neither man noticed.

After the shockingly tall waiter arrived with their entrées, Poppy simply focused on her roasted Scottish salmon and garlic shrimp. Normally, she would avoid garlic while on a date, but tonight she had requested extra garlic, hoping it might be an impediment to any of Buddy's awkward advances post-meal. She was certain Iris could take care of herself, easily discouraging any unwanted moves from Farley with a devastating taunt or, if need be, her hammy German fists.

Poppy knew they were here on a mission, and with time elapsing, she racked her brain to try to come up with a smooth, subtle way to steer the conversation toward the recent spate of break-ins at the Palm Leaf Retirement Village.

In the end, she needn't have worried.

Iris took the reins with a far more direct approach.

"Hey, Farley, did you break into your ex-wife's house and steal her jewelry?"

Farley instantly stopped talking about the time he flew to Hawaii to appear in *The Jim Nabors Polynesian Extravaganza* and nearly picked up Pat Benatar at the bar in the Hilton Hawaiian Village, and shifted in his seat toward Iris. "I beg your pardon?"

"You heard me. Where were you on the seventeenth of last month?"

There was an awkward silence.

Poppy stabbed at her last garlic shrimp with her fork and popped it in her mouth.

"I don't know. . . . I don't keep a diary . . . ," Farley said, suddenly flustered. "Why do you want to know?"

"Because as a temporary resident of the Palm Leaf, I don't want some burglar plundering my valuables, so if it's you, I want to know now."

"Why on earth would you think I'm some kind of thief?"

"Because you keep answering my questions by asking questions and not giving any answers, and quite frankly, I find that highly suspicious," Iris said, her eyes boring into him.

"And I thought Poppy was the detective," Buddy cracked.

"What?" Farley sputtered.

Poppy sighed.

She was hoping Buddy had forgotten about that little tidbit when they met at Shirley Fox's cabaret act.

Her cover was now blown, and Farley appeared ready to bolt.

Iris quickly grabbed his hand and raised it to her face. "Yes, she may be, but I'm the one who wants to know. Can you blame a girl for wanting to know if I'm dating a criminal?"

Farley raised an eyebrow.

Dating?

He was suddenly intrigued.

But he was also a bit more than a little tipsy at this point and had no idea how to respond. He sat at the table like a little boy who'd been scolded by his teacher for acting out in class. "I want to reassure you, Iris, but honestly, I don't know where I was last night, let alone last month. . . . But I can promise you I was nowhere near—"

"I'd just feel more comfortable knowing it's not you," Iris said, suddenly a seductive tone in her voice. "That way, after dinner, I won't have any inhibitions when we get back to your place."

Poppy nearly choked on her garlic shrimp.

"Yes, ma'am, and I want to put your mind at ease . . . but honestly, I don't recall. . . . When was it?"

"The seventeenth," Iris said.

"The seventeenth," he repeated. "That was what day . . . ?"

Iris checked the calendar on her phone. "It was a Saturday—"

"Farley, you were with me!" Buddy interrupted. "That was the weekend we hung out at the Spa Resort Casino and played the slots with those two divorcées from Toledo!"

"That's right!" Farley said, slapping his forehead with the palm of his hand. "Now I remember!"

"How late were you there?"

"All night . . . well, until about three in the morning, when we got separated from the girls . . ."

Ditched was probably a more accurate description.

"Then we both took an Uber home."

The burglary was discovered long before 3:00 a.m.

"Do you have witnesses?" Iris asked.

"Well, you can call the Toledo broads, but the number they gave me·didn't work when I tried to call them the next day to invite them to lunch."

Big surprise.

"We will check the casino's security camera footage," Iris promised.

"Fine. Go ahead," Farley said, shrugging. "In the meantime, you're just going to have to trust me."

He reached over and tried grabbing Iris's hand one more time.

And once again she slapped it away.

Hard.

But he was too drunk to feel the pain.

So Farley's alibi was airtight.

Or at least Poppy expected it to be.

They didn't seem at all worried that the Spa Resort Casino's security cameras would tell a different story.

Now the challenge was, how could they ditch these two drooling, obnoxious lotharios, like those tourists from Toledo obviously did?

Poppy was impressed to discover that Iris had that detail already covered.

Suddenly, Violet appeared at the table, her face flushed with anger. "Farley, how could you?"

"I'm sorry. . . . Who are you . . . ?" Farley asked.

"I suppose I shouldn't be surprised you don't remember. You were as drunk as a skunk the other night, when you told me that you loved me!" Violet wailed.

"I . . . what?"

Iris played along. "You told this woman you loved her? And all along I thought you and I shared something special."

"We do . . ." Farley said, fumbling for what was left of his drink.

"We met at the Spa Resort Casino last week, and he said he had never met a woman like me! He told me he wanted to marry me," Violet sobbed.

"What? Farley, how could you?" Iris wailed. "All these stories about all the women you've dallied with over the years. I thought what you were really trying to tell me was that they meant nothing to you, that they were just a bit of fun until you met that special one! How could you be so cruel? You made me believe I was her, the one you had long been waiting for, ever since our eyes first met in Germany, and now we were finally reunited after all these years apart!"

"I've never seen this woman before in my life . . ." Farley bellowed, pointing at Violet, utterly confused. "I swear!"

"So I meant nothing to you!" Violet screamed, loud enough to turn heads at the surrounding tables. "I should have known better than to get involved with someone in show business!" Violet marched over to him and slapped him hard across the face with the back of her hand.

This time, Poppy guessed, he felt it.

He rubbed the red welt on his left cheek with his fingers.

Violet stormed off.

Iris stood up. "I had such high hopes for tonight. And once again, you've left me heartbroken, Farley."

She followed Violet out.

"What just happened?" Farley asked, truly perplexed.

Poppy pushed back her chair and grabbed her purse.

"Wait . . . Where are you going?" Buddy asked.

"Home."

"But I didn't do anything."

"No, but I can't say I'm impressed with the company you keep. Good night, Buddy."

Poppy raced to catch up with Iris and Violet.

The host with the face full of nips and tucks intercepted her. "No dessert?"

"Not tonight," Poppy said before turning and pointing to Farley and Buddy, who sat dumbfounded at the table, wondering how their romantic evening had suddenly gone so violently off the rails. "They're ready for the check."

She ran out to Violet's car, which was where Iris and Violet were waiting for her.

And for the first time, Poppy felt like her trio of mature lady detectives was working together as a very effective team.

Maybe there was hope for the Desert Flowers Detective Agency.

Chapter 29

The iconic Plaza Theatre in downtown Palm Springs was once host to the world-famous *Fabulous Palm Springs Follies* show, a Broadway-caliber production celebrating the music, films, and television programs of the forties, fifties, sixties, and seventies, with a cast old enough to have lived through every period to which they paid tribute. The seasoned performers included dancers from *The Carol Burnett Show*, retired showgirls from the Vegas Strip's early days, still doing high kicks well into their seventies; and old-timer comedians whose last TV appearances were on classic seventies game shows like *Match Game* and *Hollywood Squares*. *The Follies* was reliably hosted by popular performers from yesteryear, like Maureen McGovern, who would perform her crowd-pleasing pop hits, such as "Can You Read My Mind?" from *Superman: The Movie* and "The Morning After" from *The Poseidon Adventure*. The theater, a historic landmark, closed in 2014 and now was rented only sporadically for special events, such as today's tribute to the career of Shirley Fox for her friends and fans.

Shirley had at first resisted such a tribute because, after all, she wasn't dead yet, but a small but rabidly loyal Shirley Fox fan club, still going strong after all these years, had insisted and had raised the money to pay for renting the theater, so she had finally succumbed to their relentless begging.

In the lobby, attendees lined up at the cash bar, while inside the theater, on the large screen, a compilation of clips from all of Shirley's classic films unspooled to raucous laughter and enthusiastic applause from the barely half-full theater. Following many of her best scenes from her short but impressive list of musical films, the tribute reel highlighted her work on her popular TV series from the 1970s and displayed a few scenery-chewing scenes from a handful of issue-oriented TV movies.

Immediately following the screening, an endless parade of Shirley's former costars, writers, and directors were introduced to tell their own personal anecdotes about Shirley. It was a who's who of the Hollywood directory from forty years ago, at least those still healthy and spry enough to make it to the theater. One by one they filed up on the stage and stood in front of a podium and microphone. Poppy was interested in hearing from the first three, but then, as they kept coming for what seemed like an eternity, the stories began blending together, and she could tell the audience was getting bored and restless.

The evening hit a low note when one crazy-eyed, heavily made-up actress with a giant pink bow in her hair, who was well known for her dumb blond roles, bounced up on the stage. She had costarred with Shirley in one of her more modest hits, *Senator Hot Pants*, in which Shirley played a ditzy beautician who on a whim runs for senator and actually wins and then storms Washington with her wild ideas to make America Beautiful Again and winds up marrying the president. Not a classic on par with *All the President's Men*, but it did garner Shirley a Golden Globe nomination for Best Actress in a Comedy or Musical. The speaker on-stage at the Plaza Theatre played Shirley's teenage apprentice at the beauty shop and disappeared from the movie after the first ten minutes. Still, she had a lot of stories to tell, and all of them were about herself. She had been talking now for twenty-two minutes, and she still hadn't mentioned Shirley.

As the over-the-hill starlet droned on and on, Poppy prayed the power would go out in the old dusty theater and they would have to wrap up the tribute early, any excuse to stop listening to this self-involved crackpot, who at the moment was detailing how her twelve-step program saved her life. Luckily, Violet was the one who answered Poppy's prayers as she scurried down the aisle, excusing herself as she stepped past the audience members filling the row, until she reached Poppy and plopped down next to her.

Violet leaned into Poppy and whispered in her ear. "I just came from the management office that handles the Palm Leaf."

"Were they willing to talk to you?"

"Yes. I told them I was an insurance investigator working with several home owners who have policies with my company."

Poppy stared at Violet, dumbfounded. "When did you become such a good liar?"

Violet chose to ignore her. "The management company always does extensive background checks on all their employees, their maintenance crew, pool cleaners, the waitstaff and bar staff at the clubhouse, and none showed any signs of criminal activity. Most of them have been working there for years."

"What about the visitors' log?"

"The company insists they have very tight security at the complex, and they make copies of the driver's licenses of all visitors entering the property, to keep track of who comes and goes. They've run through all of those and didn't come up with any red flags. The woman I spoke to firmly believes that the thief is someone who has regular access through one of the residents."

"But if it's the daughter or son or grandson or third cousin of one of the permanent residents, that still wouldn't explain how he or she got inside all those houses with no sign of forced entry."

"I mentioned that to her, and she's as baffled as we are," Violet said.

They suddenly heard a throat clearing from up on the stage and slowly turned to see the bouncy blonde with the caked makeup and pink bow in her hair glaring at them. She could obviously hear them whispering and was not amused that she did not have everyone's full attention.

Poppy and Violet, who were huddled together, both pulled away from each other and snapped back in their seats, pretending to be riveted on the blonde's sleep-inducing anecdotes.

After a brief pause to make sure everyone in the

audience was focused on her, pink-bow blonde continued with her story. Now she was in Nepal, in search of the Dalai Lama.

Out of the side of her mouth, Violet said in a hushed tone, "If the management company and the staff are in the clear, then someone who lives at the Palm Leaf or is there every day must have found a way to bypass all the alarm codes and has somehow gotten copies of everyone's house keys!"

"How is that possible?" Poppy muttered under her breath.

Violet shrugged.

After telling one last excruciating tale of a fateful encounter with Warren Beatty and how he encouraged her to go back to acting—and now she was looking for an agent to jump-start her career and would be in the lobby after the tribute to talk to any producers or agents who might be interested—pink-bow blonde finally wrapped it up.

She looked visibly disappointed by the mere smattering of applause for her speech, although Poppy clapped her hands as hard as she could, because she was so grateful that the woman was finally exiting the stage. The host, an affable middle-aged man with bushy brown hair, which, Poppy suspected, was a toupee, and who was one of Shirley's biggest fans, bounded over to the podium. After talking about the biography he was working on with Shirley's blessing, he finally got to the business of introducing the guest of honor.

"Shirley has touched so many lives during her long and celebrated career, and we've only begun to scratch the surface today when it comes to detailing her plethora of accomplishments as an actress, a singer, a dancer, and a humanitarian. But it's finally time to hear from the living legend herself, so without further ado . . ."

Before Shirley had a chance to stand up and make her way to the stage, Olivia Hammersmith blew past her, glass of champagne in hand, and stumbled up on the stage. She nearly pushed the host out of the way as she took her place behind the podium and in front of the microphone, a tote bag slung over her shoulder.

She took a generous swig of champagne.

Definitely not her first glass.

"I suppose you all know me . . ." Olivia slurred, obviously blotto.

Polite applause from the nervous audience members, who were on the edge of their seats, waiting for what was about to happen.

"I'm Olivia Hammersmith."

A few people clapped again, in case she hadn't heard them the first time.

"I missed a lot of the speeches because I was out in the lobby, enjoying my bubbly, but I could never forgive myself if I missed out on the opportunity to say a few words about my dear friend Shirley."

Poppy's eyes fell on Shirley, who was seated several rows down toward the front, and she could see her visibly tense up.

First Buddy at the Purple Room and now Olivia at the playhouse.

Shirley had been plagued by hecklers lately.

The host stood skittishly a few feet from Olivia, eyeing her with growing concern, desperately trying to figure out a way to give the old bag the hook without looking like a bully.

"You know, Shirley, standing up here, in front of these bright lights, suddenly I'm drawing a blank. I'm at a loss for words," Olivia said.

An audible sigh of relief from the audience.

Olivia reached into her tote bag and pulled out a thick manuscript with an elastic band wrapped around the middle. "Luckily, I have this to jog my memory."

The welcoming sense of relief was quickly replaced by a palpable tension.

Everyone suddenly expected the worst.

And Olivia Hammersmith did not disappoint.

She dropped the manuscript on the podium with a thud and plucked her reading glasses from the pocket in her skirt and then gave the audience a big smile before she began reading.

"Nineteen sixty-nine. What a year of upheaval and unrest, so full of significant events. The first man on the moon. The Vietnam War raging on. The Beatles' last public performance. The horrific Manson murders. And then there was Barbra Streisand, so woefully miscast in the movie musical *Hello, Dolly!*"

Olivia glanced up from her manuscript and looked down at Shirley, her reading glasses perched on the tip of her nose. "She was way too young to play that role, don't you agree, Shirley?"

Shirley sat frozen in her seat and refused to respond.

"I remember another film that came out that same year, as well. Your first role, I believe as a young ingenue, in a musical called *Let's All Dance*. Not an auspicious beginning for you, as I recall."

Olivia flashed Shirley a devious smile and then continued reading. "*Let's All Dance* was MGM's last gasp from the past, a time when movie musicals dominated, but now with more socially relevant films emerging in the culture, when it was released, it was scorched by critics and ignored by audiences. But it is remembered mostly for one thing—the debut of future star Shirley Fox as a coat-check girl at the Coconut Grove, with big dreams of stardom!"

Poppy held her breath.

Was Olivia actually going to take the high road?

Was she going to pay an honest tribute to the guest of honor?

No such luck.

"Despite the dated feeling of the whole film, Shirley made an indelible impression. The question on everyone's lips was, 'Where did this girl come from?' No one had ever heard of her. I mean, she came out of nowhere! Of course, the gossip around town at the time was that the director, Frank Collins, had spotted her in a seedy bar downtown, and that Shirley's skills unrelated to acting were what sealed the deal for a screen test, but that's unfair. I know for a fact Shirley never slept with her director on that film."

Another round of audible sighs of relief.

"What got Shirley the part was her undeniable raw talent."

An appreciative round of applause.

"And, of course, she boffed the producer of the film, Harvey Cohn."

Absolute silence.

"Cohn was sixty at the time. Shirley was twenty-five. I'm sure many might cringe at the ick factor over the age difference. But who cares? A star was born!"

Some uncomfortable shifting in seats.

Olivia looked up from her manuscript and then raised her champagne glass.

"You've come a long way, Shirley! Here's to you, still singing for your supper after all these years!"

And then she downed the rest of the champagne.

Shirley remained in her seat, not moving a muscle.

"You can read more about it in my upcoming memoir, which will be out next spring! I have four whole chapters dedicated just to you, Shirley!"

And then, the host, unable to take any more, sprang forward, took Olivia forcefully by the arm, and escorted her off the stage and down the steps to the aisle, where he handed her off to an anxious usher, who hustled her out. The host speedily returned to the podium and spoke into the microphone, his mouth too close, which caused earsplitting feedback.

"Now, again, without further ado . . . Shirley Fox!"

The audience exploded with encouraging applause, but the damage had already been done. The devastated screen legend was already racing up the aisle and out of the theater, covering her face to hide the flood of tears.

Chapter 30

After the flummoxed host swiftly wrapped up the proceedings following Shirley Fox's dramatic exit, Poppy and Violet hurried out of the theater together. Outside, they spotted Olivia Hammersmith on the curb, swaying back and forth, trying to fish her car keys out of her purse.

"She's in no condition to drive," Poppy said to Violet. "I'll see you back at the Palm Leaf."

"Okay," Violet said, watching with concern as Olivia, her eyelids at half-mast, tried desperately to press the button on her key to unlock her firehouse-red Chevy Malibu.

Poppy skittered over to Olivia to intercept her before she managed to climb behind the wheel.

"Whoa. Hold on just a minute, Olivia. Why don't you let me drive you home?"

Bleary-eyed, Olivia stared at Poppy with suspicion. "Why would I want you to do that?"

"I think you may have had a bit too much champagne."

"Why, that's the most ridiculous thing I've ever

heard," Olivia slurred. "I am perfectly capable of driving myself home."

Reasoning with her wasn't going to work, so Poppy decided to try another tack.

"If you come with me, I'll fill you in on a little dirt I heard about Shirley Fox that would be a perfect addition to your tell-all book."

That got Olivia's attention.

"What kind of dirt?"

"I'll tell you on the way," Poppy said, gently taking Olivia by the arm and guiding her safely away from her Chevy Malibu.

Poppy plucked the keys out of Olivia's quivering hand and surreptitiously pocketed them.

Olivia craned her head back around toward her Chevy Malibu. "What about my car?"

"It'll be fine parked here overnight, and I promise I will come around and get you first thing tomorrow morning and drive you back here to pick up your car. Deal?"

Olivia mumbled something unintelligible.

Right after Poppy got her situated in the passenger's seat of her own car, Olivia's head drooped back against the headrest and her mouth hung open. She had passed out.

Poppy obviously had nothing dishy to report about Shirley Fox, but the ruse had worked, and she had successfully prevented Olivia from attempting to drive herself home while heavily under the influence of alcohol.

Tomorrow Olivia would probably have no memory of their conversation and Poppy's promise to pass along some delicious gossip.

Poppy drove them back to the Palm Leaf in twenty minutes and was able to rouse Olivia enough to get her inside her house and into bed. She didn't bother trying to undress her and just pulled the comforter up to her chest to keep her warm, since Olivia apparently liked to keep her home at a chilly sixty-eight-degree temperature.

And then Poppy tiptoed out of the room and soundlessly closed the door behind her.

True to her word, the next morning, after an energetic power walk around the Palm Leaf golf course, followed by a hot cup of coffee and one of Violet's homemade sweet cranberry-orange scones, Poppy drove the few blocks from Betty's house over to Olivia Hammersmith's house in order to drive her back to Palm Springs to retrieve her car. Poppy hoped enough time had passed for her to sober up to the point where she could safely drive, but just in case, she brought along a hot, steaming paper cup of black coffee with a plastic lid on the top to keep it from spilling.

When she arrived at the house and rang the bell, there was no answer.

Was Olivia still passed out in bed?

She banged on the door with her fist and waited.

Still no answer.

Perhaps Olivia was already up and out of the house.

Maybe she found a neighbor to drive her back to Palm Springs.

But there was a gnawing feeling in the pit of Poppy's stomach that she just couldn't ignore.

She knocked on the door again.

Something seemed wrong.

She had nightmarish visions of Olivia getting sick in her drunken stupor and choking on her own vomit.

She kicked herself for not staying with her overnight to make sure she recovered from her bender.

Poppy jiggled the door handle.

The door was unlocked.

She entered the house.

She followed the raspy voice of Elaine Stritch singing "The Ladies Who Lunch" on an old CD player into the living room. And then she spotted something out of the corner of her eye.

Turning her head, Poppy gasped, then struggled to steady herself as she stared at the body lying facedown on the floor, next to a cracked coffee table.

A small pool of blood seeped slowly into the pristine white carpet.

Olivia Hammersmith was on the floor, dead.

Chapter 31

When Detective Lamar Jordan and his officers finally arrived on the scene, Poppy's heart was beating so fast, she thought she was going to faint. After all her months of going through the process to become a bona fide private detective, the one thing she had never considered was discovering an actual dead body during the course of one of her cases. She knew enough to know that she should not disturb the body in any way, but during the interminable wait for the police to arrive after she called 911, she did carefully step around the body and kneel down to inspect it thoroughly, making mental notes of her observations. Her on-the-fly inspection came to an abrupt end when she heard the wailing screams of a police siren fast approaching Olivia Hammersmith's house.

There was loud banging on the door, and Poppy opened it without delay, then ushered Detective Jordan and his intrepid band of detectives inside the house.

"Where's the body?" Detective Jordan asked, eyeing her distrustfully.

"In here," Poppy said, then led them into the living room, where Olivia remained facedown on the white carpet.

Detective Jordan, who hadn't encountered many murder cases in this sleepy, arguably dull retirement community, kept a poker face, but Poppy could easily surmise from his stiff countenance that he was somewhat shaken. He ordered his officers to keep at bay any nosy neighbors and passersby outside. They scurried off, leaving him alone with Poppy and the poor victim lying at their feet.

Detective Jordan glanced once more at Poppy. She was expecting him to request that she exit the house immediately, but after a moment, he turned away from her and left her standing by the fireplace, awkwardly out of the way but still very close to Olivia's lifeless body.

He circled Olivia, carefully studying the scene, then leaned over the coffee table to inspect a small crack near the edge. He then got down on his hands and knees to observe Olivia's forehead, which sported a deep gash that had obviously bled out onto the carpet.

He peered up at Poppy.

"You didn't touch anything, did you?"

"No," Poppy sighed.

Detective Jordan popped back up on his feet and continued his examination. "Was there any sign of forced entry when you arrived?"

"The door was unlocked, so I let myself in. That's when I found her. . . ."

He nodded curtly, then stared down at Olivia.

"You told the nine-one-one operator she had been drinking?"

"Yes. We were at an event in Palm Springs yesterday afternoon, and she had consumed way too much champagne and was too impaired to drive, so I gave her a lift home, and then I came around this morning so I could drive her back to retrieve her car."

"How was she when you left her?"

"Barely conscious, but I managed to get her into bed, and she fell right to sleep, so I left."

"Seems to me that she must have woken up sometime during the night and come out of the bedroom to get a glass of water or something, and she was still intoxicated and tripped or stumbled and fell. . . ." He pointed to the crack in the wood of the coffee table. "She probably hit her head on the coffee table on the way down, and it was the blow that killed her. . . ."

"Like William Holden," Poppy said.

"Who?" Detective Jordan stared at her blankly.

"William Holden. The movie star? *The Bridge on the River Kwai? Sunset Boulevard?* Won the Oscar for *Stalag 17*?"

"Sorry. I'm not much of a movie buff. More of a sports fan myself."

Plus, he was barely forty, so a silver-screen legend like Bill Holden was way before his time.

"He died in a similar fashion. He was heavily intoxicated, slipped on a rug, lacerated his forehead on a teak bedside table, and bled to death."

Detective Jordan was not impressed with her knowledge of Hollywood history. He barely acknowledged her as he shrugged and went back to inspecting the body.

"Overall, I'm thinking we're looking at a tragic accident," he said.

"Really?"

Detective Jordan stared at Poppy with a raised eyebrow. "Yeah. Why?"

"Well, I just noticed a couple of things, that's all."

"Like what?" Detective Jordan said, glaring, challenging her.

"There's a display case over there that has some photos and memorabilia from Olivia's acting career. If you look inside, you will see a couple of framed pictures and awards have been knocked over."

He stared her down for a few seconds before turning on his heel and marching over to the display case and peering through the glass.

"Do you see?"

"Yes," he hissed, mad at himself for not noticing this detail before.

"It appears that there may have been some kind of struggle."

"Or maybe Ms. Hammersmith was just so drunk, she bumped into it on her way into the living room. Did you think of that?"

"Yes, I did," Poppy said. "But if you look closely at her fingernails, you'll find what looks like tiny pieces of skin underneath."

"Wait just a minute, Ms. Harmon!" Detective Jordan barked. "I thought you said you didn't touch the body."

"I didn't! I swear! But you'll notice the palm of her hand is turned out and her nails are really long, so I was able to get down on my hands and knees and get a really good look."

Detective Jordan did a slow burn before turning his back on Poppy, walking over to the body, dropping down to his knees, and then bending his frame over, one eye closed to thoroughly observe the long, sharp, pink-painted nails.

He jumped back up. "You can't be one hundred percent certain that's human skin there."

"I said it looked like skin. I didn't say I was positive."

"Look, I know you're having fun playing this little game of pretending to be a detective. . . ."

"Actually, I'm licensed with the state of California. . . ."

"I thought you were just a secretary."

"I can send you my certificate, if you don't believe me."

"Fine. Whatever. You're a detective. But just because you found a few items out of place and something that may or may not be human skin underneath the victim's nails, that doesn't necessarily make this a crime scene."

"I was just sharing a couple of observations."

"And I appreciate it, Ms. Harmon. But this is my case, not yours, and I am not going to make any assumptions until I have my CSI guys comb this place. They're trained in determining whether or not any foul play is involved here, and so I don't need you doing their job for them."

"I understand completely."

"So why don't you go home, and if I have any further questions for you, I will give you a call, okay?"

"Yes, Detective Jordan," Poppy said. "Thank you."

Poppy glanced down at Olivia Hammersmith's

body one more time before nodding sadly at the detective and heading out the door.

Detective Jordan was right.

Poppy was an amateur.

The highly trained crime-scene investigators were far more skilled than she was when it came to determining a cause of death.

And by the following morning they had issued their findings.

Olivia Hammersmith's death had been ruled a homicide.

Chapter 32

Panic permeated the Palm Leaf Retirement Village after word spread that Olivia Hammersmith had been found murdered in her home. It quickly became clear to all the residents that not only was a brazen thief with unexplainable access to all the targeted homes still on the loose, but also his or her crimes had suddenly escalated from simple nonviolent burglary to murder. Suddenly, the happy hour mixers at the club were like a ghost town, as residents stopped socializing and remained locked up tight in their homes, some with guns at hand in case the killer decided to prey upon them in the middle of the night.

There was also a small faction of gossipy folks who pointed fingers at Shirley Fox as Olivia's obvious killer. After all, she had good reason to want to see Olivia dead. Perhaps she was willing to go to extremes to keep Olivia's tell-all memoir from ever seeing the light of a bookstore display window.

The police finally released a statement, reporting that Olivia had indeed died from the traumatic blow to her head when she hit the coffee table as she fell to the floor, but that there were also signs of a physical struggle. The killer had either pushed her too hard or intentionally banged her head against the table.

Poppy was not entirely convinced that Olivia's murder and the rash of burglaries were necessarily connected, but since there had been next to zero crime in the Palm Leaf prior to the first break-in, it would seem logical that perhaps the thief believed Olivia was not home when he decided to strike, and when she surprised him, he panicked and killed her.

Shirley Fox had been lying low ever since Olivia's death became public, canceling her remaining shows at the Purple Room and avoiding reporters camped outside the Palm Leaf residents' gate, hoping to get an interview with her.

Which was why Poppy was surprised to receive an urgent call from Shirley's personal assistant, Jayden, requesting a meeting between Shirley and Matt at the Desert Flowers garage office in Palm Springs as soon as possible.

Poppy was able to catch Matt, who was leaving to drive to Hollywood for a commercial audition, and he swung by on his way to play his Matt Flowers, PI role for their client.

Matt insisted on wearing a fedora for the meeting just to make himself look more the part, and he stood in a corner, making strange noises, which he called his vowel groups, to warm up for the show.

The noises irritated Iris to the point where she

plugged a headset into her computer and played selections from Mozart to drown him out.

When Shirley Fox—dressed in a wide white hat with black trim and a matching suit right out of Alexis Carrington's closet from *Dynasty*, a pair of oversize black sunglasses shading her eyes—finally breezed into the office forty-five minutes late with her assistant Jayden in tow, Matt was ready to perform.

Curtain up.

With a concerned look on his face and a somber tone, Matt greeted Shirley, taking her hand in his and bringing it up to his beating heart. "I am so sorry about your tragic loss, Ms. Fox. I know you and Olivia were close friends."

Shirley stared at him, not sure if he was joking or not.

Poppy had e-mailed Matt a full dossier on where they stood with the case, all the residents they were investigating, and the contentious feud between their client and Olivia Hammersmith. He clearly had forgotten or had neglected to read it.

"He means you were close friends once," Poppy interjected. "Way back when."

"Yes, I'll admit, there was no love lost between me and that woman," Shirley spit out. "And everyone knows it. That's why I'm here."

"Poppy, why don't you fill Ms. Fox in on what we have so far regarding our efforts to recover her jewelry," Matt suggested.

Because he had absolutely no idea.

She would scold him later for not doing his homework.

Shirley and Jayden sat down in chairs and looked at her expectantly.

"Yes, well—" Poppy said, rifling through some notes as Violet brought two cups of coffee from the mini-kitchen for Shirley and Jayden.

"I don't care about that anymore," Shirley interrupted. "I want you to change the focus of my case."

"You don't want us to find your jewelry?" Matt asked, dumbfounded.

"If you do, that's fine. But I would prefer you concentrate your talents on clearing my name, Mr. Flowers."

"I'm not following . . ." Matt whispered.

Poppy sighed and gingerly stepped forward. "I believe Ms. Fox would like you to help her prove she did not kill Olivia Hammersmith."

"Oh," Matt declared, as if lightning had finally struck.

But, alas, it hadn't, because he still sported a screwed-up, confused look on his face.

"Your secretary is right, Mr. Flowers. Most of the residents at the Palm Leaf were at that tribute for me the day before Patsy here discovered Olivia's body. . . ."

"Poppy . . ." Matt said.

"I'm sorry?"

"Her name is Poppy, not Patsy. And that's Violet and that's Iris over there," Matt said, beaming. "They're all named after flowers. Isn't that the cutest damn thing you've ever heard?"

Shirley Fox was not amused.

"And they were all witnesses to Olivia publicly humiliating you, and now everyone is convinced that her crashing the tribute was the motive for you to murder her," Iris said, impatient that it was taking so long to get to the point.

"That's correct," Shirley said, sipping her coffee. "I am a lot of things, but I am not a violent person. I would never harm anyone . . ." Shirley said before adding, "Physically."

There were a lot of ex-husbands, past lovers, and mistreated costars who might argue about Shirley's penchant for mental abuse.

"If that's what you want us to do, then that's what we're going to do, am I right, ladies?" Matt asked, turning to his team of "assistants" hovering in the background.

They all nodded and smiled.

"Then I won't take up any more of your time, so you can get started," Shirley said, reaching out for Jayden to help her up on her feet.

Matt gallantly took Shirley by the arm to assist in escorting her to her Rolls-Royce parked outside, but they had not quite made it to the door when it suddenly burst open and Heather stormed into the office.

"Heather, I thought you were working . . ." Matt said softly.

"I'm on a break!"

"Have you met . . . ?" Matt asked weakly, gesturing to Shirley, who had been startled by Heather's sudden and dramatic appearance and was at the moment trying to catch her breath.

"Nice to meet you," Heather barked without waiting for a proper introduction. "I saw all your movies when I was a kid! But I'm not here to get a selfie with a celebrity. I'm here to put a stop to this ridiculous charade!"

Matt's bulging eyes pleaded with her to keep

her mouth shut, while Poppy, Iris, and Violet stood next to each other, frozen in place, afraid their very first case was about to explode in their faces.

Before she could get another word out, Matt grabbed her forcefully by the arms, pulled her into him, and planted a big sloppy, wet kiss on her face, effectively sealing her lips shut and preventing her from talking anymore.

He held his mouth in place for what seemed like an eternity, but soon realized Shirley and Jayden were not going anywhere. They were too curious to know just how long this kiss was going to last.

Finally, Matt released Heather, who gasped for air as Matt continued to quickly usher Shirley and Jayden out to her Rolls.

"Hold that thought, honey. I'll be right back," Matt cooed before turning to Shirley, whom he quickly led out the door. "My girlfriend. We're very much in love."

"I can see that," Shirley said.

Jayden just smiled at Matt lustfully, as if he was picturing himself on the receiving end of one of Matt Flowers's long, deep kisses.

There was an awkward silence while Matt was outside.

Heather refused to make eye contact with her mother.

"Can I get you some coffee, dear?" Violet offered, attempting to break the tension.

"No, thank you," Heather answered in a clipped tone.

"I'm sorry I haven't called, Heather. I've been very busy lately," Poppy said.

Heather half nodded, then looked away again.

Matt bounded back into the garage office.

"Man, that was a close one! I thought Heather was going to blow our cover!" Matt cried, laughing with relief.

"That was my intention before you stopped me," Heather said.

Matt moved in to kiss her again. "I'm glad you're here."

She pushed him away.

"Heather . . ." Poppy admonished.

Heather still did not look at her mother. She kept her eyes trained on Matt. "I know my mother is a lost cause. She's never going to stop putting her life in reckless danger just to make a quick buck. I can beg her until I'm blue in the face, and she's never going to listen to me. Whoever murdered Olivia Hammersmith could have been still hiding in the house, but she just blundered in there on her own, without any thought to her own safety."

"To be fair, I wasn't expecting to find a dead body when I entered the house, Heather . . ." Poppy argued.

But Heather ignored her.

Which, in Poppy's mind, was a cruel slap in the face.

"I have no control over her actions, that's for damn sure," Heather growled as her eyes bored into Matt's. "But you, you I can at least reason with. I want you to stop this big fat lie about you being a world-class detective. I don't care if it's some kind of cool acting challenge, and I don't care that you're doing this as a favor to my mother. . . ."

"Heather, just let me get through this one case, and then I'll hang up the Matt Flowers character forever."

Poppy knew by the look on his face that he could never stop now.

He was having way too much fun.

Matt crossed his heart with his hand. "I promise."

"That's not good enough," Heather said flatly. "Either you give up this ridiculous, foolhardy enterprise right now or we're finished."

Another long, awkward pause.

Interrupted only by Iris slurping her coffee, riveted on the showdown like she was engrossed in watching a really good TV drama.

Matt's head drooped forward, and he sighed.

"I'm sorry it's come to this, but you leave me with no choice," Heather said, distraught. "If you're not outside in five minutes, I'm leaving. For good."

And then she walked out.

Matt stared at the floor for a long time and then slowly turned to Poppy, Iris, and Violet, who were still glued in place, having watched the whole ugly scene unfold.

He smiled sadly and said, "I'm so, so sorry, ladies, but I love Heather too much to let her go."

After a melancholy tip of his fedora, he walked out of the garage office.

"So what do we do now?" Violet wanted to know.

"We're going to recover Shirley Fox's valuables, solve the murder, and get justice for Olivia Hammersmith," Poppy said with a charged vehemence. "With or without the great Matt Flowers."

Chapter 33

Poppy immediately went into overdrive on her mission to clear Shirley Fox before the story that she brutally killed her archrival, Olivia Hammersmith, began to firmly take root in the Palm Leaf complex. The following morning, she drove straight to Shirley's house, where Dash greeted her at the door.

"You're early. Shirley's not quite ready yet," Dash yawned, bare-chested and wearing only white boxer shorts.

"May I come in and wait, please?"

Dash thought about it for a moment, then shrugged and stepped aside, allowing her inside the house.

The place was exquisitely decorated with expensive art pieces from Shirley's many world travels. Unlike Olivia, Shirley chose not to flaunt the awards she had received from her acting work. If she still possessed the trophies, it appeared they were stuffed in a closet somewhere.

Dash padded into the kitchen, leaving Poppy standing in the foyer. Not bothering to turn his head, he asked, "Want some coffee?"

"No, thank you."

Dash puttered in the kitchen for a few minutes before roaming back to Poppy, coffee mug in hand, scratching his tousled hair on top of his head. "So why didn't Flowers come himself?"

"He's busy questioning other potential suspects," Poppy lied.

In fact, Iris and Violet were out canvassing the neighborhood and doing all the necessary legwork.

She hadn't heard from Matt since he left their garage office, chasing after Heather, tail between his legs.

Dash sized Poppy up and down. "You know, you're still a very attractive woman."

"Thank you, I think," Poppy said, racking her brain for a way to quickly change the subject.

"Very fit," Dash said with a wolfish smile as he kept stepping into her personal space.

"I do Pilates."

"Is that all? You have a rocking body for a woman in her sixties. What other kinds of exercise do you like to do, Poppy?"

The subtext was obvious.

He wasn't talking about exercise.

Poppy's skin crawled as she deliberately inched away from him.

Dash relished the idea that he was making her uncomfortable, and advanced ever so slowly, getting closer and closer, backing her almost up against the front door in the foyer.

Poppy checked the time on her phone.

"Shirley better hurry up, or we're going to be late."

"It's no secret I'm a big fan of older women."

"Older women or their purse strings?"

"Ouch," he laughed, raising a hand to his heart. "You hurt my feelings, Poppy."

He then extended the hand from his heart toward her face, and she recoiled, disgusted.

"If you don't get out of my personal space, I'm going to knee you in the balls," Poppy said coldly.

"I consider that foreplay—"

"Sorry I'm late," Shirley interrupted, putting on a diamond earring as she entered from the bedroom. "It takes me a lot longer to put on my face these days."

She stopped suddenly at the sight of Dash practically on top of Poppy by the door, but she chose not to comment and simply let it go.

"You look beautiful, darling," Dash said, playing the dutiful husband.

Shirley wasn't buying any of his bull and just rolled her eyes. "Is Matt meeting us at the police station?"

"No, I'm afraid not. He sent me as your escort today so he can be free to follow up on some other leads," Poppy said.

Shirley paused, thought about it, decided to buy the excuse, and then nodded, turning to Poppy. "Okay, let's get this over with."

"Do you know what you're going to say to Detective Jordan?" Poppy asked.

"Yes. That I was here with Dash, having dinner, on the night Olivia was killed. I was very upset about what had happened at the tribute earlier in the day, and Dash was doing his best to comfort me, and then, after watching the local news, we went to bed."

"Do you need me to come with you and corroborate your story?" Dash asked.

"No, Dash," Shirley said. "This is *my* statement. If the police want to talk to you, they'll contact you. You just stay here and do what you do best. Lounge by the pool and get drunk."

He ignored the slam. "I'll be here waiting when you get back."

He gave her a peck on the cheek and then did an about-face and ambled off to the sliding glass door that led to the pool outside, winking at Poppy as he left.

"They'll probably want to take a DNA test to prove the skin that was found underneath Olivia's fingernails doesn't belong to you," Poppy said.

"I'm happy to do anything to prove my innocence."

"Once the results come back, Iris . . . I mean Matt, has a reporter friend at the *Desert Sun* who we can get to write about the mountain of evidence the police have that excludes you as a suspect."

"I'm very impressed with how Matt is having us go on the offense like this," Shirley said as they headed out the door.

"Yes, he's very good," Poppy said, smiling to herself.

Shirley insisted they go in her Rolls-Royce.

Poppy was too nervous at the thought of getting behind the wheel of such an expensive car, so Shirley drove them to the police station in Palm Springs where Detective Jordan worked.

After they signed in and waited almost an hour, a

heavyset police officer whom Poppy recognized from the crime scene after she had been attacked by the intruder waddled out and accompanied Shirley back to a private room where she could provide a DNA sample.

"I'll wait for you right here," Poppy said.

Shirley didn't respond or look back. She was either too nervous or was uninterested in conversing anymore with one of Matt Flowers's lowly employees.

Forty-five minutes passed.

Poppy plucked her phone out of her bag and called Iris, who answered gruffly, "What?"

"I'm still at the police station with Shirley."

"Good for you. Is that all?"

"Am I getting you at a bad time?"

"Yes. I'm at the office, talking to Shirley's assistant."

"Jayden? What's he doing there?"

"He wanted to go over Shirley's alibi with me so we can share it with the cops and get her name cleared."

"That's not necessary. I've already heard everything from Shirley, and she's giving her statement to Detective Jordan now."

"Oh, well then, this is a total waste of time," Iris sighed. "So you were with her until what time?"

"Eleven thirty," Poppy heard Jayden answer on the other end of the phone.

"Eleven thirty at night?" Poppy asked.

"This was p.m.?" Iris asked.

"Yes," Jayden answered.

But that didn't make any sense.

Shirley's official story was that she spent the whole evening alone with Dash, who commiserated with her about the embarrassing scene earlier in the day, at her tribute. She never mentioned Jayden being there.

"Iris, ask him what he and Shirley were doing until eleven thirty."

"What were you two doing?"

"Going over her upcoming concert dates in Hollywood next month, which have now been canceled, after all my hard work getting them set up in the first place," he said, frustrated.

Poppy could picture him pouting.

Another call began beeping in.

It was Violet.

"Iris, I have to go. I'll meet you at the office after I'm finished with Shirley and drop her off at her home."

Iris began to mutter something, but Poppy was already off the call and was now talking to Violet.

"Violet, what have you got?"

"Something potentially big."

"What?" Poppy gasped.

"I was hanging out at the clubhouse, grilling the locals, and who should turn up for breakfast but my old friend Esther."

"The one with the grown son still living with her?"

"Yes. Sammy. She told me she and her son were out walking their dogs around six o'clock on the night Olivia was killed, and they saw her arguing with a young man in her driveway. It got so heated, Esther sent Sammy over to make sure Olivia wasn't in any kind of danger. Well, the second the man saw Sammy, he got spooked and ran off. Apparently, when Esther asked if Olivia was okay, she just brushed it off and went back inside her house."

"Did Esther recognize the young man who was arguing with Olivia?" Poppy asked.

"No, but she described him as African American, around twenty-three or twenty-four years old, about five feet nine inches tall, lean, and wearing a bright orange, expensive-looking shirt."

Jayden Emery.

Or someone who sounded an awful lot like Jayden Emery.

And at the moment, Jayden was nailing down his alibi with Iris under the guise of wanting to clear his boss, Shirley Fox.

But his story was at direct odds with what Shirley and Dash were claiming.

Which begged the question.

Why would Jayden lie?

Unless he had something really big to hide.

Chapter 34

Chill Bar was one of the new bars on Arenas Road, the epicenter of the gay scene in Palm Springs. Violet had tailed Jayden Emery the previous evening, and his first stop was the bar's outdoor patio facing the street, where he hugged and kissed nearly every patron sipping a cocktail during happy hour. He was obviously a regular here, and so it quickly became clear to Violet that if they were going to find out more about him in order to shed some light on why he had lied about his alibi for the night of Olivia's murder, this club might be the best place to start.

Poppy knew the young men who frequented Chill may not be so anxious to gossip about a buddy with three old biddies they had never met before, so she hoped they would be more open to talking to a strikingly handsome man who was fun and engaging and off the charts sexy. Unfortunately, the only man she knew who came close to that description was Matt, but he was no longer on the team. Still, she had texted him earlier in the day, explained how she needed him for just an hour, one drink, and some flirty conversation in order to loosen the lips on the boys at Chill, but she had heard nothing back. She had tried calling him in the afternoon with her plan to show up at the bar around 6:00 p.m., but she had just got his voice mail.

Finally, at around 5:30 p.m., the ladies piled into Violet's car and drove to Palm Springs. After finding one last spot in the adjacent parking lot, they entered Chill, which was packed with a bevy of chatty, excitable, sharply dressed boys barely over the drinking age, along with a handful of older, distinguished men, who were perched at the bar or on the long leather banquette that ran along the wall and were ogling all the beautiful men socializing before the blazing hot desert sun even had a chance to descend below the San Jacinto mountaintops.

It took almost ten minutes for Poppy to flag down the wiry bearded bartender with a red ball cap on his head that read MAKE AMERICA GAY AGAIN. She immediately liked him. He was sweet and polite, paying deference to the fact that she was a woman and an elder, and suggested his world-famous special frozen cosmo. Poppy ordered three and paid with a twenty-dollar bill. She even got some change back. God bless happy hour prices.

The women took a seat at a table near the patio and watched as the surrounding young men chatted and laughed and danced. Poppy had known many gay men in her life as an actress in Hollywood and as a philanthropist in Palm Springs, and she had always marveled at how they always seemed to know how to have a good time. No won-

der so many female bridal parties crashed gay bars
to dance and celebrate. They could never repli-
cate the same joyous, freeing feeling at a straight
bar.

"Okay, so what's the plan?" Violet asked.

"Maybe we should fan out and start some conversations," Poppy suggested.

"That is not going to work. Nobody wants a
woman old enough to be their grandmother interrupting their conversation," Iris barked.

"So what do you suggest we do?" Poppy asked.

"You need to get them to come to you," Iris said
matter-of-factly.

Several patrons wandered by, not giving them a
second glance.

An older Japanese man, tiny in stature but big in
voice, was on the makeshift stage, singing "Stand by
Your Man" with a karaoke microphone, the lyrics
spelling out on all the TVs that hung on the walls
of the bar.

Iris stood up, guzzled the remainder of her
frozen cosmo, and then crossed over to the man in
the DJ booth, who was handling song requests. She
scribbled something down on a piece of paper,
handed it to him, and then returned to the table.

"Back in Germany, I was what you called a gay
icon. The boys loved me," Iris boasted.

The Japanese singer wrapped up his song to a light
smattering of applause, and then the DJ announced
over the speakers, "Next, we have Iris singing a Doris
Day classic, 'Perhaps, Perhaps, Perhaps'!"

No one paid much attention as Iris made her
way to the stage, swiped the microphone from the
smiling Japanese man, who was stepping down,
and then turned her back to everyone.

As the song began playing, Iris slowly turned her head and began singing. Poppy and Violet exchanged stunned looks. Her voice sounded so assured and professional. She swiveled her hips like a dancer and hit the notes perfectly, completely comfortable in the role of seductive songstress. The boys were slow to notice at first, but when they did, they stopped their conversations and herded in the direction of the stage.

"Perhaps, perhaps, perhaps . . ."

Poppy looked around. Even the bartenders had stopped serving drinks to watch Iris's show-stopping rendition.

Iris flounced around the small stage, pointing at a different boy every time she hit the word *perhaps*, and they ate it up. Every last one of them. And when she hit her final note, giving it 100 percent, she was as mesmerizing as if they were watching Judy Garland at Carnegie Hall. The entire bar erupted in thunderous applause.

Poppy and Violet could only watch, slack jawed and totally impressed.

One impossibly tan young man in a salmon Izod shirt and khaki shorts raced forward and held his hand out to help Iris down off the stage. She shot him a sweet air kiss as a thank-you and then made her way back to Poppy and Violet, who clapped their hands wildly at her unexpectedly powerhouse performance. Iris gracefully sat down, surrounded by a gaggle of adoring boys who were paying her gushing compliments, and she made sure to get every one of their names memorized as she accepted their offers for drinks.

"Now we're all friends, and we can ask them whatever we want," Iris said.

As the boys eagerly crowded in beside them, chatting and wanting to know more about Iris and where she came from, Poppy managed to pick one or two off from the herd and pepper them with some direct questions about Jayden.

"Oh, sure, I know Jayden," the kid in the salmon Izod said as he swirled his glass around, watching the ice clink against the sides. "He comes in when he's not working. But that battle-ax Shirley Fox keeps him pretty busy, so it's usually just one night a week or really late on a weekend, after she's passed out from too much bourbon."

This kid liked to dish.

And he seemed to know quite a lot.

So Poppy decided to keep her focus on him, even though the rest of the boys around the table were full of information about Jayden, too.

How he had a taste for skinny, blond, white boys.

How he had his own dreams of becoming a screenwriter in Hollywood someday, if he could get his firm butt out of the desert.

How he came from an oppressively religious family from Alabama who kicked him out of the house when they discovered he was gay.

But nothing they said suggested Jayden was capable of murder.

In fact, a few mentioned how he had admitted to being a bigger fan of Olivia Hammersmith than of Shirley Fox, a blasphemous statement, if his current employer ever heard him breathe a word about it.

But the boy in salmon had suddenly become noticeably quiet. He watched his gay brethren tattle and prattle and howl with laughter, and shrank away from the conversation, as if he didn't want to share any more dirt on his pal, for some reason.

He caught Poppy looking at him.

"What?" he said.

"You seem like you have something you want to say."

The boy reacted, surprised. "No, I don't."

He was clearly lying.

He had some dirt, and he was purposely not sharing.

And despite the cadre of fans Iris had accumulated from her sensational karaoke debut at Chill Bar, salmon boy was going to remain tight-lipped.

Suddenly, everyone's attention was drawn to a man who had just burst into the bar in tight white shorts and a dark blue, short-sleeved, button-up shirt that pressed against his bronzed, hairy chest. There were titters and gasps from around the bar. The man's eyes sparkled as he flashed a wide smile and nearly blinded everyone with his mouthful of perfect white teeth.

After spotting Poppy, Iris, and Violet, he waved cheerfully as he crossed over to them.

Matt Flowers had arrived at Chill Bar.

"Sorry I'm late, ladies," Matt said, deepening his voice for effect.

The boys around the table swooned.

"I just checked my phone on my way over. Seems like there was some kind of German Streisand show here that's trending on Twitter," Matt said.

"I killed it," Iris bragged.

"Hi, boys! My, you're all looking fresh faced and adorable," Matt said, winking. "Thanks for taking care of my girls in my absence."

The man sure knew how to flirt.

He had them all in the palm of his hand.

Poppy leaned in and whispered in his ear. "Thank you for coming. Does Heather know you're here?"

"No, and I'd like to keep it that way."

"Got it."

"What do we have?"

"The boy in the salmon shirt next to you knows something, but he's suddenly not talking," Poppy whispered in his ear.

"I'm on it."

Matt instantly cranked up the charm meter to redline levels and moved in for the kill, looping an arm around salmon boy's shoulder, drawing him in, relentlessly captivating him with his bewitching personality.

In less than fifteen minutes, when salmon boy skipped to the bar to buy everyone a round of drinks, Matt turned to Poppy.

"There's a big rumor going around town that Jayden's been embezzling money from Shirley for months."

Poppy sat back in her chair, speechless.

Both from the shocking new revelation about Jayden and from the record amount of time it took Matt to ferret it out of his newfound admirer.

Chapter 35

"You want to go to Detroit and do what?" Poppy asked Violet's grandson Wyatt, who sat glued to his computer at the garage office, eyes laser focused on the screen, fingers wildly tapping on the keyboard.

"Become human," Violet answered while hovering over her grandson, watching him work.

"I'm not following any of this," Poppy said, exasperated.

"It's a video game," Wyatt said flatly, still concentrating on what he was doing on his computer. *Detroit: Become Human.* It's all about artificial intelligence and humanity's future. It's set in the near future in Detroit, which has become the manufacturing hub for artificially intelligent robots that look exactly like human beings."

"Okay," Poppy said, her left eyebrow raised at Violet.

"It actually sounds like a really good story. It follows one female robot named Kara who wakes up from servitude and demands her freedom," Violet added.

"And it's a game, not a movie?" Poppy inquired.

"Yes," Violet answered.

"And Wyatt wants us to buy it for him?"

"Yes."

"Why?"

"As payment for the work he's been doing for us."

"And how much does it cost?"

"Way less than the salary you should be paying me," Wyatt said, turning his computer screen around for Poppy and Violet to see. "Look at this."

"Please don't tell me you hacked into another Web site!" Poppy moaned.

"Okay, I won't," Wyatt said, flipping the screen back toward himself and blocking Poppy's view. "But if I had, I might have found some really interesting financial info concerning Jayden Emery."

Poppy struggled not to ask him for any details.

It would be unethical for her to do so and also against the law.

Wyatt's grandmother had no such worries, however.

"What did you find, dear?"

"Violet!" Poppy cried.

"Well, it's too late now. He's already done it," Violet reasoned.

"Did you know the FBI has very capable cyber agents working around the clock to capture lone-wolf hackers like you, Wyatt?"

Wyatt chuckled. "Yeah, but I'm too smart to leave a trail of bread crumbs. Trust me, they'll never catch me."

"I refuse to listen to any information you obtained illegally . . ." Poppy announced emphatically.

Poppy covered her ears as she marched toward the door.

"I've gone over the statements for Jayden's checking and savings accounts, and there was a series of cash transfers that occurred every month around the same time for the same amount of money from Shirley Fox," Wyatt called out to her.

Poppy stopped at the door, lowered her hands from her ears, unable to resist hearing more.

"Perhaps he receives his paychecks from Shirley as a direct deposit," Violet offered.

"Yes. Makes perfect sense," Wyatt said, nodding. "But here's the thing. Over the past few months, there were a few random deposits in varying amounts. One for five thousand, one for fifteen thousand and, just last week, one for almost twenty thousand."

"That's a lot more than what a personal assistant usually makes in a month," Violet said, rubbing the top of her grandson's head. "You're such a talented boy."

Poppy's hand was on the doorknob. She was almost out of there, free and clear from any further criminal activity.

But then she sighed, knowing she had just lost her internal ethics battle, and spun around. "So the rumors appear to be true. Jayden found a way to steal cash from Shirley's accounts and deposit it into his own."

"Which is pretty stupid, if you ask me. It's easily traceable," Wyatt scoffed. "I would have laundered it through an account I set up out of the country, like in the Cayman Islands."

"How old are you again?" Poppy asked.

"Twelve."

"You seem much older."

"I hear that a lot."

"We have him red-handed, Poppy," Violet exclaimed, excited and breathless.

"Not necessarily. We can't print out his bank statements and hand them over to the authorities. We'll all be arrested."

"Oh . . . right . . ." Violet said, folding her arms, suddenly concerned.

"And it still doesn't prove he had anything to do with the break-ins at the Palm Leaf, or that he actually murdered Olivia Hammersmith, despite what your friend Esther and her son Sammy saw."

"So where does that leave us?"

"Jayden seems to be a young man harboring a lot of secrets, so maybe we can use this information to squeeze some of those secrets out of him," Poppy said, her mind racing.

"See? You're not the Goody Two-shoes you pretend to be," Wyatt said, laughing.

Poppy glared at him. "Do you want a copy of *Detroit: Become Human* or not, kid?"

Wyatt threw his hands up in the air in surrender and then, without missing a beat, said, "We can order it right now on Amazon. Grandma has a Prime membership, so it can get here by tomorrow."

Poppy knew in her gut this enterprising kid wasn't going anywhere. Like it or not, he was going to remain a permanent member of the Desert Flowers team.

Which made Violet a very happy and proud grandmother.

Chapter 36

Poppy knew what she had to do.

She placed a direct call to Shirley Fox, who at the moment was wrapping up a show at the Gardenia Restaurant and Lounge in Hollywood. She had previously canceled her dates at the Purple Room in Palm Springs to avoid the gossipy locals but had decided at the last minute to keep her concert dates out of town.

Dash answered the call.

"Hello, Dash. This is Matt Flowers's assistant Poppy. May I speak with Shirley?"

"She's removing her makeup now, and we have a dinner reservation. Call back later."

"It's important. It's about the case she's hired our firm to solve. Please, could you just put her on? It's vital that she hear this."

She could hear Dash begrudgingly hand the phone to Shirley. "It's Flowers's secretary," he said.

"Yes?" Shirley asked gruffly.

"It's Poppy Harmon, Ms. Fox."

"Yes. I know. What do you want?"

"I have some information about your personal assistant, Jayden Emery, that you need to hear about."

"We're driving back first thing tomorrow morning. Can't it wait until then?"

"I have reason to believe he's been embezzling money from you."

There was a long pause on the other end of the phone.

"Did he steal my jewelry, too?"

"We're not sure about that. But I believe . . . I mean, Matt believes that if we get him in a room with you, like one of those interventions, he won't be expecting it and won't have time to make up a story, so he'll be more likely to spill everything he knows."

"We'll leave in ten minutes," Shirley said. "He texted me earlier to say he'd be working at my house tonight. Have Mr. Flowers meet me there at eleven o'clock."

"Uh, he may be tough to reach right now since he's working another case, but he provided me with all the proof we need to confront Jayden. He personally uncovered this evidence himself."

"I see. Well, tell Mr. Flowers he is a very good detective, but he should be a bit more available to his clients."

"I most certainly will, Ms. Fox. I will meet you and your husband at your house at eleven o'clock."

"Fine."

She heard Shirley addressing Dash on the other end of the phone. "Cancel our reservation at Rosaline. We're heading back to the desert tonight."

"What?" Dash protested in the background.

And then Shirley hung up.

Poppy debated with herself about whether or not she should include Iris and Violet, who were at the moment waiting for her to return to Betty's house in the Palm Leaf, but she decided to handle this one herself. Jayden would already be on the defensive with Poppy, Shirley, and Dash surrounding him. He didn't need two more people, especially the naturally intimidating Iris, crowding him and making him even more nervous.

Poppy waited two hours before leaving the garage office and driving straight over to the Palm Leaf, arriving at Shirley's house at around five minutes to eleven. Cars were parked all along the street and the house was lit up and she could hear loud music playing inside. She pulled in behind a beat-up Honda Civic with the license plate PARTY BOY.

She marched up the cement walkway, her heels clicking against the concrete pavement, but before she could knock on the door, it flew open, and she was face-to-face with a handsome, young, inebriated man in a bright yellow tank top and tight white shorts, who clung to the door and frowned when he noticed she was empty-handed.

"Where's the booze?"

"I didn't bring any."

"What? No booze? Aren't you the delivery lady from the liquor store?"

"No, I'm afraid not. I'm looking for Jayden."

The young man stepped, or rather stumbled, aside and dramatically waved her into the house.

Poppy nodded and said curtly, "Thank you."

When she entered, she could hear Selena

Gomez crooning one of her recent pop hits from an Amazon Echo speaker atop the mantel above the gas-powered, glass-enclosed fireplace.

Several young men, mostly clothed only in brightly colored Speedos, lounged around the living room, cocktail glasses in hand, chatting and laughing.

Poppy approached two of them.

"Can you tell me where I can find Jayden?"

They stared at her glumly, trying to assess what she was doing there, before one of them pointed toward the pool outside.

Poppy headed out the sliding glass door and stopped suddenly when she realized the five or six young men splashing and frolicking in the swimming pool were completely nude.

One of them was Jayden.

He jumped out, shook off water, before scampering toward the deep end. He climbed up on the diving board, did a quick run right off the edge, and landed in the water in the cannonball position before playfully emerging and dunking the head of one of his friends under the water. The friend used his free arm to splash water in Jayden's face, and both of them erupted in a fit of giggles.

Poppy moved closer to the pool's edge and hollered "Jayden!"

He turned to see who was calling his name, and at the sight of Poppy, his smile instantly evaporated.

"What are you doing here?" he asked warily.

"I suggest you put some clothes on and clear this place out, because Shirley is on her way here right now."

"No she isn't. She's not due back until tomorrow."

"There was a sudden change of plans."

"What?" he squeaked, panic stricken.

He hopped out of the pool and stood in front of Poppy, utterly unaware of the fact that he was flashing his privates right in her face.

Poppy turned to two young men in Speedos who were sitting in cushioned patio chairs, sharing a joint. "Could one of you please hand me a towel?"

Annoyed, the boy closest to her picked up a towel off the pile on the table and handed it off to her.

Poppy threw it at Jayden.

"You better dry off fast. She'll be here any minute."

"I don't understand . . . ," he said, wrapping the striped green towel around his waist.

"Do you want to explain what's going on here, Jayden?"

Jayden's face fell.

Poppy hadn't asked him the question.

It was his boss, Shirley Fox.

She stood a few feet away, near the sliding glass door, her hands clasped to her hips, her face red with fury.

Behind her was Dash, snorting like a bull ready to charge at the waving red flag in the ring.

"I'm going to mess you up good, you little pissant!" Dash pushed past Shirley and ran at Jayden, his big hands poised to throttle him.

"Dash, no!" Shirley cried.

But Dash was in the zone, and Poppy feared he was going to do serious bodily harm to the poor man, so realizing she had to find a fast way to cool him down, she thrust her foot out in front of him.

He tripped over it and went hurtling into the swimming pool.

"Party's over, boys! Time to go home!" Poppy announced to the gaping young men on the patio, who were watching the whole messy scene unfold.

Poppy turned to Jayden. "Say good night to your pals, Jayden. We have a lot to discuss."

Jayden nodded, defeated.

Shirley passed them to retrieve her soaking-wet and embarrassed husband, who was now climbing up the metal-rung ladder of the pool and whining about how his cell phone in his back pocket was probably ruined.

A half hour later, the house was empty of young men except for Jayden, who sat forlornly on the couch in the living room. Dash sat across from him in a chair, glaring at him, while Poppy and Shirley stood in front of him like a pair of prosecuting attorneys.

Outside by the pool, three young men remained, but they were behaving and were talking quietly among themselves, so Shirley declined to eject them, at least for now.

Jayden kept his eyes fixed on the floor and talked in a low, contrite tone. "Yes, I used my access to your accounts to make a few deposits, but I was going to pay you back, I swear!"

"What did you spend the money on?" Poppy asked.

Jayden squirmed a bit and whispered, "I have a

new boyfriend, and I wanted to impress him, so I took him on a few weekend trips."

"You stole almost forty thousand dollars!" Poppy exclaimed.

Jayden shrugged, not looking up at them. "He has very expensive taste. I just wanted him to like me."

Shirley folded her arms, eyes narrowing, her former impression of her devoted employee irreparably and irrevocably changed. She then shook her head, disgusted.

"I'm calling the police right now!" Dash bellowed, springing to his feet.

Shirley whipped her head around in the direction of her husband. "Dash, don't make things worse. Just go make me a drink."

Dash shrank back like a scolded puppy and then stormed out of the room to the kitchen.

Shirley rotated back to Jayden. "Did you steal my jewelry, too?"

"No! I would never . . . ," Jayden protested. "I know I don't have a lot of credibility at this point, Shirley, and it looks really bad, but I know how much that jewelry meant to you . . . the sentimental value. . . ."

She scowled at him, sad and disappointed.

He went on. "That's why I encouraged you to let me hire a detective agency to find the stolen pieces. . . . You've been so good to me. . . . I've always idolized you . . . and I hated seeing you so upset. . . . I had to do something to help. . . ."

"But you didn't think twice about filching my cash," Shirley spit out.

"I . . . I honestly didn't think you'd even miss

it . . ." he said weakly and then wiped away a tear that had streamed down the side of his face. "And I never dreamed that when I hired Mr. Flowers, he would find out about the missing money. . . ."

"What about Olivia Hammersmith?" Poppy asked, stepping forward.

Jayden finally looked up, perplexed. "What about her?"

"I found a witness . . . I mean, Mr. Flowers found a witness who saw you arguing with her outside her house on the night she was killed."

Jayden's mouth dropped open as he realized the severity of Poppy's insinuation. He shook his head, and his hands were shaking. "No . . . I didn't. . . ."

"Do you deny going over to her house?"

"No . . . I did go see her. I was worried about Shirley. I saw how upset she was after the tribute, and so I went over there and begged Olivia not to write about Shirley in her memoir, but she refused to listen to reason. She was really mean and just laughed at me. She took such great pleasure in the fact that she was going to trash Shirley and there was nothing anyone could do about it. I got so angry."

"And what happened when you got angry?"

"Nothing! That creepy neighbor, the mama's boy, Sammy, showed up, and so I left! And Ms. Hammersmith was very much alive when I did! I swear, I never touched her!"

"If you are so innocent, then why did you feel compelled to lie about where you were that night? You claimed that you were with Shirley, but according to her, she was home with Dash and you were never there. Why didn't you just tell the truth if you didn't cause any harm to Olivia?"

Jayden sighed. "I wasn't trying to cover for myself. I didn't want Shirley having to deal with the stress of being a murder suspect, so I lied in order to protect her, not me! I didn't know Dash was home with her that night. He rarely is. . . ."

Shirley appeared stung by the comment but tried not to show it.

"I didn't kill Olivia! I'll take a DNA test! Anything! You have to believe me! I'm not some cold-blooded killer!"

"Just a conniving thief," Shirley said.

Dash returned with a bourbon on the rocks and handed it to his wife, still sore from being summarily dismissed from the conversation.

The sliding glass door opened, and a blond young man in a patriotic red, white, and blue Speedo rambled into the room. "Am I interrupting? I saw that cocktails are being served. Can I get one?"

"And just who are you?" Shirley snarled.

"I'm Christian, Jayden's boyfriend," he said proudly, winking at a deflated Jayden. "Everything all right, honey?"

Jayden nodded solemnly.

"No, everything is not all right! I'm about to call the cops and have your boyfriend's ass tossed in the slammer!" Dash roared.

"Oh, come on! Jayden's a sweetheart!" Christian cooed. "He was just trying to keep me happy! What's so bad about skimming a tiny little bit off the top? Everybody does it! It's not like you were ever going to miss it!"

"Which, as it turns out, isn't true, because here we are!" Shirley barked.

"I suppose you encouraged him," Poppy said with an accusing tone.

Christian grinned, almost proud of himself. "What can I say? He loves me and would do anything for me."

Poppy suddenly noticed that Christian was wearing a leather bracelet with a silver clasp engraved with the initials CH.

She gasped.

Her face went a ghostly white.

"Are you all right?" Shirley asked.

Poppy gaped at the shiny silver clasp, which was the center-piece of the bracelet. "What does the CH stand for?"

"Christian Hartley. That's my name."

"Where did you get that?" Poppy demanded to know.

"Jayden had it made for me. Wasn't that sweet of him?"

Poppy spun around to face Jayden. "That clasp is made from a cuff link! How did you . . . ?"

Jayden nodded. "I know. I found it in Shirley's bedroom. I didn't steal it! She said I could have it."

Poppy's stomach began churning.

She felt as if she was going to be sick.

She turned to Shirley, whose face was now ashen.

Poppy's bottom lip quivered. She took a deep breath and then said in a whisper, "That cuff link belonged to my husband, Chester Holloway. CH. I bought him those cuff links for his birthday last year and had his initials engraved on them. How on earth did one wind up in your bedroom?"

Chapter 37

Shirley Fox was at a loss for words.

Christian put a protective hand over the cuff link on his bracelet, as if he half expected Poppy to reach over and try to snatch it away from him.

Dash stared at his wife, confused and dumbfounded, waiting for her to refute such an unexpected and wild accusation.

But Shirley was stuck.

The evidence was staring all of them in the face. Her thieving assistant, Jayden, had just inadvertently exposed what had been up to this point a very well-kept secret.

Poppy's face felt hot.

A wave of nausea overcame her.

But she managed to stand her ground, patiently waiting for Shirley to answer her question.

"Well?" Poppy managed to choke out.

Shirley averted her gaze from Poppy to Dash.

"I'm sorry . . ." she said.

As reality set in, Dash's nostrils flared, and he stormed out of the room in a huff.

Jayden hopped to his feet and murmured, "We're going to go now, Shirley. I'll call you tomorrow. And please, believe me. I will pay back every cent I took. I promise."

Shirley ignored him.

Jayden nabbed his boyfriend, Christian, by the arm and hustled him out the door, leaving only Poppy and Shirley standing in the room. They could hear the muffled laughter of the two young men who had remained after the party and who were still poolside, oblivious to the dramatic events unfolding a mere few feet away.

"How . . . ?" Poppy asked.

"I can't . . . I can't do this now," Shirley babbled as a flood of tears burst forth, and she ran from the room to her bedroom, where her crushed and infuriated husband awaited her.

Poppy was alone now.

Her mind raced.

When did it start?

How did their paths cross?

Why was she finding out about it only now?

Her whole body was numb and she felt dizzy as she quietly walked out the door to her car. She climbed in and pressed the ignition button, and the car roared to life. She was about to start the drive home when a conversation that had happened months before unexpectedly popped into her head.

She reached for her phone and called a number from her list of contacts. After two rings, a man's tired and scratchy voice answered.

"Poppy, it's past midnight. . . ."

"I apologize for calling so late, Edwin. . . ."

It was her lawyer, Edwin Pierce.

The man who had broken the news about her dire financial circumstances shortly after Chester's funeral.

And who, she instinctively knew, also had more secrets he had been hiding from her.

"Did you know, Edwin?"

"Know what?"

"About Shirley Fox."

There was an interminable, agonizing silence on the other end of the phone.

She waited.

She had all the time in the world.

"Yes . . . ," he finally groaned.

"Why didn't you tell me?"

"I didn't want to add to your grief," he cried.

"Were there others?"

"Poppy . . ."

"I deserve to know, Edwin. Chester's dead and buried. There's no reason to keep anything from me anymore."

"Yes . . ."

"How many?"

"I don't know. Three, maybe four."

"Good night, Edwin."

She ended the call and slumped over the wheel of her car and sobbed until she became too tired to cry anymore.

And then she drove straight home, found the other cuff link with her husband's engraved initials on it, and tossed it in the trash.

Chapter 38

"What is it, Mother? Just come out with it," Heather said, standing in the kitchen of her second-floor apartment.

Poppy sat at the small table in the breakfast nook, staring down at the yellow flower-print cloth covering it. She took a deep breath and raised her head and beheld her daughter, whose facial expression was a mix of curiosity and trepidation.

Matt hovered behind Heather, worried and anxious. Whatever news Poppy was about to spring on them couldn't be good.

"Are you sick?" Heather asked.

Poppy shook her head. "No, I'm fine. . . ."

"Oh, thank God!" Matt cried. "I was afraid you were going to say the C word! I just couldn't handle you having cancer!"

Heather shot Matt a look, silently ordering him to keep his mouth shut and allow her mother to speak.

"I don't have cancer," Poppy sighed.

"Then what is it?" Heather asked.

"It's about Chester. . . ."

"What about him?"

"It's recently come to my attention that during the last year or so of his life, he was unfaithful to me. . . ."

Poppy waited for Heather to react, but she remained still, listening, before nodding calmly.

"He was cheating on me with Shirley Fox."

"Our client?" Matt yelled before catching himself. "I mean, your client?"

"Yes. And apparently, there were other women, at least according to Edwin."

"Who's Edwin?" Matt asked.

"Mother's attorney. He was also Chester's best friend."

"Wow . . ." Matt murmured under his breath.

Poppy studied her daughter, who placidly approached her, bent down, and gave her a comforting hug.

There was something off about her actions.

They were too considered and rehearsed, as if she had been waiting for this moment to come.

Poppy pulled away and looked her daughter straight in the eye.

"You knew, didn't you?"

Matt gasped. "What?"

Heather hesitated, tossing another peeved look at Matt, who decided it best if he just stepped back and did not continue to participate in the conversation.

"I had my suspicions."

"How?"

"Does it really matter?" Heather lamented.

"Yes, it does," Poppy said. "It matters to me."

"I ran into him at Billy Reed's last winter, dining

at an out-of-the-way corner table, away from the main dining room. It was pure happenstance that I saw him. I took a wrong turn toward the ladies' room, and there he was."

"Was it Shirley Fox?"

"No, a woman I didn't know. A redhead, very pretty. She's a winter resident, I think. Just in the desert during the seasonal months."

"What did you say to him?"

"Nothing. He introduced her as a friend of his. Fran something or other. I don't recall her last name. I was so flustered. I managed to make some small talk, and then I turned around and made a beeline back in the direction of the ladies' room. When I came out, Chester was waiting for me and spent five minutes still trying to convince me that she was just a friend, but even he knew how utterly unconvincing he was, and so then he changed tactics and begged me not to say anything."

"And you agreed?"

Heather nodded. "Yes. He swore that she was the only woman he had ever strayed with and that he was trying to end it, because he didn't want to jeopardize his marriage with you, and I believed him."

"Well, he lied."

"I know that now."

"Why on earth didn't you tell me about this?"

"Because I loved Chester. He always treated me like I was his real daughter, and I didn't want to see the two of you get a divorce."

"That was my choice to make, not yours."

"I was trying to protect you!"

"By hiding the truth from me?"

"Mother, you can't blame me for Chester's past indiscretions. . . ."

"I don't. . . ."

"I did what I did out of love for you."

"I know. . . ."

Poppy could tell Matt wanted to run to her and envelop her in a big bear hug and tell her everything was going to be okay, because he instinctively knew Poppy was hurting, but he couldn't, because he had to remain loyal to his girlfriend. But Poppy also knew Matt had grown fond of her, as she had of him, and it was killing him that he couldn't be a more comforting presence to her during this extremely difficult time.

Poppy stood up from the table.

"Well, I guess I made the trip over here for nothing. You already knew," Poppy said, shaking her head.

"Mother, don't be like that," Heather scolded.

Poppy was trying her best not to break down.

She wasn't angry at her daughter for keeping such a devastating secret, and she certainly didn't blame Heather for any of the pain she was suffering from the revelations.

She understood Heather had just been trying to shield her from a broken heart, but what bothered her the most, what rubbed her so raw, was that she was suddenly a boring cliché.

A role she had played on screen but never in real life.

The unsuspecting wife.

Blithely skipping through life, oblivious to what everyone else knew was going on around her.

The last one to know.

And it made her feel like such a fool.

Poppy gave her daughter a perfunctory hug and offered a cheerless smile before nodding to Matt, who appeared to be on the verge of tears himself as he watched her wander out the door.

"Call me when you get home so I know you made it safe," Heather called after her.

Poppy raised her arm as she descended the steps of the apartment building to the parking lot below, and gave a little wave to acknowledge her.

She got out of there as fast as she could, because she thought she might start to cry again.

But she didn't.

Her emotions were firmly in check.

And by the time she reached her car and was driving back to the garage office at Iris's house, where she had called an emergency meeting with her two Desert Flowers partners, she wasn't feeling sad or distressed.

Instead, she was full of grim determination.

Chapter 39

"Well, there is only one course of action," Iris announced. "We drop Shirley Fox as a client!"

There was a brief moment of silence in the garage office as the Desert Flowers detectives pondered this.

Violet finally broke the silence. "That strikes me as a tad extreme."

"What part of 'She was sleeping with my husband' did you not hear Poppy say, Violet?" Iris bellowed.

"It's terrible, I know, and if Poppy wants to drop the case, that's her prerogative, and it would be totally understandable, but . . ."

"But what?" Iris snarled.

"Maybe this situation is not so black and white. . . ."

"Yes, it is! That slut was having an affair with Chester behind Poppy's back! We should have nothing to do with her!"

Poppy listened to her two best friends as they argued in front of her, still thunderstruck and confused by all the recent revelations that had come to light.

"It wasn't just Shirley Fox. There were others . . ." Poppy mumbled.

"What?" Iris bellowed.

"Oh, Poppy, dear, I am so sorry. . . ." Violet cried.

"You ought to be sorry, Violet, for taking Shirley Fox's side!" Iris bellowed.

"I did no such thing!" Violet cried.

"Violet's right. We should think about this before we act recklessly and abruptly drop Shirley as a client," Poppy said.

"What is there to think about?" Iris demanded to know.

"Chester is the sole reason why I find myself in such dire financial circumstances. And it's because he was a world-class liar and had a whole other secret life that he kept me completely in the dark about."

"Shirley is not blameless! It takes two to tango!" Iris argued.

"I know that. But right now she seems to be a big part of the solution to my problems. She has already paid a tidy sum for a deposit, with the promise of a whole lot more if and when we retrieve her jewelry and officially clear her name."

"There is something called standing on principle!" Iris barked.

"There is also something called paying your rent on time," Poppy said. "And, at the moment, she's the best chance I have to fight my way back to solvency."

"I agree . . ." Violet said, more forceful since she now knew that Poppy was on her side.

Iris threw up her hands. "Fine. What do I care? She wasn't cheating with my husband!"

"Now, we may receive a call from Shirley any second, firing us, but until that happens, I say we just move forward with the case and try to make as much progress as we can so we have something concrete to report to her," Poppy said calmly.

"We can call her right now, because I have some good news she will want to hear," Violet said, smiling, as she printed out a file from her computer.

Poppy rushed over to the printer to retrieve the pages. "What?"

"I have the results from the DNA test Shirley took at the police station," Violet said, barely managing to contain her excitement.

Poppy snatched the pages from the feeder and eagerly flipped through them. "And?"

"She's in the clear. The skin found under Olivia's fingernails is not a match."

"Violet, how did you . . . ?" Poppy's voice trailed off.

Violet smiled demurely. "I have my ways."

"Please tell me you did not have Wyatt hack his way into the Palm Desert Police Department's computer system."

"No . . . Well, I asked him if he might be able to, and he called me back a few minutes later and said they had surprisingly tough security and he couldn't breach their firewall."

"Thank God!"

"So I did the next best thing. I called Gladys Hackett."

"Who is Gladys Hackett?" Iris asked.

"One of the women I play cards with. Her grandson Cleve works at the lab where the Palm Desert PD sends all its samples for testing."

"And he sent you the results, just like that?" Poppy asked, incredulous.

"Well, not exactly. You see, Gladys owed me because I covered her bar tab at the club last month, and so she put in a call to her grandson Cleve. It turns out Gladys promised to leave Cleve some of her property when she passes on, so he has a good reason to keep his nana happy. . . ."

"I get it. Nice work," Poppy said as she plucked her phone off the desk and placed a call.

She took a deep breath.

After a few rings, she heard the unsteady, anxious voice of Shirley Fox.

"Yes?"

"Hello, Shirley. This is Poppy Harmon with the Desert Flowers Detective Agency. . . ."

"Poppy, I don't know what to say. . . ."

"You don't have to say anything. I'm the one who called you. I have some very good news. Matt got his hands on a copy of the results from your DNA test, and I'm happy to report that you are one hundred percent in the clear for Olivia Hammersmith's murder."

"Oh . . . thank you. . . . I'm so glad he convinced me to cooperate with the police. . . ."

"Now he is going to focus all his attention on recovering your missing jewelry," Poppy said, striking as professional a tone as she could possibly muster.

"I appreciate that. Please tell him how grateful I am that he is working so hard on my case."

"I will," Poppy said.

"Poppy, I just want to say . . ."

"He will be in touch as soon as he has more information," Poppy said. And then she hung up on her.

Iris and Violet observed her with trepidation, waiting to see if she was going to crumble after that very difficult call.

But Poppy knew she was going to remain strong and persevere.

She had to because it was her only option at the moment.

She needed to be successful and solve this case.

Despite the heart-wrenching curveballs that kept flying at her out of nowhere.

Chapter 40

The last name Poppy expected to hear again so soon was Gladys Hackett, Violet's drinking pal and the grandmother to a lab tech for Riverside County, but that was exactly whose name popped up on her phone when Violet texted her, telling her to drive over to Gladys's home immediately. That text was followed by another text with an address and directions. When Poppy texted back to inquire as to what this was all about, Violet instantly responded by writing, **Big break in the case!**

So wasting no further time, Poppy jumped in her car and drove from Betty's house straight across the Palm Leaf property to Sunny Dale Drive and the third house on the left, as instructed.

An older woman with bleached blond hair piled high on her head, thick painted red lips, and an extreme face-lift that gave her a permanent look of surprise opened the door.

"Gladys?"

"Yes. Please come in," she said in a high-pitched,

girly voice as she pumped Poppy's hand up and down a few times before pulling her inside.

Poppy entered to find Violet clearing some plates with remnants of pie and empty coffee cups from the dining room table.

"I want to thank you for helping us out yesterday, Gladys," Poppy said.

"My pleasure. My grandson Cleve will do anything for me. He has to because he wants me to leave him my lake house in Big Bear. He's a sweet kid but a greedy son of a—"

"Well, I'm very grateful," Poppy interjected, cutting her off.

"I'm sorry the place is a mess, but I just had some ladies over to play cards."

Poppy knew all about Violet's biweekly card game with the girls. They met at a different house every two weeks so that none of them had to end up hosting all the time. Violet had mentioned that it wasn't the card game with very small stakes—dimes and quarters, for the most part—that stoked their competitive side, but the baked goods that were served. They all considered themselves to be master chefs, and each woman spent the days leading up to the game when it was her turn to host whipping up tasty sandwiches and interesting salads and baking cakes, pies, and cookies to show up the food served at the last game.

"Can I get you a cup of coffee and a slice of my homemade coconut cream pie, Poppy? It went over very well with the other girls," Gladys cooed.

"No, thank you," Poppy said, smiling, before noticing the stricken look on Gladys's face, or what appeared to be one. It was hard to tell from her severe face-lift.

"Oh . . . okay . . ." Gladys moaned.

Violet signaled Poppy to just accept a piece of damn pie.

"You know what, Gladys? I've changed my mind! A piece of your pie sounds absolutely delicious!" Poppy declared.

Brightening, Gladys shuffled off to the kitchen.

When she was gone, Poppy turned to Violet.

"What's this all about?"

"Esther Hamilton. The woman you met at the party we threw at Betty's house. The one in the wheelchair, with the germaphobe son," Violet said.

"Yes, I remember. What about her?"

"Well, she was here playing cards today, and I overheard her talking to Gladys about how absent-minded she can be and how she is always locking herself out of the house when she goes grocery shopping or golfing, so she has to keep a spare key hidden outside, under a flowerpot."

Poppy shrugged.

"Okay. That's not unusual. . . ."

"And so Gladys offered up her own secret hiding place for her extra house key."

"So you think Esther was purposely luring her into revealing that information?"

"Not at first. It sounded like a completely inno-cent conversation, but then Esther excused herself to go to the bathroom, and she was gone a really long time, and so I went to see if she might need some help, given her handicap, and I caught her wheeling out of the spare bedroom at the end of the hall, which Gladys uses as an office."

"Did she take anything?"

"She had a small piece of paper in her hand and she appeared really nervous when she saw me. Esther claimed she had just been looking for a pen in the office to write herself a note. She said she needed a few groceries and wanted to write them down so she wouldn't forget before she called Sammy to go to the store. Well, I pretended to believe her, but when she returned to the table, I doubled back to the office and saw that the paper in her hand was from a notepad on the desk. I could barely make out the impression left on the pad of what she had written, so I colored it in with a pencil to get a clearer picture and it was *not* a grocery list!"

She handed a piece of paper to Poppy.

On it was scribbled the numbers 41692.

"Four-one-six-nine-two?"

"My grandson's birthday," Gladys answered as she entered with a dessert plate with a heaping piece of coconut cream pie on it. She handed it to Poppy, along with a tiny silver fork. "Here you go."

"Thank you. It looks yummy." Poppy ignored the slice of pie. "Why would Esther be writing down the date of your grandson's birthday?"

"It's also the password to turn off the security alarm in the house," Violet said solemnly. "Gladys has it written down in the owner's manual she keeps . . ."

"In her office," Poppy said.

"In the top left drawer of my desk," Gladys said.

Poppy's mind raced as she put the pieces of the puzzle together, until she noticed Gladys staring at her with disappointed wide eyes and that disconcerting perpetual look of surprise.

It took her a moment to figure out why Gladys appeared so sad.

Poppy hadn't bothered to try her pie yet.

Poppy cut herself a healthy piece and stuffed it in her mouth.

"Oh, Gladys, it's scrumptious!"

"Really?"

"Yes. This is one of the best pies I've ever tasted!"

"Aw, you're just saying that. . . ."

Poppy shook her head. "No, I'm serious."

Finally, after a few more minutes of Poppy fawning over Gladys's baking talents, they managed to get back on topic.

"So after everyone left, Gladys and I sat down and went over who hosted the card games over the past few months, from when the break-ins started," Violet recounted breathlessly. "And get this, Abigail Rogers hosted in April, and a week later her house was robbed. In June it was Dolores Connelly, in August it was Sylvia Whitfield, and then, this past September . . ."

"Shirley Fox!" Poppy gasped.

"Bingo. It was Shirley's first time hosting," Violet said. "It's been hard to nail her down with her busy show schedule."

"It was also the mother lode for the thieves, since she had so much expensive jewelry lying around," Poppy said.

"My guess is that Esther attends the card games held at houses in the complex and sizes up the layout of the houses and finds out how they can gain access without resorting to forcible entry or setting off a burglar alarm," Violet said.

"And then she has her son Sammy carry out the actual burglaries!" Poppy said, the excitement inside her growing as the details fell perfectly into place.

"Yes! We're dealing with a mother-and-son team of thieves!" Violet cried, clapping her hands. "We cracked the case!"

"This is a cause for celebration! I'll get us some more pie!" Gladys said before swiveling her wide hips around and dashing back into the kitchen.

"What about Olivia Hammersmith?" Poppy asked.

"She played with us only once, most notably when Shirley was out of town, but she looked bored the whole time and never came back."

"So she never hosted a game?"

"No, never."

"So maybe Esther and Sammy found another way to gain access to Olivia's house and somehow didn't expect her to be home at the time. She could have surprised Sammy, and he panicked and perhaps pushed her away or something, maybe a little too hard, and she tripped and fell and hit her head on the coffee table and died," Poppy said.

"Which would make Esther and Sammy guilty of murder."

Chapter 41

Poppy was unprepared when Iris slapped her hard across the face in front of everyone in the clubhouse bar at the weekly Palm Leaf Friday night mixer.

She reached up to rub her stinging cheek and then, boiling over with rage, shouted, "How dare you? Get away from me!"

Iris stood her ground, steely-eyed and determined. She held her hand out. "Give me back that necklace now!"

The necklace in question was a Blue Nile signature floating diamond solitaire pendant in platinum from Tiffany, which Poppy had borrowed from an old pal, the ex-wife of a major Hollywood studio mogul. The woman had divorced the studio mogul in 2003 and had walked away with roughly twenty-five million dollars. This pendant was worth about five grand. Upon hearing that Poppy needed an expensive piece of jewelry to help solve a case she was working on in her new career as a private detective, the wealthy pal was more than happy to lend the necklace. She found this whole crime-solving enterprise of Poppy's exciting and was just dying to be a part of it. Poppy promised to take good care of the pendant, because she knew if it got lost or destroyed, she had no means to replace it.

"I told you, this was a gift. It doesn't belong to you," Poppy said, gingerly backing away from Iris.

The crowd huddled around as the dramatic scene unfolded, watching in awe as the two women carried on with their very loud and public show-down.

Iris advanced toward Poppy, who threw a hand over the pendant to prevent Iris from literally tearing it off her neck.

"He had no right to give it to you! That was a gift to me on our tenth wedding anniversary!" Iris said, seething.

"He told me he bought it while on a business trip in Paris! When he saw it in the window, he knew he wanted me to have it!"

"Well, the bastard lied to you! He promised me I could have it when he filed for divorce, but then he stole it, and I've been trying for years to get it back."

"That's not my problem," Poppy sneered. "You should've taken better care of it."

"You smug, greedy, two-faced bitch!" Iris wailed as she charged at Poppy.

Violet hurtled herself forward, inserting herself between the two raving, furious women. "Ladies, please, let's just calm down and talk about this."

"There's nothing to talk about. She'll never accept the fact that I've found love with her ex-husband . . . ," Poppy responded.

Gasps from the riveted onlookers.

Adrenaline racing, Poppy glared at Iris, nostrils flaring, and delivered the final blow. "Face it, Iris, you never could satisfy him."

Iris looked as if she was about to blow.

But instead, she shrank back and dissolved into a puddle of tears.

Violet put a comforting arm around her and led her out of the bar.

Poppy couldn't help but admire Iris's commitment. She had delivered a stellar performance. Perhaps she should have taken that up-and-coming director's offer to make her a star more seriously back in Germany all those years ago.

Violet was convincing, as well, which was admirable, considering Poppy was the only actress among the three of them.

Iris may have worked as an exotic dancer and print model back in the day, but she had no formal training, and yet she was so believable playing the woman scorned. Poppy wondered if she might have gone through some real-life experience. Iris was always so tough and resilient, and she rarely showed any signs of vulnerability.

Of course, Violet was naturally adept at playing a loyal and supportive friend, because that was exactly what she was.

As for Poppy, it felt good to be acting again.

Even if it was just for a case.

Poppy glanced over at Esther Hamilton, who had leaned forward in her wheelchair by the bar, her White Russian in hand, and had watched the scene with rapt attention.

With her audience still engaged, even though

Iris and Violet had left the bar, Poppy marched straight over to Gladys Hackett.

"Clearly, I'm no longer welcome at the house I'm sharing with Iris and Violet, so at the risk of being an inconvenience, could I stay with you for a few nights, Gladys, just until I find my own place?"

"Of course, Poppy," Gladys said. "I'm so sorry you had to go through that. I'm certainly not surprised by Iris's inexcusable behavior! I never liked her!"

Poppy resisted a smile.

Even Gladys was enjoying her small but pivotal role in the melodramatic saga.

The entire scene had been carefully staged and rehearsed beforehand in Gladys's living room.

And the curtain had been scheduled to go up at the height of happy hour during the Friday night mixer so they would have a full crowd.

But they were really playing only to an audience of one.

Esther Hamilton.

Esther already knew where Gladys kept her spare key, and she also had the pass code to Gladys's alarm system, so there was little question that Gladys Hackett's home was next in line to be targeted.

And if Esther set her sights on Poppy's pricey diamond pendant and knew it would be ensconced in Gladys's house, at least for the next few days, she might move up her timetable and strike sooner rather than later.

And by the look on Esther's face, it appeared as if Poppy's plan had worked. She was already excitedly on her cell phone, immersed in a whispered conversation. Poppy could only assume that Esther's son Sammy was on the other end of the line.

Mother and son were spiritedly plotting their next move.

And Poppy was banking on the fact that it was going to happen within the next twenty-four to forty-eight hours.

Which was why she had already reserved a room at the world-famous Two Bunch Palms, a resort and spa in Desert Hot Springs, for Gladys for the weekend and had gifted her with a deep-tissue massage, an exfoliating facial, and a mud bath. She wanted to be sure Gladys was safely out of the way when the thieves struck. Poppy, however, had every intention of hiding out at Gladys's house all weekend. Ready and waiting.

Chapter 42

Poppy was a pulsating ball of nervous energy as she sat in the dark with Iris and Violet that night, quietly waiting. She had made a very public pronouncement at the mixer the previous evening that she was having dinner tonight with the gentleman who had so generously gifted her with that Tiffany pendant, and she'd also added that she did not plan on wearing her prized piece of jewelry to dinner. She then had stressed that given the fact that a whole week had passed since she and her lover last saw each other, she would undoubtedly be out on the town very late, probably not arriving home until well past midnight, if at all.

Gladys had also made a big show of leaving town for the weekend to visit her niece in Phoenix. However, in reality, she was already ensconced in a comfy room at the Two Bunch Palms spa and resort, once home to famed criminal Al Capone, and was probably at this moment relaxing in the mineral pool after her soothing mud bath treatment.

Poppy sat at the dining room table and gripped her phone, finger at the ready, poised to dial 911 if or when Sammy did indeed show up. Iris and Violet sat across from her. Violet's face was taut, and she clasped her hands together in uneasy anticipation. Iris was next to her, full of stoic determination and holding a baseball bat, just in case a weapon was needed.

The silence was unnerving, and every time the lights from a passing car outside flashed through the window, all three of them jumped. And then, as darkness engulfed them again, they tried their hardest to relax.

Finally, Violet spoke up.

"The more I think about this, the less I like it! I mean, what if he's got a gun and panics when he sees us and shoots one of us, maybe all of us!"

"We've been over this dozens of times, Violet. We are not going to confront him. If he does show up, we are going to very calmly get up and walk out the back door and call the police and wait for them to arrive and arrest him while he is still inside the house."

"Are you sure he's going to enter through the front door?" Violet asked.

"Yes. He knows where the spare key is hidden. Once we hear him outside, we leave immediately."

"And if something goes wrong and he tries any rough stuff, I have this, and I am prepared to use it," Iris promised, holding up the baseball bat.

"I wish you would put that away. You're not going to need it," Poppy said.

They waited another hour.

It was now close to eleven o'clock.

Poppy could see Iris's eyes drooping.

She was fighting to stay awake, but the late hour was making it harder and harder, and just when it appeared she was about to topple over in a face-plant, she let go of the baseball bat and it clattered to the floor, startling her.

Iris bent over, scooped the bat up off the floor, and tried to remain alert. But then, after a few minutes, her eyes slowly fluttered and then closed again.

Violet had reached over to gently shake her arm when suddenly they heard a rattling sound.

It wasn't coming from the front door, as expected.

Someone was jiggling the door handle to the back door off the kitchen.

Poppy sprang to her feet, alarmed, and whispered urgently, "He's coming through the back door!"

She couldn't understand what had gone wrong.

She had been certain Sammy would enter the house easily, using the key after retrieving it from where Esther had told him it would be, and then would deal with the alarm, the control panel for which was located right in the entrance, just past the front door.

The door handle shook more violently this time, as the intruder continued trying to get inside the house.

Iris snapped awake and sat frozen, the baseball bat in her hand.

The fear was crippling.

Finally, Poppy snatched the baseball bat from

Iris, raised it above her head, and cautiously moved through the kitchen toward the back door.

As she approached, she noticed the intruder had stopped fiddling with the door handle.

Had he given up and gone back around to the front of the house?

She waited almost a minute.

Staring at the door handle.

Expecting it to rattle again.

And then, once she was confident the intruder was no longer on the other side of the door, she carefully reached for the lock on the door and turned it to the left quietly to unlock it. She waited another few seconds and then whipped open the door, ready to strike with her bat.

But there was no one there.

She heaved a sigh of relief.

And then someone tapped on the kitchen window from the outside, and Poppy screamed at the top of her lungs.

A flashlight temporarily blinded Poppy, and then a figure appeared at the back door, dressed all in black. Poppy began swinging her bat like Derek Jeter at an all-star game and connected with the intruder's right shoulder.

He yelped in pain and went down on one knee, then covered his head with his hands.

"Please, not the face! I'm an actor! My face is my fortune!"

The voice was instantly recognizable.

"Matt! What the hell are you doing here?" Poppy screamed, dropping the baseball bat to the floor.

Violet and Iris raced in from the dining room,

breathless and scared. They settled down only when they saw Matt's handsome face after Violet snapped on the light.

"I couldn't stay away. I was worried about you ladies confronting this guy on your own. So I lied and told Heather I had a callback for that national commercial audition back in LA, and came right over."

"How did you know we were even here?" Poppy asked.

"I told him," Violet said sheepishly. "I thought he'd want to know. And technically, he is our boss."

"No he is not, Violet!" Iris roared.

"I'm glad you did call me, Violet. There's safety in numbers," Matt said. "We don't know how dangerous this Sammy Hamilton can be."

"But you made your choice," Poppy said. "I thought your relationship with Heather was more important than playing a detective."

"I adore your daughter, Poppy, and I want to make my relationship with her work, but I also love doing this, and I don't think it's fair that I have to choose between one or the other. After I dropped out, I couldn't stop thinking about you three, and how we make a great team, and I really want to help solve this case, because it's our very first one, so . . . here I am."

Poppy dreaded the tense scene ahead when Heather was inevitably told that Matt had willfully defied her ultimatum.

But she had to admire his unbridled tenacity and his puppy dog devotion to her budding detective agency, and she was deeply touched by it.

Matt went in for a hug.

Poppy let him grab her and squeeze her like a homesick child reunited with his mother after two weeks at summer camp before gently pushing him away. Then he did the same to Violet, mauling her and telling her how much she meant to him. By the time he got to Iris, she had reclaimed possession of the baseball bat and aggressively used it to hold him at bay. So he got only two out of three hugs.

Suddenly there was a beeping sound.

It was the house alarm warning that the front door was open and someone had entered the house. They heard someone pressing a code on the alarm panel, and the beeps stopped.

All four of them remained still in the kitchen.

They heard footsteps approaching.

And then the footsteps stopped.

The trespasser had probably noticed the light on in the kitchen and was now wondering if someone was home.

Poppy slowly raised her phone to call 911, but before she had a chance, without warning, a man in black jeans, black T-shirt, black sneakers, almost identical to Matt, except with a black wool hat pulled down over his face, with two holes cut out in the center for his eyes, rounded the corner and came face-to-face with the four people huddled in the kitchen, one brandishing a baseball bat.

He turned to make a run for it, but Matt lunged forward, grabbed a fistful of his T-shirt, yanked him back. The burglar elbowed him in the eye in order to wrestle free, but Matt held on, howling in pain, and the two fell to the floor, then rolled across the linoleum floor until the burglar got the upper hand and managed to wrap his hands around Matt's throat.

Iris whacked him in the back with the baseball bat, and he cried in pain at the top of his lungs, toppled over, and landed facedown on the floor, moaning. As Poppy finally got out the call to 911, Violet found some large trash bag zip ties in a drawer and used them to bind the burglar's hands together behind his back as he writhed on the floor in agony.

"My back . . . I think it's broken . . ." he wailed.

"You'll be fine!" Iris yelled. "Don't be such a pussy."

Iris yanked the wool hat off his head, and just as they expected, underneath it was Sammy Hamilton.

Once Sammy was under control, Violet rummaged through Gladys's freezer, pulled out a frozen piece of steak, unwrapped the plastic, and then tenderly placed the steak over Matt's bruised eye.

Matt tried acting calm and collected but kept checking himself out in a small hand mirror he had plucked from his back pocket, to make sure the blow wouldn't leave any permanent damage to his face.

After giving the 911 operator all the required information, Poppy asked Violet for Esther Hamilton's phone number and placed a call to her.

"Yes?"

"Hello, Esther. This is Poppy Harmon. I'm at Gladys Hackett's house, and we have your son here. He was attempting to break in and rob the place, but I'm sure you already knew that. You should also know the police have been called and are on their way."

There was a long silence on the other end.

"Esther? Are you still there?"

"Tell Sammy I'm calling a lawyer and he shouldn't say a word to anyone!"

"I certainly will," Poppy said, then ended the call.

She looked down at Sammy.

"Your mother said the best thing you can do is confess."

"No . . . she wouldn't . . ." Sammy moaned, trying to lift his head. "Please let me sit up. . . . The floor is so dirty."

The poor germaphobe.

Matt reached down and lifted him up until he was sitting on the floor, his back against the stainless-steel refrigerator.

"Your mother's right, Sammy," Matt said, patting him on the head. "It will be better for you if you just tell us everything you know."

Sammy was scared, and he was a mama's boy, and, unfortunately for him, she wasn't here to direct him with her orders, so he suddenly felt alone and vulnerable, and it worked to their advantage.

He confessed to the burglaries.

"Did your mother put you up to it?" Poppy asked sharply.

He didn't answer.

"And did she tell you to write that warning in lipstick for me on the bathroom mirror when she found out I was investigating your crimes?" Poppy asked.

"No . . ." Sammy protested weakly. "I did that on

my own. . . . Mother wasn't happy about that. . . .
She said it was too risky. . . ."

"And did you kill Olivia Hammersmith?" Poppy
demanded to know.

Sammy gasped. "What? No!"

"You didn't break into her house and discover
she was there and accidentally push her too hard?"

"No! No! No! I would never kill anyone!"

"Was it your mother?"

"What? That's crazy! My mother is wheelchair
bound! How could she do any harm?"

Sammy fought his bonds, panic stricken, suddenly fearful he would be charged with murder.

He was already going to prison for years.

But at least he wouldn't have to face the death
penalty.

If he was telling the truth.

Poppy stared at his frightened, skittish face. He
had probably committed all these crimes in a desperate attempt to take care of his invalid mother,
knowing the spoils of their haul would keep her in
comfort for the remainder of her years left on
earth.

Sadly Poppy knew that despite Esther Hamilton's advanced age, she would soon be arrested
for her part in the burglaries.

But when Poppy looked at Sammy, she didn't
see a killer. She saw a little boy anxious to please
his domineering mother.

And he was right about Esther.

It was a stretch to imagine her physically getting
the upper hand on Olivia Hammersmith. Or anyone else, for that matter given her handicap.

Which meant, if her gut feeling was right, the
real killer was still out there.

* * *

When Detective Jordan and his officers arrived
and were quickly brought up to speed on what exactly had happened, they were far less inclined to
believe Sammy Hamilton's pleas of innocence
when it came to the murder of Olivia Hammersmith. The detectives conveniently concluded that
Sammy was lying to avoid a murder charge.

What they did firmly believe, however, was that
private detective Matt Flowers had heroically solved
the case. They pushed Poppy, Violet, and Iris out of
the way in order to clap him on the back, glad-
hand him, and offer their enthusiastic congratula-
tions.

Matt was happy to take the credit.

Which he did fervently.

In front of the officers who were placing Sammy
Hamilton under arrest.

And before the swarm of reporters who showed
up in front of Gladys Hackett's house after hearing
about the collar on their police scanners and live-
streaming Web sites.

Matt did offer a perfunctory nod in front of the
cameras to his three loyal and dedicated assistants
for their backup support, but at the end of the day,
the Palm Leaf break-ins were officially solved because of one man—Matt Flowers.

The press was also eager to believe that Sammy
Hamilton had brutally murdered Olivia Hammersmith during a botched burglary, despite the fact
that Olivia had never hosted a card game, so it was
unlikely her house had ever been a target.

As Matt winked at a fawning, blond, female TV
reporter who had gushed about his prowess as an

expert crime solver, he declared while smiling directly into the camera, "Case closed!"

Poppy was too busy running the remaining suspects through her mind, determined to find out who had actually killed Olivia Hammersmith, to take much offense at Matt, who was bordering on becoming a fame whore.

Chapter 43

Poppy could hardly blame Matt for so greedily soaking up all the attention after the arrest of Esther Hamilton and her son Sammy.

After all, he was an actor.

Actors took to publicity like a trout to a running stream.

And the whole Matt Flowers scheme had been her idea.

But because of his movie-star good looks and disarming easy charm, the press quickly turned ravenous for pictures of Matt and interviews with him and decamped in front of Iris's house in order to capture the perfect image of his gorgeous mug and toss out an endless stream of inane questions about his dating life, instead of making any serious inquiries about his crime-solving techniques.

Iris, who had become quite fond of the baseball bat she had wielded on the night they caught Sammy Hamilton breaking into Gladys Hackett's house, waved it menacingly at the reporters who dared trample the small flower garden she had so lovingly attended to out in front of her house.

In order to calm down Iris, who was now livid and was shouting four-letter words at the reporters, Matt swaggered out of the garage office, strolled down the walkway to greet the gaggle of reporters, and promised to answer all their questions if they would only back up and away from Iris's prized garden.

They dutifully obeyed the suave local celebrity's simple request and then greedily snapped pictures and shouted out more questions.

"Is there a woman in your life, Matt?" One reporter asked as she stepped off a crushed desert marigold in the garden.

Poppy, who was watching the circus from inside the garage office, saw him smile brightly. She waited for it to suddenly dawn on him that the actual woman in his life had been purposely kept in the dark about his continued role in the Desert Flowers Detective Agency, and that all this relentless positive press about his heroics in solving the crime would surely find its way to her attention.

Any moment he would realize what a mistake he had made by grabbing the spotlight, and would wish he could take it all back, all his humorously entertaining sound bites, his bright, toothy smiles for the cameras, his flirtatious banter with the prettier female reporters.

Poppy saw the KMIR-TV news truck parked across the street. They were among the swell of reporters and cameras rapturously recording Matt's every thought and move. Heather watched KMIR religiously, especially in the morning, when she made her coffee and whole-wheat toast with butter and jam. They were broadcasting live.

Poppy swallowed hard.

She tried to warn Matt with a frantic wave through the window, but he was so inebriated by the cameras and the attention, he didn't notice her.

He just recklessly answered more questions and posed for more pictures, intent on getting his publicity fix.

And he was about to pay for it dearly.

Because rounding the corner at the moment was Heather's beat-up car, and it was racing down the street at an unsettling speed.

For a moment, Poppy feared her angry daughter was going to plow right into the crowd of reporters.

But she hit the brakes just in time and squealed to an abrupt stop.

The driver's side door flew open, and Heather emerged, wearing black leggings and a gray T-shirt, her hair pulled back in a ponytail with a scrunchie. No makeup. Fuming.

Poppy cringed as Heather stormed through the press, pushing them out of the way to get to Matt.

When he finally saw her, his face fell.

She shouted at him in front of everyone.

Poppy couldn't hear what she was saying, but her boiling rage told the whole story.

There were lots of clicking cameras.

Red-faced, Matt took her forcibly by the arm and guided her up the cement walkway, past Iris's flower garden and toward the garage, so they could have a semiprivate discussion.

The reporters tried to follow, but Iris kept

swinging her bat in their direction, and fearing serious bodily injury, they ducked and scurried back to the edge of the sidewalk.

By the time Heather and Matt entered the garage through the side door, Poppy had moved to the other end of the office, wishing she was invisible.

Heather spotted her immediately but chose to ignore her as she laid into Matt. "You blatantly lied to me and made me look like a fool!"

"I'm so sorry, sweetpea. I know it was wrong, and I've been a bad boyfriend, but just hear me out—"

"I've listened to your crap long enough, Matt! I'm sick of it!"

"I really wanted to abide by your wishes, but this role, it's a once-in-a-lifetime opportunity—"

"I don't care! We're through!"

This stopped Matt in his tracks.

Poppy swallowed a surprise gasp, afraid that if she let it escape her lips, she would only draw attention to herself.

And right now that was the last thing she wanted.

"What?" Matt whimpered.

"You heard me! Done! Finished! We're breaking up!"

"I know I fibbed, and that was wrong, but do you really—"

"Yes! I can't take it anymore. I tell you honestly how uncomfortable it makes me for you to take part in my mother's shenanigans, and so instead of respecting me, you choose to lie and scheme behind my back! With my own mother! It's just ludicrous!"

"Your mother had nothing to do with my decision—"

"Oh, please! She was the one who got you into this whole mess! You know what the irony is?" She glanced at Poppy, who averted her eyes away from her daughter and stared guiltily at the floor. "It was my mother who once said to me, 'I will support any decision you make in your life, but please, God, just do me one favor. Never, ever date an actor!' "

The words stung Poppy as they were thrown back at her.

Mostly because they were true.

"It's probably the only time I should've listened to her!"

Matt stepped toward her. "Heather, please . . ."

She backed away from him, throwing up her hands to stop him from getting any closer. "No, I don't want to hear anything else you have to say. I never want to see you again."

And then she fled out the door.

Matt started after her but thought better of it and gave up. He bowed his head, and he looked as if he was about to cry.

"She's right," Poppy said sadly. "This is my fault."

Matt wiped his eyes with his shirtsleeve and sniffed. "Nope. You are not taking the blame for this, Poppy. This was all me."

His whole body was slumped over, crushed and defeated.

It was obvious from the broken posture, the hand over the face to hide the tears, and the weak, distraught tone of his voice that Matt Flowers loved Heather deeply.

And he had just lost her for good.

Despite Matt's denials, Poppy knew in her heart that she had played a very critical role in the eventual dissolution of the relationship.

And that made her want to cry, too.

Chapter 44

Poppy stepped through the metal detector, retrieved her purse on the conveyor belt on the other side, suffered through an additional pat down by a severe-looking female officer, and then was escorted by another officer to a private room with peeling paint, a scuffed table, and one hard, uncomfortable metal chair. She waited about five minutes before the door opened and a third officer wheeled Esther Hamilton into the room.

Esther was in an orange jumpsuit and looked tired. Her gray hair was long and stringy and unwashed; there were dark circles under her eyes, as if she hadn't slept in days; and her gaunt face was free of makeup. She was wearing handcuffs, which the officer unlocked and removed before he parked her wheelchair across from Poppy.

They sat in silence until the officer left and locked the door behind him.

Esther waited another moment and then sighed.

"Thank you for coming, Poppy."

Poppy nodded.

She had debated whether or not she should visit Esther in jail when she received the call that Esther wanted to see her. But in the end, her curiosity had gotten the best of her.

"What did you want to see me about?"

"I know my son Sammy is in real trouble. . . ."

"As are you, Esther . . ." Poppy said, gesturing to their surroundings. "You're in jail, and you're going to be charged with multiple counts of trespassing and burglary."

"I know. I don't care what happens to me. I'm just worried about Sammy. I understand he pleaded guilty to the break-ins but not to the murder of Olivia Hammersmith."

"I read the district attorney is going to go for first-degree murder," Poppy said solemnly.

"He didn't do it, Poppy! I know my son! He's not capable of killing anyone!"

"If that's so, what can I do about it?"

"The cops have already closed the case in their minds. They're convinced it was Sammy. They're not going to look at anyone else. But your agency can. Talk to your boss. Have him keep investigating."

"Shirley Fox got her jewelry back. That's what we were hired to do. We're no longer working for her."

"I have some money left in my savings. I can get it to you before the lawyers get their grubby hands on it." Esther's hand shook as she reached out and touched Poppy's arm. "Please. I'm begging you. . . ."

Poppy's own intuition had been telling her Sammy Hamilton wasn't the one who killed Olivia Hammersmith.

And so she was inclined to believe Esther.

"I don't want your money, Esther."

Esther broke down and sobbed. "I don't know what I'm going to do now. You were my last hope. . . ."

"No, I will keep looking at suspects for you, but I'm not going to accept payment. You're going to need that money for your defense."

Esther cried harder, with tears of relief.

She grabbed Poppy's hand and wouldn't let go of it, clutching it tight like it was her only lifeline.

"Do you have any idea who might have wanted Olivia dead?" Poppy asked.

Esther sat back, sniffed, and wiped her nose with the back of her free hand before she nodded. "Yes. Dash."

"Shirley's husband?"

Esther nodded again. "I may have gotten a little carried away after the first few burglaries. I used some of the money we received after fencing some of the more expensive items we stole, and I bought some designer clothes and a few expensive pieces of jewelry and a new car for Sammy. Well, it didn't take Dash long to notice, and he came right up to me at one of the club mixers one Friday night and asked me point-blank if I had come into some money. I told him a wealthy cousin of mine had died recently and left me a small fortune. Of course, I couldn't tell him the truth. Well, after that, Dash began to flirt shamelessly with me and tell me how pretty I looked and how he'd always been attracted to older women."

"Did you believe he was sincere?" Poppy asked.

"I'm a seventy-year-old woman in a wheelchair. I knew exactly what he was up to. He smelled the perfect opportunity to bilk a lonely old woman out of a big chunk of her newly expanded savings account."

"So how did you handle it?"

"Very carefully," Esther said. "The last thing I wanted was to make him mad. I didn't need an enemy paying close attention to what Sammy and I were up to, so I just thanked him for being so kind and flattering me and avoided making any plans with him to meet for a drink sometime, which he kept pushing. After a while, he got bored and moved on."

"Moved on?"

"To Olivia Hammersmith."

"You know that for sure?"

"He moved in on her like a shark to chum. With such a steady focus, it was chilling. Lord knows how many other women he's juggling behind Shirley's back," Esther said, shaking her head.

"Did Olivia fall for his charms?"

"I would say so. Sammy took me out for a stroll in my wheelchair early one morning so I could get some fresh air, and we saw Dash leaving Olivia's house around six in the morning."

"So you think Dash is romancing other women in the Palm Leaf in order to con money out of them? But why? Shirley has plenty for both of them."

"I hear he's a big gambler and has accrued a mountain of debt, and so he's been trying to raise enough money to pay it off without Shirley ever finding out."

"If that's the case, then perhaps Olivia refused to pay up when Dash came calling for cash, and he got angry and pushed her hard enough to kill her."

"That's exactly what I think."

Poppy finally extricated her hand from Esther's viselike grip.

"So you'll talk to your boss?" Esther asked, a hopeful look in her eyes.

"Yes. I'm sure he will try to help clear Sammy," Poppy said as she stood up.

Esther cried some more, burying her face in her veiny, dry hands. "Thank you, Poppy. Thank you. . . ."

As Poppy knocked on the locked door and waited for the guard to open it for her, she prayed Shirley Fox's check had already cleared, because if the Desert Flowers Detective Agency was able to prove that her husband, Dash, had killed Olivia Hammersmith—which would send him to prison for life, without the possibility of parole—then Shirley certainly was not going to be writing a positive Yelp review for their budding detective agency as a satisfied client.

Chapter 45

Poppy couldn't take her eyes off Shirley Fox's hands shaking as she held the paper and stared at the list of names written on it. She recognized some people on the list, knew others well, but a handful drew a blank. But there were enough of them to cause her distress, and finally, after tearing her eyes away, she crumpled up the piece of paper and tossed it to the floor.

"I'm sorry," was all Poppy could think of to say in the moment.

She felt so bad for Shirley, who had thought the case was finally neatly wrapped up after the arrest of Esther Hamilton and her son Sammy for all the Palm Leaf break-ins, and after her jewelry was returned, once it was recovered from a pawnshop in Desert Hot Springs and the police declined to impound it since they were already swimming in evidence.

But sadly, nothing was over.

Olivia Hammersmith was still dead.

Murdered, according to the police.

And if Esther and Sammy were to be believed, the real killer was still at large.

The names on the list—exhaustively compiled over the past twenty-four hours by Poppy, Iris, and Violet, who had fanned out and talked to as many women in the Palm Leaf complex as possible in order to find out just how many women had been targeted by Shirley's gigolo of a husband, Dash—numbered twenty-three and included Olivia Hammersmith.

And that was a conservative estimate.

They all had admitted to falling under Dash's spell, some reluctantly at first, some more enthusiastically. None of them had denied writing Dash big checks for his promising new business ventures, although none of them had been the least bit fooled by his insistence that they would see their investment come back twofold. No, all these ladies had been around the block enough times, and they all had been well aware what they were really paying for, and Dash had been only too happy to satisfy the carnal needs of some very lonely women. It had just seemed much less offensive to be investing in Dash as a businessman rather than in his far more impressive talents in the bedroom.

Poppy half expected Shirley to accuse these women of lying and to claim they were just jealous of her marriage to a sexy, charming, much younger man. But Shirley didn't have the energy. She knew it was pointless to try to salvage any shred of dignity. Because she had always known what Dash was, and had willfully chosen to ignore the dark side of his nature.

Matt, who had been hovering behind Poppy,

dreading this meeting, because he never liked to see anyone in his orbit sad or upset, stepped forward, passing Poppy, and walked over to Shirley and kneeled down in front of her. He took her hands in his.

"I know this is hard, and we are so sorry to put you through this, but we felt you should know . . ." he said.

"Why? Because you believe he killed Olivia?"

"We don't know that," Poppy said. "He has a firm alibi. According to you, he was here at home with you on the night Olivia was killed. That's what you told us, and that's what you told the police."

Shirley nodded. "I lied."

Matt's mouth dropped open.

Poppy was far less shocked by the admission.

This was the outcome she had been hoping for, since she had suspected right from the beginning that Shirley Fox had lied about that night.

Now she knew why.

"Did Dash ask you to lie for him?" Poppy asked.

"No, I was the one who coerced Dash into claiming he was home with me, because the fact was, I was here alone . . . all night. I was afraid that if I told the police I was at home by myself, with no one to back me up, they would continue to believe I was the one who had murdered Olivia, so I panicked and begged Dash to give me an alibi."

"Which gave him an alibi, too!" Matt exclaimed.

"The irony is, he hasn't even spoken to me since the revelation came to light about my affair with . . ." Shirley's voice trailed off.

She looked as if she wanted to kick herself.

She hadn't meant to bring his name into the conversation.

Poppy's jaw tightened.

Chester.

She was talking about Chester.

Poppy had managed to bury all her rage and disappointment and sadness in order to carry on with the case, but now she could feel it all about to come to a boil all over again.

There was an agonizing silence.

Shirley kept her eyes fixed on the floor, not sure how to continue, so Poppy made it easy on her by finally speaking.

"Did he ever tell you where he was all night?"

Shirley shook her head. "No. And I didn't ask. I just assumed he was at the Spa Resort Casino, gambling away my money, as usual."

"We can check the security cameras at the casino to see if he was there," Matt said.

"You can, but why bother?" Shirley said quietly, defeated. "I think we all know where he really was that night."

Shirley didn't come out and say it.

She didn't have to, because they were all thinking it.

Dash was probably at Olivia Hammersmith's house.

Trying to squeeze more cash out of her in exchange for sexual favors.

And when she refused to give him any more handouts, he got angry and knocked her head into a coffee table and killed her.

Chapter 46

There was no question Dash was in tip-top shape as Poppy and Matt watched him bench-press over three hundred pounds in the small workout gym located near the clubhouse and main swimming pool in the Palm Leaf complex. He was by far the youngest one in the gym. Two wispy, frail ladies in their eighties chattered while slowly and steadily walking next to each other on side-by-side treadmills. An elderly man with a hunched back and a few strands of gray hair combed over his otherwise bald head was on the floor, on his back, trying his best to do a few crunches. And then there was Dash, shirtless, muscles bulging, sweat streaming down his face, full of youthful vigor and an overabundance of testosterone, showing off by lifting those giant round weights.

Shirley had guessed they would find Dash at the gym. It was the only regular appointment he bothered to keep during the day. She was right. At the sight of Dash, defined arms glistening and wide chest heaving, Matt obviously hesitated in confronting him. If things got heated, the slim, unintimidating actor didn't stand a chance. He was about four inches shorter than Dash and fifty pounds shy of Dash's formidable body weight.

Poppy pushed past Matt, who was still trying to work up some bravado before alerting Dash to their presence. She stopped next to the bench where he was on his back, ready to do one more rep, and looked down at him with a polite smile.

Dash sighed, and instead of lifting, he carefully placed the metal bar back in its slot and sat up, then scooped a white towel off the floor and wiped the beads of sweat off his face.

"What now?" he asked gruffly.

"We spoke to Shirley," Poppy said.

"Yeah, and?"

"And she told us you were not with her on the night of Olivia Hammersmith's murder, like you said."

Dash scowled as he eyed Matt, spoiling for a fight.

Matt tried hard not to shrink away, summoning as much acting skill as possible to play the part of Poppy's brave protector but falling short of a truly convincing performance.

Poppy wasn't the least bit concerned about Dash going on the attack and beating up Matt. There were too many witnesses.

Dash looked around. The two old ladies were still engrossed in their own gossipy conversation, and the feeble man had given up on finishing his sit-ups and was now bent over the water fountain, slurping loudly to rehydrate.

Dash turned his attention back to Poppy.

"I said that only because Shirley wanted me to."

"We know. So where were you?"

Dash paused, thinking over what he should say, and then said flatly, "I was at the Spa Resort Casino all night. I was never anywhere near Olivia's house."

"Yes you were," Matt said.

Dash stood up and puffed out his chest. "You calling me a liar?"

Matt's lip quivered a bit and his face went slightly pale, but he held his ground and continued. "We got ahold of the security footage from the casino on the night in question. You were seen entering at nine forty-five and not leaving until almost four in the morning."

Dash stared at them evenly. "Okay." He tightened his grip on the towel in his hand, as if he was going to roll it up and snap it at them. But he didn't. He just kept it taut in his grip, ready to strangle somebody, which was mostly just an intimidation tactic.

Matt bravely went on.

"And we also checked the security cameras at the Palm Leaf. You were seen driving onto the property at six o'clock that day, after the tribute for Shirley at the Plaza Theatre in Palm Springs. And then you were seen driving off the property again at nine o'clock."

"See? I wasn't even at the Palm Leaf when Olivia was killed!" Dash yelled.

"But you were," Poppy said. "The police believe Olivia was killed sometime before ten o'clock. They're still waiting for a more exact time from the coroner, but regardless, that puts you in close proximity to her house near the time of the murder."

Dash finally flinched as he realized he'd been caught.

"If you weren't at your house, where were you? No one saw you at the gym or the clubhouse. We questioned all the special friends you have at the Palm Leaf, all the ladies you often drop by to say hello to, and none of them said they had entertained you on that day, so that really only leaves Olivia Hammersmith," Poppy said, eyes locking on Dash.

"You can't prove anything!" Dash wailed.

Poppy pointed a finger in his face.

"We have two eyewitnesses who saw you leave Olivia's house early one morning, so we know you two had some sort of relationship"

"Who? The old broad on wheels and her screwed-up son? I saw them watching me that morning. Last time I checked, they were both in jail for a series of burglaries, so what they say isn't exactly credible."

Dash turned to walk away, but Matt advanced quickly and grabbed his arm. Dash froze in place, slowly turned his head, and glared down at Matt's hand gripping his bicep. "You best let go right now, little man, or I'm going to pick up that barbell over there and crush your head with it."

Matt stayed in his tough guy character, giving it his all, although Poppy could tell he was terrified on the inside. "You can get hyped up on your steroids and threaten me all you want, big guy, but we both know you are in a heap of trouble."

"We haven't told the police yet about your little side hobby, romancing the wealthier ladies of the Palm Leaf, Dash," Poppy said. "But we've gotten rather friendly with a Detective Jordan of the Palm

Desert Police Department, and I am sure he would love to hear all about it."

Dash's bluster and bullying tone suddenly faltered just a bit. He dropped the towel he had been holding.

The idea of falling under the spotlight of the police obviously frightened him.

"Okay. Fine. I was there that night."

"At Olivia's?" Poppy asked.

"Yes. I went over there around eight thirty. I needed some cash to gamble with at the casino. Anyway, I didn't want to ask Shirley, and so I figured Olivia, who I had gotten rather close to, would be happy to help me out."

Poppy knew exactly what he meant by *close.*

"But she refused. Can you believe that? I guess I hadn't been paying her enough attention. These women, they can be so needy. Whatever. We argued, and I may have gotten a little loud and angry, and she was worried the neighbors might hear, so she finally relented and stuffed an envelope full of cash and handed it over just to get rid of me."

"Which you happily accepted," Poppy said, disgusted.

"Sure. I had a great night at the casino, too. Came out ahead playing blackjack."

"So you're saying she was still alive when you left?" Matt asked.

"Of course she was! I never touched her! Well, she wanted me to, but I needed a casino fix and didn't have time to spend my whole night making that silly drunk old broad happy. So I promised to come back the next day and curl her toes, if you know what I mean."

"Yes, unfortunately, I do," Poppy said.

"But I never got the chance, because the next day it was all over the news that she was . . ." Dash's voice trailed off.

"Dead," Matt said.

Dash shook his head. "It's so sad. . . ."

"You're actually going to miss her?" Poppy asked, incredulous.

Dash chuckled and then spat out, "Not her. Her checkbook."

Poppy really wanted to hit him.

But she refrained.

She still wasn't convinced he was telling them the truth.

But she certainly wasn't as sure as she had been before that Dash was without a doubt their killer.

Chapter 47

Poppy had really hoped that Dash was guilty of Olivia's murder. Not for any noble reason, like finding justice for Olivia Hammersmith. No, if Shirley Fox's husband was put away for murder, in Poppy's mind, that would be some kind of karmic punishment for the fading star for sleeping with her husband. She hated herself for thinking that way, but she couldn't help it. Despite her resolve to remain impartial until the case was solved, she just couldn't entomb her fury and resentment. It bothered her that she was so easily capable of such angry thoughts.

The fact was, it wasn't Shirley's fault that Chester had cheated on her. She was merely a willing participant.

The blame for Chester's betrayal was solely the responsibility of Chester, who had proved himself a liar already by hiding the state of their finances before his death.

But as Poppy stared at the police report addendum that Violet's grandson Wyatt had co-opted,

her secret desire that Shirley watch her husband
go to prison for murder slowly began to fade away.

Because once the coroner typed up his final au-
topsy report and delivered it to the police, it had
quickly become apparent that, true to his word,
Dash was in the clear.

The blow to Olivia's head, which was most
likely from falling into the coffee table and which
caused severe head trauma, had occurred at ap-
proximately nine thirty in the evening, give or take
a few minutes.

The coroner continued to insist that Olivia's
death was a homicide, based on the angle from
which she fell. There was nothing in the vicinity
for her to trip over, and even if she had stumbled
over her own two feet, given the exact location of
the impressions on the shaggy area rug from her
slippers, it would have been impossible for her
head to connect with the edge of the coffee table
where it did. She would have had to have been
much closer, and there would have to be distinct
impressions of her footprints to prove it. There
was a great deal of medical speak in the report that
Poppy barely understood as she hovered over
Wyatt's computer, reading the file, but the gist of
the coroner's conclusions was crystal clear. The
coroner, although not with 100 percent certainty,
strongly believed that someone had given Olivia
Hammersmith a powerful shove that sent her col-
liding into that coffee table.

And since there were no other foot impressions
on the rug besides the victim's, and those were too
far away from the coffee table to support a "trip
and fall" theory, the coroner believed the killer

had to have been standing several feet away from the table, somewhere on the hardwood floor.

It just wasn't Dash.

On security footage Dash was clearly seen driving away from the Palm Leaf complex at 9:00 p.m. The security cameras at the Spa Resort Casino had him entering there at 9:45 p.m., which would make sense since it was about a half-hour drive from Palm Desert to the Spa Resort Casino in Palm Springs, and taking into account the time it would take to park and walk to the entrance, Dash would have arrived some time around 9:45 p.m., which was what the cameras clearly showed.

They played the Palm Leaf security cam video again—all of them, Poppy, Matt, Violet, Iris, and Wyatt—watching carefully to see who drove onto the property and who drove off, trying to identify any recognizable cars or faces that passed underneath the bright floodlights at the main gate.

Finally, Iris rubbed her eyes and walked away. "This is a waste of time. If the killer is someone who lives at the Palm Leaf, they won't be seen coming or going. There are no cameras on the individual streets, so someone could have driven or just walked over to Olivia's house and not been seen by anyone."

"Iris is right," Violet sighed. "If the killer was already on the property at the time of the murder, we may never know who it is."

"We can't give up yet, ladies," Matt said, trying to be encouraging. "Let's watch it back one more time and see if we missed something."

Poppy appreciated his determination.

She knew he was trying his best to keep her

from collapsing in a flood of tears, but he needn't have worried. She was done crying.

She just wanted this whole nightmare to finally be over.

But as Poppy gazed at the footage on the computer screen and saw a car entering that she instantly recognized, it suddenly became clear that the nightmare was just beginning.

"Wyatt! Go back!" Poppy cried.

Wyatt, startled, scratched his face and then hit a button. The footage reversed, and a beat-up Subaru backed into frame just enough so the person driving was briefly caught in the light.

"There! Stop!"

The time code froze at 9:11 p.m.

Nineteen minutes before the murder.

Matt leaned in, his eyes squinting. "Is that . . . ?"

Poppy's heart was in her throat.

She couldn't speak.

Iris and Violet returned to the desk and peered at the screen, curious to know what they were seeing.

Violet gasped.

Poppy managed to gather herself long enough to pick up her phone and make a call.

When the person on the other end answered, Poppy spoke in a shaky voice. "I need to see you right now. Where are you?"

Chapter 48

They stood facing each other in the parking lot of a popular yoga studio in Palm Springs.

Her hair was pulled back in a ponytail, and she looked trim and fit in a light purple high-low tank, a maroon sweat jacket, and black leggings. Underneath her arm was a rolled-up yoga mat, the same color as her top. Her sneakers matched, too. She had always had a definitive style and sense of fashion.

Her face was drawn and defeated, and her shoulders slumped forward, as she stared solemnly at her mother.

"I had a feeling the second you called that you knew . . ." she said softly, glancing from Poppy to Matt, who stood re-solutely behind Poppy, mouth agape, devastated, still trying to process what they had just learned.

Iris and Violet had wisely chosen to stay behind at the garage office so as not to overwhelm her with a crowd during the confrontation.

"Heather, why did you come to the Palm Leaf that night if not to see me . . . ?"

Heather gazed guiltily at them and sniffed back tears that desperately wanted to push their way out of her eyes and down her cheeks. "I went to see her."

"Olivia Hammersmith?" Poppy whispered.

Heather nodded.

"Why?" Poppy asked.

Matt was too broken up to speak.

"Because of the book she was writing. She was threatening to blab everything she knew about Shirley Fox's love life and expose all her past lovers."

Poppy gasped as the realization hit her. "Including Chester."

"Yes . . ." Heather said, unable to hold back the tears any longer. "Mother, I was trying to protect you. I didn't want to see you go through any more pain."

"Oh, Heather . . ." Poppy cried.

"I didn't go there planning to do her any harm, I swear. It just happened. It was a horrible accident. I begged her to omit Chester from the manuscript, I even offered to pay her what little I could scrape together from my savings, but she refused. She was so rude and dismissive. We argued. Things got heated. She was drunk and belligerent and kept yelling at me to leave, but I just stood there, trying to reason with her, which just made her madder, and then she came at me in a boozy rage and slapped at me and tried to physically push me out the door, and then I don't know what happened, but I shoved her to get her away from me. . . ."

"Hard enough to send her flying into the coffee table . . ." Poppy murmured, in a state of shock as the hard reality of what had happened slowly sank in and settled into a sense of dread.

"I heard this loud crack as her head hit the edge of the coffee table, and she was facedown on the floor. I kept apologizing to her, but she didn't answer me, and then I saw a pool of blood forming on the carpet, and I panicked. I didn't know what to do, so I just ran out of there . . . and I've been guilt ridden ever since."

"The skin under Olivia's fingernails belongs to you," Poppy said.

Heather nodded and then bunched up the fabric of the maroon sweat jacket she was wearing, revealing remnants of scratches on the back of her left arm.

"I wasn't a suspect, so they never requested a DNA sample."

"It was self-defense," Matt offered, trying to make the best of a miserable situation.

"I still killed her, and I'm going to have to live with that for the rest of my life," Heather cried.

Poppy finally snapped out of her stunned state.

She couldn't allow this to happen.

Her daughter had already been through enough emotional trauma.

The shocking discovery of her beloved stepfather's infidelities.

His sudden death only a few months earlier.

The total loss of her inheritance, which clouded her entire future.

No.

Poppy was not going to let her daughter suffer anymore.

She was going to figure a way out of this mess.

She tried to think.

There had to be an answer.

"Mother . . ."

Poppy held up a hand to silence her daughter. She was busy racking her brain.

Maybe if they just kept quiet about the whole unfortunate incident, the police would never have to know what really happened.

That was probably the best course of action.

Yes, she could get Matt, Iris, and Violet, and even Wyatt, if they bribed him with enough video games, to make a pact and keep the secret.

"Mother . . ."

A police cruiser with its lights flashing pulled into the parking lot.

Poppy stared at her daughter.

"Heather, what have you done?"

"After I received your call, I knew the truth was about to come out, and that you would try to stop me from making a full-blown confession to the police, so I took the opportunity while I was waiting for you to get here to call them. I told them everything."

"Heather, no!"

Two officers, a man and a woman, stepped out of the cruiser and slowly crossed over to them.

"Heather?" the female officer asked gently.

"Yes, that's me," Heather said, holding out her hands.

The male officer extracted a pair of handcuffs from his belt and snapped them on her wrists behind her back, and then both of the officers led Heather away and placed her in the back of their squad car.

Matt placed a comforting hand on Poppy's shoulder as she dissolved in a flood of tears and called out,

"I'll call Edwin! He'll find us a good criminal lawyer!"

She could see Heather sitting in the backseat of the cruiser, her head down, no doubt contemplating what lay ahead of her.

Poppy couldn't stop crying as Matt took her in his arms and hugged her as tightly as he could.

Chapter 49

Heather was indicted for involuntary manslaughter.

Despite Heather's initial misgivings, her lawyers, convinced it was self-defense, insisted she plead not guilty, which she finally did, and a trial date was set.

When Poppy heard the charges at the arraignment, she was inconsolable. She couldn't help but feel responsible for her daughter's state of mind leading up to the death of Olivia Hammersmith. If she hadn't been so persistent in making a go of this private detective agency, perhaps her daughter would not have been so on edge, so wound up, to the point where she would actually drive to Olivia's house and confront her about what she was planning to write in her memoirs about the beloved stepfather Heather had held up on such a pedestal.

Iris and Violet were insistent that Poppy was acting utterly ridiculous. None of what had happened was remotely Poppy's fault, in their unvarnished opinions. But still, Poppy could not shake the crushing guilt and considered shuttering the whole agency, like her daughter had initially wanted. But the Desert Flowers Detective Agency was now a well-sought-after business after busting Esther Hamilton and her son Sammy for the series of burglaries at the Palm Leaf Retirement Village.

By the end of the first week after the *Desert Sun* did a front-page story on the agency's successful case, there were nine voice-mail messages inquiring about hiring the agency for various assignments.

And Poppy needed as much money as she could raise for Heather's bail and legal defense.

Poppy didn't seriously believe Matt was going to stick around for long after Heather's arrest. She half expected him to blow town to escape the bad publicity. But he didn't, although she had heard he was planning a move to Hollywood to more aggressively pursue his dream of being a successful actor and just to put this whole nightmare behind him.

Which was why she was so surprised when he showed up on a Sunday morning at Heather's apartment, where Poppy was now residing, having taken over her daughter's bills and obligations and was looking after her daughter, who had been mercifully released on bail until after the trial.

Heather was still asleep in her bedroom when Matt arrived, so Poppy ushered him into the kitchen, where they spoke quietly.

"How is she?" Matt asked.

"Okay. Some good days, some bad days. But we'll get through this."

"She hasn't returned any of my calls."

"She's not talking to anyone. I keep telling her she has a lot of people who love her and want to support her, but she's too ashamed at this point. I'm sure with time she'll let you back in."

"I hope so."

"When are you heading to LA?"

"I'm not."

"But I heard . . ."

"I thought about it. But I decided I'm going to stay for the trial. I want to be here for her."

Poppy was truly surprised.

However, during this whole detective agency adventure, she had begun to see different sides of Matt, sides that called into question her first impression of him as just an egotistical, self-absorbed actor.

"Plus, I have no plans to leave you in the lurch."

"What do you mean?"

"Matt Flowers, at your service."

"No, Matt. It's unfair to you to have to keep playing this role just so we can lure more clients. . . ."

"By helping you, I'm helping Heather."

Her instinct was to argue with him, convince him he was holding himself back by hanging out with three old . . . older women in the desert, instead of going to Hollywood to focus on his career.

But she could tell from his steely resolve that there was no point in arguing with him.

He had made up his mind.

All she could do at this point was to hug him and say, "Thank you."

"Besides, I've grown fond of you three ladies."

"Even Iris?"

"Even Iris," he said, laughing.

He kissed her on the cheek. "Now, if you'll excuse me, I'm off to meet with a client."

"You don't waste any time, do you?"

"We have bills to pay!"

And he was out the door.

Poppy sat down at the small kitchen table and counted her blessings. Despite the events of the past year, and the fact that her entire life as she knew it had been torpedoed, the Desert Flowers Detective Agency had thrown her a lifeline, and as hard as the next year was going to be, she was convinced that she would be able to stay above water with the help of her friends and new business partners, Iris and Violet and, yes, even Matt.

She could make this work as long as she didn't have to deal with any more surprises.

No, absolutely no more surprises.

There was a knock on the door.

Poppy thought Matt must have forgotten something.

She stood up and crossed through the living room quietly, trying not to wake Heather, and opened the door.

"Sam . . . ?"

Sam Emerson stood there with a sexy, laconic smile on his face. "Hello, beautiful."

"How did you know I was here?"

"I showed up at your office, and a very sweet lady told me where I could find you."

Violet.

Definitely Violet.

Iris would have slammed the door in his face.

"What are you doing here? Do you want to hire

us for a case? You didn't have to come all the way down from Big Bear."

"Uh, no, I don't want to hire you," he said. "I came to ask if I could take you to dinner."

His eyes twinkled naughtily as he gave her a wink.

Poppy unexpectedly changed her mind.

Maybe she could take one more surprise.

For retiree-turned-PI Poppy Harmon, spending her golden years running the Desert Flowers Detective Agency is far from the glamorous life she once knew. But becoming ensnared in two twisted Palm Springs crimes might be her worst look yet . . .

If Poppy didn't believe she was in too deep as the only female juror in a high-profile assault case involving an infamously hot-tempered crooner, she's sure of it upon meeting blast-from-her-past Rod Harper. A former TV co-star from her short-lived acting days, Rod is as dashing as ever, and now he wants to partner again—this time to locate his missing daughter . . .

Returning a pampered songstress with a penchant for running away back home unscathed shouldn't be too challenging. But dodging Rod's charms while on the job is another story—and so is finding a dead body! When Poppy discovers a fellow juror face down in a swimming pool, she's unwittingly thrust into a murder investigation with sinister parallels to the troubled chanteuse's disappearance . . .

As Poppy struggles to survive a steamy love triangle while deciphering the connection between two seemingly unrelated cases, the Desert Flowers Agency must outsmart a ruthless killer who will do anything to keep hideous secrets hidden away . . . including ensuring Poppy becomes the next forgotten ex-actress to bite the dust . . .

Are you ready for more Poppy?
Then please turn the page for an exciting sneak peek of
POPPY HARMON AND THE HUNG JURY
coming soon wherever print and e-books are sold!

Poppy pressed a call answer button on her steering wheel and had to roll up the driver's-side window so the whipping desert winds didn't drown out the sound of the caller's voice.

"Hello, this is Poppy."

"Is this really Poppy? Poppy Harmon?"

It was a man.

His voice sounded vaguely familiar but she couldn't quite place it.

"Yes, who is this?"

"Alden Kenny."

The name didn't ring a bell at first.

She remained silent repeating it over a few times in her head.

Alden Kenny.

Who is Alden Kenny?

The voice on the other end of the call finally answered the question for her.

"I was a juror with you on the Tony Molina trial."

Of course. The young, arrogant holdout who was solely responsible for the unfortunate mistrial. She wanted to wring the little bugger's neck at the time and had very little interest in ever speaking to him again, especially now with her mind preoccupied with worried thoughts about her daughter.

"How did you get this number?" Poppy asked coldly.

"I was sitting next to you when we were filling out the jury forms and I just happened to glance over and I saw you writing down your phone number."

"That was two weeks ago. How on earth did you remember it?"

"I kind of have a photographic memory."

Poppy wasn't sure if she should believe him, but she had no reason at the moment to doubt him, either, so she decided not to challenge him.

"What do you want, Alden?"

"I really need to see you."

"What for?"

"I don't want to discuss it over the phone. It's better if we talk in person."

"I'm sorry, but I'm very busy, and I'm not about to drop everything just because you say you want to talk to me, and you refuse to tell me what it's about."

There was a long pause and Poppy thought he had hung up. But then he spoke and there was a sudden urgency in his voice. "It's about the Tony Molina trial."

"What about it?"

"*Please . . .*" he said, sounding fidgety and nervous.

He was pleading with her. He sounded desperate. And that's when her curiosity was finally piqued. She took a deep breath and made a decision.

"Where are you?"

"At home. I live in Cathedral City."

"I'm about twenty minutes away. What's your address?"

He rattled off a number and street address and she promised she would drive there straight away. After ending the call, she repeated the address to Siri, who mapped out the fastest route. In less than twenty minutes, she was pulling up in front of a modest nondescript house in a run-down area south of the 111. As she got out of her car, she looked around at the neighboring houses and empty lots, the whole area still years away from gentrification. The house next door was abandoned with busted windows and wildly overgrown palm trees out front.

She walked up to the door of Alden's house and rang the bell. She heard nothing inside. She pressed the doorbell one more time. Again, no sound. She assumed it was broken and so she rapped on the door with her knuckles. Still no answer. She waited a few moments and then banged on the door with her fist.

Poppy was starting to get annoyed. Alden Kenny had sounded so desperate to see her and now he wasn't even answering the door. She did an about-face and started marching back to her car when suddenly she stopped. Perhaps he was in the backyard and hadn't heard her knocking. She turned around and saw a dilapidated metal gate that led around the house to the back. She debated with herself but decided to at least take a peek since she had driven all the way out to Cathedral City.

Poppy walked back, unlatched the gate, and headed to the backyard, which was much larger than she had anticipated. There were several palm trees, an outdoor bar, and some patio furniture with colors faded from the intense desert sunlight.

There was even an impressive large kidney-shaped swimming pool, given the small-scale size of the house.

And then, suddenly her eyes fell upon something floating in the pool.

It was a body.

Poppy screamed.

She could tell it was a man.

He was floating facedown, but from what she could remember about his height and frame and blond hair when they had served on the same jury, she was certain it was Alden Kenny.

Connect with Us

Visit us online at
KensingtonBooks.com
to read more from your favorite authors, see books
by series, view reading group guides, and more.

Join us on social media

for sneak peeks, chances to win books and prize packs,
and to share your thoughts with other readers.

facebook.com/kensingtonpublishing
twitter.com/kensingtonbooks

Tell us what you think!

To share your thoughts, submit a review,
or sign up for our eNewsletters, please visit:
KensingtonBooks.com/TellUs.